A Scottish Love Story

A Scottish Love Story

GWEN KIRKWOOD

JOFFE BOOKS

Joffe Books, London
www.joffebooks.com

First published in Great Britain in 2025

Cover art by Jarmila Takač

ISBN: 978-1-80573-336-2

For my good friends Gill and David Stewart
and the late Dot Lumley (my agent)

Chapter 1

2001

'We may need to contact you later and I'm sorry I forgot to take your details,' the stressed young policewoman said. 'Can you give me your name and address now, please?'

'Of course. I am Roxanne Carr. My home is at Willowbrook Farm in Derbyshire, or, er . . . that is . . . I-I did live there. My brother, Tommy, is still there. I am on my way to start new employment. If you do need to contact me, my address will be with Mrs Amynta Baxter, Oaklands View, Thornielee, Dumfriesshire, Scotland. At least, I hope it will be if she still wants to employ me by the time I arrive,' Roxie added anxiously, glancing at her watch. She would be at least two hours late. 'I can't get a signal on my mobile phone to let her know I've been delayed.' She hated letting people down.

She had yet to meet Mrs Baxter. Her interview had consisted of two letters and one very long telephone call, plus references of course. Consequently, all she knew of her employer was she was incapacitated in some way and that Roxie was to be her 'companion and chauffeur, with other duties as required'.

'The accident has caused queuing in all directions,' the policewoman said with concern. 'It's such a busy roundabout anyway and there are no convenient diversions.'

'We are all so helpless in a situation like this,' Roxie said quietly, reflecting with horror how terrible it was for the couple in the crashed car and their young family. At least she was still alive. Even if she did lose her job, it was not the end of the world for her, not like that poor young woman and her little girl. She shuddered at the memory of them lying on the road.

'I-I was on my first traffic duty training today but we were the nearest when the accident call came in,' the young policewoman confessed in a shaky voice.

Could even the hardest heart ever get used to witnessing such tragedy? Roxie wondered. She glanced towards the car, and the lorry that had crashed into it. It was only two vehicles in front of her own. She trembled at the thought of the lives of the little family being shattered.

'Other crews are coming to assist but even the fire crew are having difficulty getting through,' the policewoman said in troubled tones. 'My sergeant has had to try and control everything until they arrive. He said I had to do the best I can until he was free to come and assist when the others arrive. I am truly grateful for your help with the baby boy. I had no idea what to do with the poor wee scrap, and his cries were upsetting the driver. The medics are working to save his life now. They think he is probably the baby's father. They asked me to pass on their thanks to you,' she added with real sincerity.

'It was a small thing in the circumstances, cuddling him until the paramedics arrived. At least the poor little boy is safe now.' Oblivious to the terrible upheaval in his young life, she thought sadly.

Roxie took a moment to reflect on her own life. She couldn't deny she was stricken with grief at her father's death so recently caused, so simply, so needlessly. Her mother's death from leukaemia five years ago had left a huge gap in their lives, especially her father's; they had been sweethearts since their schooldays, but the recent upheavals were still too fresh, too raw to dwell on. They had turned her own life upside down.

Her focus returned to the scene around her. She swallowed hard and forced herself to think about her responsibilities. 'I do hope my employer isn't relying on me to provide her with food and essential care today,' she murmured aloud.

'I could ask my sergeant if he can put through a call to the Dumfriesshire police and ask them to contact your employer,' the young policewoman suggested earnestly as the idea occurred to her. 'They could make sure she is all right until you get to her.'

'Do you think that might be possible? It would be a big relief to me! I don't know if she has neighbours, or — well, or anything until I meet her.'

'I can at least ask my sergeant when he gets a moment.'

'Thank you. I would really appreciate it, if they can spare time for what must seem trivial in the present turmoil.'

* * *

Eventually the man had been freed from the tangled metal of the car, all casualties had been ferried off in ambulances and traffic had resumed in some shape or form.

Roxie was relieved to see a large sign indicating the place the policewoman had recommended as a comfort stop. Roxie parked as near to the entrance of the farm shop as she could get and hastily made her way inside, looking for the toilets. With that out of the way, she headed to the restaurant.

She ordered the ham salad and watched the young woman cut two generous slices from a large joint of succulent-looking pink ham, cooked on the bone. She also selected a fruit scone with butter and jam, and a slice of pavlova. She was so late already she felt she needed a decent meal to sustain her for whatever lay ahead.

Roxie prayed she would not find herself on her way back to Derbyshire tonight. As she'd mentioned to the police officer, she didn't even know whether the old lady was relying on her to do her weekend shopping and make her food with today being Saturday. The job description had included some cooking. The arrangement had been that she would be there by one o'clock today. It was past that time already and she was still miles from the Scottish border, and then she had to find her final destination. Roxie was glad she had thought to bring a dozen fresh eggs and a large bottle of milk in a cool bag from home. At least they could have an omelette. She enjoyed cooking and had baked with her mother since she was a young girl.

Feeling calmer and more refreshed after her meal — and two large cups of coffee — Roxie went back to the produce counter.

'Can I have one of those delicious-looking homemade pork pies, please?' She also requested a bag of tomatoes and a freshly baked loaf of bread. She selected a box containing a sponge cake oozing with fresh cream and raspberry jam, then added a tray of locally grown apples and pears. She would take the food and hope it would be accepted as an apology for her very late arrival.

Back in the car, Roxie made a determined effort to put the memory of the car crash out of her mind. Right now, she needed to concentrate on reaching her destination safely, but she knew she would never forget the sight of the young woman and her little girl lying on the road before a policeman quickly covered them. She would probably see it all in her mind over and over, but she forced herself to focus on her own driving.

* * *

Two hours later, Roxie crossed the Solway Firth into Scotland. A light drizzle made the November day seem darker, but her journey was going well now. Eventually she turned off the main road, following the directions she'd been given. She was used to country roads at home so the narrower winding roads didn't trouble her and even the rain seemed to have cleared. She saw the sign for Oaklands to her right. She hesitated for a moment, but there was a car rather close behind her. In the opposite direction she could see two tractors approaching slowly, one towing a trailer. She followed the sign and turned swiftly off. Although the road was tarmacked and seemed in good repair, she realised it was more likely the road to a farm than a public road. Sure enough, as she rounded a bend she could see a fairly large house with farm buildings behind. There was no place to pull off, or turn round, and the two tractors had also turned off and were behind her.

With no other option, Roxie followed the road as it curved around the tall, whitewashed farmhouse, but the tractors kept close behind. She stopped the car, intending to get out and ask where she could turn, but before she could open the door and stretch her weary limbs, the driver of the first tractor was standing by her car, glaring at her with angry blue eyes.

Roxie wound down her window.

'You can't stop there! Can't you see you're blocking the bloo . . . the road?'

Roxie's mouth tightened. It had been a stressful day. She was very tired. 'I realised I'd turned into a farm, but with two tractors behind me, there was no place to pull out of the way or to turn. I'm looking for Oaklands. Oaklands View, actually.'

'You're not from this area,' the man stated with a frown. 'This is Oaklands Farm. Didn't you read the sign?'

'I did. It said *Oaklands*. It did not say farm.' Roxie refused to be cowed by his bad temper.

'It didn't say "View" either. Anybody with sense would realise this led to a farm. Why are you going to Oaklands View anyway?'

'If it's any business of yours, I'm looking for Mrs Amynta Baxter. I am to be her companion and chauffeur.' The man's blue eyes almost shot out of his head. His curly red hair was already ruffled, but he pushed his fingers roughly through it, making it stand on end.

'Her companion? That can't be right! You're just a lassie. There must be some mistake.' He scowled. His bushy eyebrows came down and he glared at her accusingly. 'Unless you deliberately misled her?'

'I did not mislead anyone!' Roxie said indignantly.

'Look, can you tell me where I can turn, and give me directions? I'm already very late . . .'

'I'll say you're late. She phoned me at two o'clock to say you'd not turned up. She was convinced you'd changed your mind about the job.'

'I couldn't get a phone signal to tell her about the traffic accident and delays.'

'For three hours and more! Go tell that to the marines!'

'Marines?' Roxie compressed her lips again, holding on to her temper. She opened her car door, forcing him to move back. She stepped out and looked around. 'I don't see any marines but if they were here, *they* would do me the courtesy of believing me.'

A woman laughed. A tall, young woman, maybe a few years older than herself, rounded the corner of the house, followed by a man in smart flannels and a sports jacket. He was grinning. It did not help the mood of the furious man confronting Roxie.

'Oh, Ciaran, lighten up a bit,' the woman said with a chuckle. 'We all have bad days you know. This must be Aunt Amy's new companion.' She stepped closer and held out her hand. 'You must be Roxanne Carr? Aunt Amy is expecting you. She will be so pleased you have arrived safely. I am Jenny Pringle, and this is my husband, Donald. And *this* is Ciaran Baxter, Aunt Amy's son.'

Ciaran spluttered angrily. 'There must be some mistake! My mother is expecting a middle-aged widow.'

'No, she isn't,' Jenny said. 'It was you, Ciaran, who considered the middle-aged widow the most suitable applicant. Aunt Amy made up her own mind this time. She wants someone young and cheerful to brighten her life. She has plans—'

'She never told me that!' Ciaran interrupted her. He eyed Roxie for a moment. 'Mum particularly wanted a competent driver. The last one nearly made her a nervous wreck.'

'I'd say Roxanne must be competent enough, old boy,' Donald said. 'She has driven all the way from, er . . . Derbyshire, wasn't it?' He looked at Roxie and winked.

'Well, it's taken her long enough . . . I suppose you're not used to an early start?' He raised an ironic ginger eyebrow at her.

Roxie longed to tell him she had been up every morning by five thirty and milked a hundred and fifty cows before breakfast for several years, but she bit back the sharp retort. While he might wonder what sort of companion she was going to make for an old lady, the old lady herself had been extremely interested to hear all about her home, the farm, her work, and her life with her father since her mother's death. 'You were supposed to be here by one o'clock and it's . . .' He glanced at his watch. 'Good gracious, it's half past four! It's time I was milking. I need to get on. You'll have to move your car out of the way.'

He waved at the other tractor driver. 'Max, we need to wait while this lassie gets her car out of the way. I'll move your tractor if you want to get away home now.'

'I will move my car when you to tell me where to turn,' Roxie reminded him drily.

'Hmph.' He looked at the tractor driver who was grinning at his frustration. 'You can't turn here with two tractors in the way. You'll need to drive round the end of the house and turn right.

You'll have to go down the front drive, back onto the farm road. Then go back to the public road and turn right. Oaklands View is about a mile further along. You can't miss the sign on the right. It says *Oaklands* View.'

'Thank you.' Roxie refused to rise to the bait. She climbed back into her car and started up, driving in the direction indicated. Ahead of her was a really tight turn into a garden with an overgrown drive. She brought her car sharply round, narrowly avoiding the corner of the house. She was about to straighten up when she heard the most dreadful grinding noise as though the bottom of her car was being ripped off. It juddered. It would move neither back nor forward. She was stuck. Of course she was.

Chapter 2

Roxie wanted to put her head on the steering wheel and burst into tears. She never cried usually, but she felt totally exhausted by the strains and stresses of the past five weeks, all culminating with today's dreadful events. She had not even reached her destination yet. She was anxious. She was frustrated. She had probably ruined her little car. She had encountered the rudest, most abrupt and bad-tempered man existing on the planet. Worse, it seemed he was the son of her employer! Worse still, he had preferred some other applicant. She couldn't turn round and drive home. She couldn't drive anywhere. She shivered, remembering she didn't really have a home of her own anymore. It belonged to Tommy and his pregnant new wife, Gilda, who resented her without even knowing her.

'It's your fault, Ciaran.' Jenny called to Ciaran as he came rushing to see what had caused such a noise. `We keep telling you to shift those pesky stones.'

Roxie lifted her head to see Ciaran standing, hands on hips, mouth pursed. He strode right up to her car. She wound down the window with a resigned sigh.

'Competent driver, eh? Didn't you see the boulders? They're to stop people like you driving over the grass.'

'You mean those grassy-looking bumps in the long grass? Are they boulders?'

'Of course they're boulders — well, big stones anyway. Really big stones.'

'I'm afraid I didn't see the first one. It was a tighter turn than . . .'

'There must be something wrong with your eyesight.'

Jenny exclaimed in dismay. 'Ciaran! For goodness' sake! It's not like you to be so bad-tempered! You'll have the poor girl heading for home before she has even met Aunt Amy, and she is so looking forward to her arrival.'

'I know she is,' Ciaran muttered. 'Now I know why.'

'It's not Roxanne's fault your dairyman has broken his leg playing football and left you in the lurch. Or that the relief man has let you down at the last minute,' Jenny added in a milder tone.

Roxie groaned softly. She didn't want to cause a family row, but she was worried about the damage to her car after that awful grating noise.

'Nobody would see that first stone if they didn't know in advance,' Donald said amiably. 'It's a tight turn round this end of the house and they're all covered in moss now. Bring me your lorry jack, Ciaran, then you can get on with milking your cows. I'll jack up the car and see what the damage is. It may be possible to rock it off the stone and back onto four wheels.'

Ciaran snorted, reminding Roxie of an angry bull, but he went off in the direction of the farm buildings and quickly returned carrying a sturdy-looking jack, muttering under his breath. 'I'll do it myself. I can't imagine dental surgeons ever using a jack, no matter their strange instruments.'

Roxie had a suspicion he was swallowing a lot of angry swear words. He might have been better getting them off his chest as her brother would probably have done in the circumstances.

She climbed out of the car to lessen the weight while he worked the jack. She moved to stand beside Jenny and saw Donald wink at his wife.

'I swear I never saw a huge stone,' she said quietly.

Jenny patted her arm. 'You wouldn't have time to see it. Anyway, they're not so obvious now they're covered in moss. Ciaran placed them along the side of the drive so delivery lorries would use the entrance into the farmyard and not turn in by the front of the house.'

'The avenue is overgrown anyway,' Donald said. 'Dear Ciaran maybe a good farmer but he doesn't keep the garden very well, not like your aunt Amy used to do.'

'Aunt Amy loves her garden.' Jenny sighed. 'She made the one at the bungalow and it's beautiful, or it was until she had her accident. Do you like gardening, Roxanne?' she asked. 'I'm assuming it's all right to use your first name, is it?' She grinned.

'Of course. My friends usually call me Roxie. Yes, I like gardening but I'm no expert. My mother was the gardener in our family, when she was able. Even later, when she became frail, a walk around her flower beds always cheered her up. My father took over the vegetable garden as soon as we knew she had leukaemia. I'm not sure what will happen now as the garden is now in my brother's care and I don't think he, or his new bride, have much interest in gardening.'

'Ah, I'm sorry about your mother,' Jenny said thoughtfully. 'My mum died about six years ago. I suppose that's why you're up here to be a companion chauffeur to Aunt Amy?'

'My mother died five years ago when I was eighteen,' Roxie said. 'My father was terribly lost without her, so I stayed at home and did my best to take her place. Even when she was physically frail, she still handled the banking and the farm accounts on the computer, as well as all the records farmers have to keep these days.'

'Can you do all that sort of thing, then?'

'Oh, yes, of course. I enjoyed it, and my father loved his pedigree herd so I helped him with that too. If I hadn't had a brother, I would have taken over the farm.'

'I see . . .' Jenny exchanged a strange look with her husband. 'Does Aunt Amy know?'

'Oh, yes, of course. We had a long telephone conversation. I would never be anything but honest with her. It wouldn't have done to try to deceive her.'

'No, you don't seem the deceitful kind anyway. People always get caught out.'

'Yes, they do.' Roxie smiled ruefully, 'Believe it or not—' she gave a wry grimace — 'I even have an advanced motoring certificate.'

'Good for you!' Jenny chuckled. 'I don't suppose they take you over drives with moss-covered boulders. I'm beginning to see why Aunt Amy set her heart on choosing you instead of the middle-aged widow, or the other older applicants Ciaran was convinced she should consider. I don't believe she has told him that her youngest applicant has interests the same as her own once were.'

'Amy's are still the same, if you ask me,' Donald said. 'She always seems to know what Ciaran is busy with down here.'

'She has a good view of the farm from some of her windows and it's only a couple of hundred yards away if you cut across the fields. Unfortunately, she can no longer clamber over the garden fence or walk on the rough ground since she broke her hip.'

'Ah, Ciaran has the car jacked up,' Donald said. 'I'll go and help him, see if we can ease it off the stone and onto the drive. I reckon if it had seriously damaged the petrol tank there would be a pool by now. If you're lucky, Miss Carr, it will only have caught the exhaust.' Roxie crossed her fingers as she watched the men slowly release her little car.

'Is your father living with your brother and his wife now?' Jenny asked in her friendly manner.

'Er . . . no . . .' A look of pain passed over Roxie's face. She bit her lip.

'I'm sorry,' Jenny said quickly. 'I didn't mean to pry. I-I was . . .'

'It's all right. My f-father died five weeks ago.' She gulped. 'It was an accident. He slipped coming down the steps from the hotel after my brother's wedding. He hadn't even had a drink, except the champagne toast. There were some wet leaves lying around. My father slipped. He banged the back of his head on the edge of a step above. It was all so simple. He — he never regained consciousness. He died ten days later.

'Oh, how terrible! I am so, so sorry, Roxie. Does Aunt Amy know?'

'Yes. My application was very last minute. I decided on the spur of the moment when I saw her advert. It was just after the funeral and I knew Tommy's new wife, Gilda, resented my presence in the house. There was no point in not being honest about my reason for suddenly wanting to get away and take a job when I had never been away from home before. Gilda has finished college and was supposed to start her teacher training year but — but it seems she is pregnant. I have wondered if my father guessed, especially when they were in such a rush to get married. Tommy had not known her long. He only returned from Australia at the end of July.'

'Oh, my word!'

'I felt they needed to have their home to themselves, especially when Gilda has so much to learn about running a farm. She knows nothing about farming. Tommy, my brother, wanted me to stay and carry on milking the cows as Father and I had done, but I knew Gilda didn't want me there. Tommy didn't understand.'

'Sounds as if it would have been an awkward situation.'

'Gilda looked relieved when I told her I was taking a job until I decide whether or not I still want to go to university, as I had intended when mother was alive. If I did go, I would be a mature student now, though.'

'What would you study?' Jenny asked curiously.

'I previously had acceptances for a couple of university places to study pharmacy,' Roxie said slowly. 'I'm not sure I would do that now. To tell the truth, this spell away from everything familiar will give me a chance to find myself, to decide what I do want in the future. Your aunt knows this. I think she understands. Our solicitor at home suggested I study law, but I don't fancy that.'

'What about boyfriends? Any broken hearts left behind?' Jenny asked with a smile.

'I don't think so. I felt one of them had his eye more on the farm than on me,' she said wryly. 'That was when my brother was in Australia and we'd begun to wonder whether Tommy would ever return home and settle down at Willowbrook. Some of our neighbours thought the same. He had been to agricultural college, but felt my father was old-fashioned and set in his ways by the time he finished. We have a milking parlour and pedigree Holsteins. My brother wanted to change to robots for the milking and have a commercial herd. He had only been home from Australia for about ten days when he met Gilda. Then, in what seemed a very short time, he was getting married. Everything seems to have happened so quickly I hardly know what I want.'

'Are you two going to stand and blether all day?' Ciaran called out to them. For the first time, Roxie saw him give an attractive grin. He looked genuinely pleased as he viewed her little car now sitting on all four wheels.

'Oh, you have managed it!' she cried in relief. She could have hugged him at that moment and Roxanne Carr was not in the habit of hugging men, especially cantankerous strangers.

'We think you've been lucky. No damage to the petrol tank and I think the exhaust is still in one piece. I'll have a listen when you turn the engine over.'

'I don't know how to thank you.'

'Look, I have an inspection pit,' Ciaran said. 'If you bring it down tomorrow morning, we'll take a proper look underneath to make sure everything is all right.' Roxie opened her mouth to protest, but he held up a hand. 'I don't want you driving my mother out and breaking down,' he said.

'I will bring it then — if Mrs Baxter agrees it is convenient. I must get away. I hope the police managed to contact her or she'll think I am never coming.'

'The police?' Ciaran's brows rose up to his curly hair.

'I told you, I couldn't get a signal after the traffic accident. A policewoman offered to contact the local police station up here so they could telephone Mrs Baxter and explain the delay. I had no way of knowing that she had family living close by, or how badly she may be incapacitated. I was anxious about being so late in case she was in need of help.'

'I forgot, you've never met my aunt,' Jenny said. 'She's not actually incapacitated. I'm sure the two of you will get on splendidly. Donald and I are staying at Ciaran's for the weekend so we may see you tomorrow.'

Roxie climbed into her car and started the engine. She gave them all a big grin of relief when everything sounded normal. She drove carefully back onto the farm track and went on her way, hoping Mrs Baxter would be more understanding than her son and a lot less critical.

Chapter 3

Roxie arrived at Oaklands View without any problem now she knew exactly where to go. The short, neatly kept drive brought her to a modern bungalow, which looked to be fairly new and of a similar design to the one her father had intended building at Willowbrook, including the dormer windows using the loft space for extra bedrooms. Tommy and his bride had expected to live there initially, until her father moved in himself when he retired, or when he considered Tommy and Gilda were mature enough to take over Willowbrook completely. The wedding had been too rushed to get further than obtaining planning permission.

There was no need for a new house now. All their lives had changed overnight . . .

'It is almost as though Jim had some sort of premonition,' their elderly solicitor had remarked solemnly as he'd prepared to read the will that he had drawn up so very recently. He had known their father since he was a very young man. As they'd listened to the terms of the will, Tommy had interrupted furiously.

'Father must have made that after I insisted Gilda and I were getting married. He said we both needed to grow up before we considered marriage. I knew he was disappointed and upset when I told him we had to get married immediately.'

'It is true, he was disappointed,' Mr Robson said. 'But he said your sister had sacrificed a career of her own to care for him, and for you after your mother died.' He looked at Roxie. 'He also told me how hard you have worked, and what a great help you have been dealing with the business affairs and farm records, as well as taking an interest in the pedigrees and helping him daily with the milking. He had intended leaving the new house to you one day, to ensure you would always have a home of your own, or the money if you wanted to sell.' He looked at Tommy. `It was only as an addendum that he stipulated Roxie should have two hundred thousand pounds, plus the plot of land, if the house had not been completed. It was the money he set aside to build it. As I said, it is almost as though he had some sort of presentiment'.

'Roxie has a home with us. I could have used the money to install robots and modernise things!' Tommy said in protest.

Roxie was dismayed. She and Tommy always got on well. There was only a year between them. All she could take in was that nothing could ever be the same. Their father was dead. He was never coming back . . .

Now, Roxie looked at Oaklands View and knew she had to put the past out of her mind and take the first step into her new life as a companion chauffeur, at least for the present.

She climbed out of the car and headed to the house, but, before she could ring the doorbell, the front door was flung open and a smiling woman appeared, leaning on a Zimmer frame with wheels. Although she obviously had mobility issues and was possibly in some pain, she looked healthy, with rosy cheeks, and curly hair that was a mixture of grey, silver and traces of auburn.

'Welcome, my dear,' she said. 'You must be Roxanne, my new chauffeur?'

'I am, and I'm sorry to be so very late arriving, Mrs Baxter.'

'Please, call me Amy. "Mrs Baxter" makes me feel old. And never mind, my dear, I am relieved to know you are safe. A very nice policeman telephoned to let me know you had been delayed by a bad road accident. Are you all right yourself?'

'Yes, thank you, but I was anxious in case you were here alone and in need of help.'

'I'm fine, but I do tend to worry when things don't go as expected. There is so much traffic on the road these days and you have had a long journey. Now, do come in. I have a tray set for tea, or coffee, if you prefer. I'm sure you must be ready for a hot drink.'

'Now you mention it, I am quite thirsty.' Roxie smiled, feeling a rush of relief at the pleasant welcome. 'I did stop for the toilets as soon after Scotch Corner as I could. The policewoman recommended a very nice place and they had lovely food on display so I enjoyed a quick salad and coffee there.'

'That was hours ago. You've driven many miles since then. If you like, you can drive your car round the back. There's plenty of parking and it will be handier for you unloading. Just come in through the back door and straight into the kitchen.'

Roxie did as instructed, bringing the cool bag in with her. There was a porch with a door to a small cloakroom and toilet on one side. On the other side, the door stood open into a light, modern kitchen that seemed to stretch from front to back of the bungalow with a large window at either end.

'This is lovely,' she said spontaneously. 'So bright and airy. You have a beautiful view over the fields.'

'Yes, I usually use the table under the window at that end for dining these days. It's more convenient than carrying everything through to the dining room, except for special occasions — especially since I've been reduced to needing this pesky contraption.' Amy grimaced at the offending wheels. 'We were used to a large farmhouse kitchen where everyone congregates, so my late husband and I decided we would have one here too, including the range.'

'I understand.' Roxie nodded. 'It is so pleasant in here, anyway, it would be a shame not to use it and appreciate the view.'

'We planned this house especially so we could look down on the farm after we retired. My son farms it now.'

'Er . . . yes. We have met. I'm afraid I turned into the farm first, when I saw the sign for Oaklands.'

'Yes, a lot of people turn into the farm by mistake the first time they visit me . . .'

Presumably not with two tractors on their tail, Roxie thought.

'We named the bungalow after the farm and maybe we should have chosen something completely different.'

'I-I'm afraid I chose an inconvenient time so I was rather a nuisance to everyone.'

'Oh? Surely not, my dear?'

'I got my car stuck on a big stone at the side of the front drive. Your son and Donald had to lever it off. If — if it is convenient for you, he asked me to take my car back down there tomorrow morning so that he can put it over his inspection pit. He wants to examine it underneath to make sure it's safe before I take you out anywhere.'

'Asked or ordered?' Amy asked drily. 'Ciaran worries about me too much even though it's four years since his father died! He has been even more concerned since I broke my hip!' She sighed in exasperation. 'I know he means well, so I should be grateful. It will be a good opportunity for me to go down there with you and say hello to Jenny, my niece, and her husband, Donald. They are visiting Ciaran for a couple of days. They have always been good friends since the boys went to school together.' She broke off, her eyes widening. 'Now, what have we got here?' she asked, her blue eyes bright with curiosity as Roxie began delving into the cool bag.

'I didn't know you had family close by, or that your son has a farm, so I brought a dozen fresh eggs and a large bottle of milk from home. Mum used to show some of the hens before she was ill. Dad and I never showed them, but we always kept some of the hens for their lovely brown eggs.'

'What a kind and thoughtful girl you are.'

'After I was delayed so long with the traffic accident, I was worried in case you were relying on me to do your weekend shopping, had I arrived round lunchtime as expected. I bought a home-baked pork pie from the shop, and a cream sponge. They had no soft fruit in November as they don't import anything, but I bought some tomatoes and a tray of apples and pears. They told me these are all grown locally.'

'They look lovely and fresh. My dear child, how kind you are!' For a moment, Roxie thought she saw a glint of tears in the blue eyes. She was surprised when the elderly woman enveloped her in a warm hug. 'This will make a delicious meal for us.'

Later, Roxie discovered that Mrs Amynta Baxter rarely ran out of anything in the food line. Next to the kitchen was a roomy utility room with a washing machine and tumble dryer, and a large freezer well stocked with food, as well as a corner pantry for a supply of dry goods in case they got snowed in during the winter.

When they had finished a welcome drink of tea and biscuits, Roxie unloaded her luggage.

'I won't come upstairs with you, my dear. They are a bit narrow and the bend makes them more difficult for me now. Steps are one of the things I find difficult — and painful, if I am honest. My bedroom is downstairs, next to the sitting room. At the top of the stairs, you will see the first room has been cleared to make a sitting room. I know it is really a loft extension, but I hope it will provide a pleasant place for you when you want to spend time on your own. The other room is your bedroom with the en-suite shower room. It was intended to service both rooms as bedrooms originally. It was actually Jenny's idea to make one of the bedrooms into a sitting room to give you your own space to relax. I will leave you to settle in, my dear. The dining room is next to the kitchen, but you will find me in the sitting room. It's the largest room through there.' She indicated the door a little further along the hallway. 'You will soon find your way around, especially when you've been used to a farmhouse. They were never built for convenience or comfort,' she said with a wry smile.

* * *

The following morning, Roxie was up early, partly from habit, partly because she'd slept remarkably well despite the horrors of the day before, and also because she wasn't sure yet what her duties were. Mrs Baxter had been vague about what she expected, but she had been quite definite that she didn't expect, or want, her breakfast in bed.

'I try to keep as active as I can. I don't want to stiffen up altogether. The doctors have given me an option of having another operation, but we have agreed to wait a while to see if things improve. I have an automatic car, but unfortunately it is my right leg that is affected and I can't rely on having the strength to press on the pedals. The pain can be severe after keeping my leg in one position, or putting pressure on it if I stand still for long. Have you driven an automatic car?'

'Yes, my father preferred an automatic for travelling a distance. He enjoyed being driven so that he could survey the countryside, so I often drove when I went with him to pedigree-cattle sales or the shows. He used the Land Rover locally.'

'In that case, we shall use my car most of the time. Ciaran wanted me to sell it. I did have a driver for a short time when I first came out of hospital, but she was most unsatisfactory. She said she was sixty and had driven all her life. She was so nervous and jumpy, even in her own car. I didn't feel safe.'

'Your son fears I won't be suitable for the job — but I did pass the advanced motoring course last year.'

'Did you tell him that?'

'No . . . I couldn't. At that point my car was balancing on a huge stone I hadn't even seen.' Amynta Baxter grinned at that.

'Ciaran is having a difficult time with his workers letting him down at present,' she said. 'I expect that made him grumpy. Not that that's an excuse. Maybe he will be in a better mood today with Jenny and Donald for company. Whatever he says, I'm pleased I stuck to my own choice. I have a feeling you and I are going to get along splendidly. I do like to get out and about in the summertime. I even enjoy going to the shops in the winter as they are always warm and it gets me out of the house.'

'I can understand that.'

'I was used to a busy life before we retired. Then we enjoyed planning the garden together when we moved here. Things have seemed rather dull since my husband died.' She looked at Roxie sadly before smiling and her eyes twinkled. 'That is why I insisted on having someone young and cheerful about the house, instead of either of the two women Ciaran thought would suit me as companions. It was a relief when I received your application, Roxanne. I have a feeling we shall deal well together.'

'I do hope so.'

'I have a woman who comes in two mornings a week to do the washing and cleaning. She usually makes lunch for me on those days, but she is not a cook and she doesn't enjoy it. She cleans and washes for Ciaran at the farm two full days. I have known Iris for years. She used to help me at the farm, too. Unfortunately, she doesn't drive. She lives a mile further up the road and, come rain or shine, she cycles here quite cheerfully. At the weekends I've been making light meals for myself. Did I ask if you can cook?'

'Yes, and I enjoy cooking, and baking,' Roxie said. 'I was used to helping to do it, even before my mum died. I've looked after my father, and my brother and his friends.'

She felt a pang of homesickness when she thought of the big, warm kitchen at Willowbrook. In spite of his earlier irritation over the will, Tommy had been dismayed when she told him she'd applied for a job in Scotland. He had urged her to stay and keep on doing the things she had always enjoyed doing, but Roxie knew their old happy relationship as a family could not continue. He had a wife now, and their father was no longer here to be head of the family. She had seen the flash of relief, almost triumph, on Gilda's expressive face at the thought of her moving away.

'Iris will be relieved if I have someone else to cook sometimes. She has done her best for me but . . .' The telephone rang, interrupting their conversation, and Roxie moved to the other end of the kitchen to wash the breakfast dishes.

'That was Jenny on the phone.' Mrs Baxter smiled broadly a few minutes later. 'She has invited us to lunch, but asks if we can go down about eleven fifteen so Ciaran can check your car first?'

'Does that fit in okay with you?' Roxie asked.

'It does indeed, my dear. Jenny often cooks a Sunday roast for Ciaran when they come for the weekend and she usually asks me to join them. He fends for himself at weekends since I had my accident. Before that, he came here or he took me out for lunch.' She sighed. 'Standing aggravates my hip, or, really, it's more my thigh, to tell the truth. They gave me a new hip joint, but by the time they realised I had broken my thigh bone too, it had begun to knit together and they were reluctant to break it and reset. They only discovered the damage to my thigh after I fainted with the pain when they tried to make me stand. I had never fainted in my life.'

'That seems a dreadful mistake on someone's part,' Roxie said, aghast.

'I'm so sorry you are still having to suffer such pain. I promise to do whatever I can to help alleviate it.'

'I believe having your young and cheerful presence will be a great boon,' Amy said with a smile.

* * *

When Roxie and Amy arrived at the farm, they saw Donald and Ciaran chatting together in the yard. Donald immediately came and opened the door for Amy, and escorted her into the house. Ciaran moved to Roxie's side and she wound down the window, looking at him warily.

'The inspection pit is in that building over there.' He gave her a sheepish, almost boyish smile and pointed to a shed with two doors opened wide. He strode across and Roxie followed, driving cautiously. As she got nearer, she could see the pit but it looked quite wide. It was probably more for large vehicles and Land Rovers, rather than her small car. It would be terrible to end up with one wheel in the pit. She got out to look at it more closely.

'Everything okay?' Ciaran asked. Roxie saw the challenge in his blue eyes. She could never resist a challenge and she guessed he expected her to cry off. Her mouth firmed and she eyed him keenly.

'I think so,' she said stubbornly.'

'All right, but it is a bit narrow for a wee car,' he said. 'I hadn't thought about that. I will guide you. Stop when we have the front wheels in place and I will go to the other end and wave you slowly forward.' Roxie's heart was in her mouth as she edged closer to the pit. The bonnet of her car was not long, but she could no longer see the edges of the pit in relation to her wheels. She looked at Ciaran. His face was serious as he watched carefully, patiently beckoning her forward. Eventually he was satisfied the back of the car was over the pit. He held his hand up and grinned.

Roxie let out a long breath of relief and climbed out of the car.

'Well done,' he said, his eyes gleaming with admiration. 'I wasn't sure you'd want to attempt that when you saw the width of the pit.'

'I can rarely resist a challenge. I shall go to the house now and leave *you* to reverse it out when you've completed the inspection.' Roxie grinned.

'Spoilsport!' He teased her with a chuckle. 'Look, I'm sorry I was so bad-tempered yesterday. It had been a rough day from the beginning.'

'Apology accepted,' Roxie said. 'I didn't have the best of days myself.'

'No, I suppose not.' He smiled. 'Are you going to trust me with your precious car?' he asked as she turned to walk away. 'I thought you might wait to guide me back over the pit?' He appeared to be half serious, half teasing. Roxie turned back as he slipped into the pit.

'I thought you considered yourself an expert, but I will wait to guide you back out if you think I should?' she said uncertainly.

'Yes, I think you should,' he said with that grin. 'It won't take long.' He tapped various parts of the underside of the car and smoothed his hand over other parts. 'Hmm, considering the racket that stone made, there's no real damage done — apart from a bit of a scrape.'

Roxie breathed a sigh of relief and watched him clamber out.

'I'm serious about you guiding me out,' he said. 'I hadn't considered there would be so little room. Can you go to the front where I stood so I can see you? When you think I'm getting too near one side, raise that arm, and the other arm for the other side. Keep your eye on the rear wheels if you can and don't be afraid to shout loudly if needed. You can swear at me if you like. I promise not to tell my mother.' He chuckled.

She did as he had asked, but he was very careful. Apart from raising her left arm once when the back wheel was too near the edge for comfort, he didn't need any other help — and she hadn't needed to swear.

'I'll park it near the door and show you the way in,' he said.

He led her through a stone-flagged back kitchen. Near the door was a cupboard and a small fridge. Ciaran mentioned that he kept most of the animal medicines in those.

'Come on through. This is the back door and I usually come in this way myself, but there is a side door, as well as a front door that hardly anybody uses.' He led her into a large kitchen with a big table in the centre. It reminded her of home or the place she had always called home until now. There was an Aga with a modern electric cooker next to it and lots of cream-coloured units and work surfaces. The table was already laid with a blue-and-white checked cloth and five place settings. Jenny turned to smile at them.

'Was the car all right?' she asked as soon as they entered.

'It's fine,' Ciaran said.

'The dinner is almost ready so you may as well sit at the table.'

'If it can wait five minutes, I'll have a quick shower and change out of my dungarees.' Ciaran disappeared up the stairs.

'Don't be long, I'm ready to put in the Yorkshire puddings and you know you love them,' Jenny called after him. 'You're honoured, Roxie. He never bothers to shower for Don and me.' She smiled. 'For your information, the cloakroom is through here.' She threw open the door to the hall and then to a small room with a shower, toilet and handbasin. There were fresh towels on the radiator. In the hall itself, was a good-sized alcove for coats and boots.

They were all seated round the kitchen table when Ciaran reappeared dressed in brown whipcord trousers and a pale blue shirt, which seemed to make his eyes bluer than ever. He had evidently made an effort to smooth down his damp hair, but already it was curling round the edges where it had dried.

'My word, something smells good, and I'm famished!' he declared with an appreciative grin.

'Come on and tuck in while the soup is hot,' Jenny said.

While Roxie cleared the soup plates, Jenny placed the roast lamb and carving set in front of Ciaran, along with the pile of hot plates. He rolled his eyes and muttered. 'Don't blame me if you all end up with little bits as though the dog chewed it.'

'Your father always said it was the boss's job to carve, so it's time you started,' Amy said. 'Who does it at your house, Roxanne?'

'My — my father usually did it. I discovered it helps a lot if someone carves the roast and lets the cook get on with all the other dishes needing to be served, but I can carve if necessary.' She helped Jenny carry the dishes of mashed potatoes, carrots, roast potatoes, cauliflower, gravy and white sauce. Last came the Yorkshire puddings newly out of the oven and beautifully risen.

'My word, Jenny, you have been busy. This is a real treat for me these days,' Amy said.

'I hope you enjoy it, Aunt Amy. Ciaran, have you no mint sauce?' Jenny asked.

'Of course I have. I always have mint sauce with my lamb chops. I keep it in the fridge.'

'This lamb is delicious and so tender,' Amy said with relish. 'Is this one of your own lambs from the freezer, Ciaran?'

'Of course. You should know, Mum, because I put the other one in your freezer, all nicely jointed, along with some beef and pork roasts. The butcher did them specially for you.'

'Yes, I'd forgotten. Maybe we can use some of them now Roxanne is here. I do like my food.' She brightened as she looked at her young companion. 'Maybe we shall have proper Sunday dinners again now. You might decide to join us sometimes, Ciaran?'

He glanced at Roxie. 'Maybe.'

After a delicious pudding of lemon meringue pie, Roxie helped Jenny to load the dishes into the dishwasher and tidy the kitchen while Amy moved into the room for a comfortable seat, followed by the two men.

'I'm not sure whether I should tell you this,' Jenny said hesitantly, speaking in a low voice. 'But I think if you stay, Aunt Amy will probably mention it sometime and I want you to know that Ciaran was one of the sunniest-natured people you could have found when we were younger. Even now, he is not usually as irritable and short-tempered as he was yesterday.

'When Uncle James had a slight heart attack, Aunt Amy started making plans to build the bungalow so they could retire. She intended to leave Ciaran and Amanda — his girlfriend — here in the house, although they had made no plans to marry at that time. Eighteen months later, when the bungalow was finished, Aunt Amy kept urging Ciaran to pop the question. Eventually he agreed they would probably get engaged when Amanda came back from a skiing trip with some friends. Ciaran had meant to go too, but his father had had another heart attack, more serious this time, so he withdrew.

'While they were away, the girls fell in with a group of young men. Later, they told Donald one of them was a bit wild. He seemed determined to gain Amanda's attention. He knew she was a good skier so he challenged her to go skiing one afternoon, later than usual. There had been warnings there could be avalanches, but she went with him. It is believed they went off the main slopes. Whatever happened, we'll never know. They were both killed.'

'Oh, Jenny, how awful, and what a waste of a young life.'

'It was a waste. I wouldn't say Amanda had much interest in farming, or that she was the ideal wife for Ciaran, but she was a clever girl and she had a good job teaching French. She loved all kinds of sports. That was about six years ago now. Ciaran never mentions Amanda. He has had various girlfriends since, but they never last more than a few weeks. I think Aunt Amy would like to see him happily married while she is still around. He will be thirty next year.' She smiled. 'Come on, we had better take this coffee through.'

'I'll carry the tray of cups.'

The news was coming on as they entered the room.

'Oh look,' Jenny said, 'they must be showing news of the accident which delayed Roxie yesterday.' Roxie drew in her breath.

Surely they wouldn't show the details . . . ? She set down the tray of cups hurriedly.

Chapter 4

Amy heard Roxie's sharp intake of breath. She looked at her clenched hands. 'Come and sit beside me, Roxanne,' she said quietly, patting the settee.

The television showed the roads congested with traffic.

'Goodness! That's bloody awful!' Ciaran muttered, clearly forgetting he was not alone. He cast an apologetic glance at Roxie, then kept quiet when a reporter began speaking.

'Following our reporting yesterday from the junction of the A1 and the A66 roads where a road traffic collision between a lorry and a car at the roundabout caused at least two fatalities, we can confirm that the driver of the car, and a baby, survived. The driver sustained serious injuries and is undergoing treatment in hospital.'

'I never saw a reporter — I was looking after the baby,' Roxie muttered, more to herself than anyone else. Amy patted her hand where it lay clenched on her knee.

'No, dear, I'm sure you were doing a very good job,' she said quietly. 'Caring for that poor baby.' She chatted softly, distracting Roxanne from the television until Jenny switched it off.

'I understand now why you were so delayed,' Ciaran said. 'The roads must have been jammed for miles. I'm truly sorry for giving you such an awful welcome. I hope you can forgive me and we can start again, as friends.'

'I'm amazed that you managed to get back into your car and drive it,' Donald said. 'Especially on unfamiliar roads and coming to strangers.'

'You did well,' Ciaran nodded. 'I really do apologise for being so bad-tempered. You had still taken time to worry about my mother in case she was in need,' he added.

Amy raised her eyebrows, looking pleased at her son's genuine apology. Roxie met Amy's eyes and they shared a smile of understanding. Amy realised Jenny had wanted Ciaran and Donald to understand why Roxie had been so delayed yesterday.

'I'm so glad you were able to help with the baby, Roxie,' said Jenny.

Roxie was relieved to focus on something she could talk about happily. 'Yes, I'm just glad I could do something. I helped my best friend with her twin baby girls for a while, when she wasn't well. Her parents live abroad so weren't around. I helped her whenever I could, especially in the evenings. I would get one ready for bed while she did the other one. I am their godmother,' she added with a smile.

'There you are, Jenny! When we don't know what to do, you will be able to ask Ro—' Donald suddenly clapped his hand over his mouth. His eyes were wide with dismay as he caught his wife's accusing glare. 'Sorry, *sorree* . . .'

Roxie breathed a sigh of relief now the interest had properly moved away from yesterday's tragedy, even though she knew she would never forget it.

'What is all this, then?' Aunt Amy asked, seeing Roxie's relief at the change of topic. Her bright eyes moved from Donald to Jenny and back again. 'Do you two have some news for us by any chance?'

'What were you saying, old boy?' Ciaran asked innocently, then gave a burst of laughter. 'You may as well spill the rest of the beans now or Mum will give Jenny no peace.'

Amy persisted. 'Are you expecting a baby at last, Jenny?'

Jenny shook her head in despair at her husband.

'He never could keep a secret.' Ciaran chuckled, pretending to punch Donald in the ribs.

'What do you mean "at last", Aunt Amy?' Jenny asked. 'We have only been married two years. Anyway, we didn't mean to tell anyone until I couldn't hide it — did we, dear husband?' she added darkly, but they were both smiling.

'I am so happy for you both,' Amy said. 'I shall look forward to being a surrogate granny. I know how happy your mother would have been by your news and I know I can never take her place, but I am delighted and I will do my best to help if I can. I may not be able to get around that easily, but I shall still enjoy bouncing a baby on my good knee. So, when is the baby due?'

'Not for ages yet. Oh, well, I suppose now that Donald has let the cat out of the bag I may as well tell you. It's due at the beginning of May.'

'Are you keeping well, dear? You will not have to overdo things and you spent all morning cooking us a beautiful lunch.'

'You know I enjoy cooking, Aunt Amy, and I enjoy eating too. I shall be as big as a house if this goes on.'

'But it is good to know you are keeping well. Now that Roxanne is here, maybe we shall be able to repay you by cooking a Sunday dinner for you.' She turned to her young companion. 'I hear Jenny calling you Roxie. Do you prefer that, dear?' she asked.

'My friends all call me Roxie.'

'What do you think then, Roxie? Would you consider cooking a Sunday dinner?'

'I would enjoy that! Once I get used to your cooker and where everything is kept. Everything is so new to me yet.'

'Give the girl a chance to settle in, Mum,' Ciaran said. 'She only arrived yesterday evening.'

'Yes, I'm forgetting everything will seem strange at first, but I feel as though I have always known you, Roxie. You don't seem like a stranger in the house.'

'Thank you,' Roxie said almost shyly, and she was not normally shy. 'You have all made me welcome so I don't feel like a stranger either. I was used to an Aga cooker at home and I noticed yours is an Esse at the bungalow, so I suppose it will be a little different at first.'

'It is, but you don't need to worry about that. You can use the electric cooker if you prefer, especially if we're having guests to dinner and there's more cooking.'

'You didn't tell me you were wanting a cook, Mum, as well as a companion and a chauffeur,' Ciaran said, raising his eyebrows. He winked at Roxie, but she just smiled. She felt comfortable with Amy Baxter and she was grateful for her easy, almost motherly manner. Besides, she was used to being busy. When she had first met her new employer and realised Amy would not be needing help with washing, dressing and getting ready for bed, she wondered what she would be expected to do when they weren't out and about. The house was modern and with Iris doing the washing and cleaning, she doubted she would ever earn the generous salary.

'So, Jenny, my dear, I shall be able to start knitting baby clothes now. I wondered how I was going to pass the long winter evenings when I can't get around so easily. I will crochet you two baby blankets. Would you like them in white?'

'We shall be grateful for whatever you make, Aunt Amy. That's very kind of you.'

'Do you knit or crochet, Roxie?' Amy asked.

'I'm a slow knitter. I have never learned to crochet, but I would have a go, if you are willing to teach me. I do enjoy sewing, but I left my electric sewing machine behind. I couldn't get everything in my small car and I wanted to bring my laptop and printer. I have no accounts to do now—' her heart sank when she remembered all the things she and her father had done together — 'but I do want to keep in touch with my friends . . . that is if I can get the internet? I never thought of that! Do you have an internet connection up here?' Donald and Ciaran burst out laughing.

'We may *seem* uncivilised, but we do have the internet.' Ciaran chuckled. 'Even Mum has a connection for her computer, but she rarely uses it, do you, Mum?'

'I don't understand it very well,' Amy said grumpily.

'Maybe you might succeed in teaching her what to do when you're with her every day,' Ciaran said. 'I will come and get you connected up tomorrow.'

'Yes, Aunt Amy. I could send you emails instead of letters to keep in touch more often,' Jenny said. 'And when the baby arrives, we could send you photographs now I've got a digital camera.'

'Oh, yes, I would like that,' Amy said. 'But I fear Roxie will need to sort that out for me. I don't understand these modern gadgets.'

'I will help you,' Roxie said. 'Emails are easy.'

'You might end up with more than you bargained for, Miss Roxanne Carr,' Ciaran said with a grin. 'Cooking and driving, tutoring Mum about emails, advising Jenny on baby care . . .'

'I'm sure Jenny will not need any advice that I could give on babies,' Roxie said with a smile. She fixed her eyes on Ciaran's and added firmly, 'I prefer to be occupied and know I'm earning my wages. I have always been busy.'

'I have an electric sewing machine you can use if you want to sew, Roxie,' Amy said. 'I have scarcely used it. It has a lot of gadgets my old sewing machine never had. I bought it because I wanted to make all the curtains for the bungalow before we moved in.' She looked at Ciaran and shook her head sadly. 'That was before your father had his last heart attack, if you remember.'

'I do.' Ciaran nodded. 'You did right to have them made at the shop, Mum, whatever the cost. Dad was very content in the time you had together at the bungalow.'

'Yes, I know.' She sighed. 'Anyway, Roxie, remind me to show you my little machine tomorrow and you can take it upstairs to your sitting room and use it whenever you like.'

'Oh, yes,' Jenny said. 'That little table under the window in your room opens up.'

'Your aunt told me it was your idea to make me a sitting room, Jenny. I never expected such comfortable accommodation.'

'I did think it was a good idea, honestly,' Jenny said with a grin. 'But as it happened, we benefitted too because dear Aunt Amy gave us the bed as well as the bedside cabinets! It had been her spare bedroom, you see.'

'So that means you don't have a spare bedroom now, then?' Roxie looked anxiously at Amy.

'I don't need one, dear. Most of my friends live near enough to visit for an afternoon and that is usually long enough. Jenny and Donald were the only people I enjoyed having to stay, and Ciaran has plenty of room for them. He enjoys their company too, especially when Jenny cooks as well, don't you, son?'

'I do.'

Amy smiled happily. 'I have thoroughly enjoyed my day with you all. It is so good to be with young people again, and hear you sparring and teasing and your laughter.' She reached out and patted Roxie's knee. 'Your family's loss is my gain. I am so glad I didn't allow Ciaran to persuade me to settle for either of his choices.'

'So am I!' Jenny said fervently. 'Apart from being your chauffeur, Aunt Amy, I think Roxie and I will be friends, and you're always telling Ciaran and me we can never have too many friends. Now, I had better make a cup of tea before Ciaran has to put on his working clothes again and go to milk his cows.'

Roxie cast Amy an enquiring glance, wondering if the older woman was tired and wanted to leave, but she gave a little smile and shake of her head, indicating she was happy to stay.

'I will come with you then, Jenny, and lend a hand if I can.' When they got out of the room, she added in a low teasing voice, 'Pregnant mums are supposed to take things easy, aren't they?'

'Don't you start.' Jenny pushed the kettle onto the hot plate of the Aga to boil. 'Donald has been bad enough. He has his own dental practice and I work as his hygienist-cum-receptionist so he keeps saying he ought to get me some help. They'll be getting someone in to cover maternity leave, anyway. I'm hoping we shall be able to get a receptionist too, eventually.'

'How have you been feeling so far?' Roxie asked, setting out the cups and saucers.

'Oh, no worries at all on that front. And I don't even need to travel to work. We live in one of the old Victorian houses in the town and made two of the second-floor rooms into a surgery and waiting room. Patients come in the street door. There is another door to the rest of the house, which we keep locked. We've our kitchen-diner with glazed doors onto a large garden at the back. Upstairs we've two very large rooms for our own use as a sitting room and dining room. That leaves the four bedrooms and the family bathroom on the third floor. We like it since we gutted it all out and modernised it to suit ourselves. Though it's not been convenient for Aunt Amy, of course, these past eighteen months, with so many steps everywhere. She has managed the few stairs down into the kitchen a couple of times, though. She's a lovely lady and has always been generous to me, even when I was young and Mum was alive.'

Chapter 5

'I'm sure I shall find your aunt a lovely person to work for, Jenny. She has been so warm and kind to me already.'

'Yes, she has had troubles of her own so she is very understanding,' Jenny said quietly. 'You must never tell her you know, but she had twin daughters of her own. They died from meningitis when they were very young. That was before either Ciaran or I were born.'

'How awful!' Roxie said. 'That's so very sad. I felt sad enough yesterday seeing that little boy and thinking of his sister and his mother . . . I didn't think I'd get to sleep last night for reliving the accident, but I slept amazingly well.'

'Did Aunt Amy make you a hot chocolate with brandy for a bedtime drink?'

'Yes, she did. She insisted on making it herself for all I'm supposed to be looking after her. She said I deserved it after such a dreadful experience.'

'After I had seen the news, I phoned to tell Aunt Amy you had had a far more distressing experience at the scene of the crash than we had realised.'

'It's not easy to put such things out of your mind when you get time to reflect. You have all been kind and understanding though. I do appreciate it,' Roxie said sincerely.

* * *

Roxie enjoyed hearing about Amy's early life. She was always reluctant to interrupt when the older woman felt like reminiscing — she'd been doing lots of that over the course of the ten days Roxie had been at Oaklands. They'd lingered over lunch and Roxie had yet to clear away their pudding dishes when Amy caught sight of a car through the kitchen window.

'Oh, dear, we're getting a visit from Joan Smith. She is a new elder from our local church. It must be time for Holy Communion again. Help me through to the sitting room before you answer the door, will you, dear?' Roxie did as she asked, noticing that she had shoved her wheels out of sight behind the kitchen door. As she was leaving the sitting room, Amy said conspiratorially, 'If she asks too many personal questions, turn them aside. You will not offend me if you refuse to answer them.'

Roxie showed Joan through to the room where Amy was comfortably seated beside the fire as though she had been there for half an hour or more and had no intention of stirring. Even so, Joan held up her hand. 'Now don't get up, Amy. I know you are not very mobile these days.' Amy rolled her eyes at Roxie as the woman took a seat on the other side of the fire.

'Would you care for a cup of coffee and a biscuit, Joan?' Amy asked, knowing their visitor would stay until she had discovered details about Roxie. News always spread rapidly on the local grapevine and the elders of the church, in her experience, liked to know the gossip as much as anyone else, even if it was with the best of intentions.

'Coffee would be lovely, thank you.'

'Would you bring a tray with three coffees and a plate of those delicious raisin biscuits you baked, please, Roxie?'

While the coffee was percolating, Roxie quickly put the dishes in the dishwasher and wiped down the countertops to leave the kitchen tidy. She set a tray with the coffee mugs and a plate of biscuits as Amy had requested. Already she had learned to sense her new employer's mood. She guessed their caller was a person she could accept, but did not regard as a particular friend. Her own first impression was that Joan wanted to be one of the first to meet Amy's new companion and discover her background, so she was not surprised to be greeted with a question when she entered the room with the tray.

'Amy tells me you are her new companion? You're not from our part of the country, are you, Roxanne?'

'My home is in Derbyshire.'

'Are you from the town? Did you work in an office?'

'I come from a farm, so I'm used to adapting to all kinds of work,' Roxie answered, deliberately vague. As she passed Amy her coffee, she met the mischievous glint in the elderly woman's blue eyes and saw the faint nod of approval.

'A farm? I see. You will be able to discuss country life with Amy, then? I came from the town myself. I still find it quiet living in a village, but now I'm involved with the church I am kept busy. Do you go to church, Roxanne? Are you a member?'

'I used to attend church regularly when I was younger. Since my mother died, I usually only attend special services like Easter and Christmas, Harvest thanksgiving, plus occasional times in between.'

'I suppose you are Church of England, but you would be welcome to attend our church. I don't know whether you would be allowed to take communion though.'

'I take communion when I'm at home,' Roxie said, puzzled. She glanced at Amy.

'I'm sure you would be welcome to take it here if you wish, my dear,' Amy said. 'I believe the Church of England hold communion most Sundays? We usually have it only twice a year. That is the reason Joan is here. She has brought the communion cards for

Ciaran and myself. We hand them in as we enter the church, then the elders know how many glasses to fill with the wine. There is always plenty of bread, of course.'

'You each have your own glass of wine?' Roxie was surprised at that.

'Oh, yes, but no bigger than a thimble.' Again, Amy's eyes twinkled with humour. 'The elders bring them round in a specially designed two-tier holder. Another elder brings round a plate with the small squares of bread.'

'You could come with Amy on Sunday and see how we do things,' Mrs Smith said.

'You come when you feel like it, my dear,' Amy said. 'Ciaran usually drives me to church for communion. They're the only Sundays I can rely on him going to church,' she added ruefully. 'Although, like you, Roxie, he does attend some of the special services.'

'But if Roxanne is employed as your chauffeur companion, surely you expect her to drive you to the kirk every Sunday?'

'Roxanne is here as my chauffeur and companion, Joan, but her life, and her soul, are her own. I shall not interfere with what she chooses to do. I don't attend every Sunday myself these days,' Amy said. 'But I believe I'm as good a Christian as those who never miss a Sunday.' Roxie's eyes gleamed at the gentle challenge in her tone.

'Oh, er . . . yes, I'm sure you are. But Roxanne is young and the young need our guidance . . .'

'She is young, but she practises what many of us only preach when it comes to helping others.'

'You can't know that already!' Joan said firmly. 'Time will tell.'

'Ah, but I do know. You would know, too, if you saw the news on television and that horrific road accident . . .' Roxie was aware of Amy looking over at her and she sensed Amy wasn't about to say all she might have done because she was sensitive to Roxie's feelings. 'Both the police and the ambulance crew praised her for her help and compassion at the scene of the crash. I am proud to have her for my companion,' Amy gave a firm nod, 'whether or not she chooses to attend the kirk. As a matter of fact, when the better weather comes again, I am looking forward to visiting some of the gardens that are open to the public. Roxie and I shall enjoy our Sunday lunch out sometimes, too.'

'I see,' Joan said stiffly. 'I still believe you should be encouraging such a young person to attend the kirk on Sundays, Amy. We need some younger members. We have scarcely any under thirty-five.'

'Under thirty-five?' Amy chuckled. 'Under fifty-five would be nearer the truth.'

'Hmph. I suppose so. All the more reason we should welcome Roxanne. I will leave the communion cards with you. You don't mind if I leave Ciaran's too, to save me going to the farm?'

'I'll pass it on and remind him it's communion this Sunday,' Amy said drily.

When their visitor had gone, Roxie volunteered to cook a roast ready for when they returned from church that coming Sunday.

'We may be later when it's communion. Our present minister still gives us the full sermon, then communion makes it longer by the time the elders have been round all of us with the bread and again with the wine. It will be nearer one o'clock before we get back, so I'm warning you, Roxie,' she said with a chuckle. 'Ciaran has a healthy appetite at the best of times.'

'So that means soup for starters? What shall I cook for a roast? I see you have a variety of meats in your freezer, including venison. I am not so familiar with that, though.'

'I leave the choice to you, dear. Both Ciaran and I like all kinds of roasts and he likes Yorkshire pudding with them all, too, if you can be bothered.'

'Jenny cooked lamb for us last time, so I will choose something different for this Sunday.'

Amy smiled. 'Whatever you decide, I'm sure we shall be ready for it and we shall enjoy it.'

* * *

Ciaran Baxter arrived on Sunday, driving a rather smart dark green Volvo instead of his usual battered pickup. Roxie noticed how tanned and healthy his skin looked against his white shirt. He looked taller and very slim in a tailored dark suit, blue tie and shiny black shoes. Her pulse beat a little faster as he came closer. She knew Amy was self-conscious about needing her wheels to get around on her own, so wasn't surprised when she said she would only need her stick to go to church because she had Ciaran's arm to lean on. Amy followed up her declaration with a defiant glare. Over her head, Ciaran's eyes met Roxie's and he winked.

'Such pride for an old woman,' he said teasingly.

'I don't feel like an old woman, especially now I have Roxie for company. It's like a ray of sunshine having someone young and cheerful. We shall leave you in peace to cook the dinner, lassie.'

Ciaran grinned and warned her that he was looking forward to an enormous, tasty meal.

Roxie had decided to cook roast pork, partly because she enjoyed it herself, especially with the trimmings. It reminded her of their New Year's dinners at home. Memories of her father were still fresh and raw. She would always miss him. She just hoped that time would lessen the pain. It was always going to hurt, though, she knew that, having lost her mum. She wondered if Tommy had been back to visit the grave. She felt a pang of regret that she was too far away to visit herself.

She frowned and gave herself a mental shake. She had a great deal to be thankful for. She was enjoying getting to know Mrs Amynta Baxter. She had looked up her unusual name and discovered it meant 'protector'. Whether she was that or not Roxie didn't know, but she was certainly kind as well as generous. They had had several long, comfortable conversations, in a similar way to those she had enjoyed with her own mother, exchanging views on a variety of things. Since they had fallen into the easy way of chatting together and allowing their talk to drift from one subject to another without constraint, Roxie realised how much she had missed her mother's company, and gentle guidance. She was determined to do her best to prove her capabilities as Amy's companion and helper, especially with the knowledge she'd not been Ciaran's choice for the job. She was more settled than she had ever thought possible away from Willowbrook.

She had not explored much of the surrounding countryside yet, but even on the cold, dull days of November she enjoyed the views of the surrounding hills, especially when the winter sunset gilded their purple outline with a rim of gold. She loved walking round the garden too. Iris's husband, Joe, came to help keep the garden tidy, cutting grass and weeding in summer, and planting the vegetables in spring. It was a long garden and the bottom third was an orchard with wild flowers in the summer. Amy had told her they had planted lots of different bulbs so there would be snowdrops, daffodils, crocus, primroses and bluebells in the winter and spring. Amy said she had wanted something of interest or colour all the year round. Roxie smiled to herself at that description because even in November there were shrubs like the golden Choisya and variegated holly, periwinkle, and all the shades of green, as well as Robinia with glossy reddish leaves on the ends of many of the branches. Among the fruit trees she had seen a rowan, although the birds had eaten most of the red berries. There were still a few lingering orangey-red crab apples clinging to the branches and many more for the birds still on the ground. In the spring there would be apple and pear blossom, and plum too, so long as late frosts didn't damage it. Around the flower garden the viburnum was already clothed with small clusters of pinkish flowers, reminding her of a Christmas tree with lots of candles.

It was later than Roxie had expected by the time she heard the car turning into the drive. The table was set and the soup was ready to serve, along with hot garlic bread. The batter for the Yorkshire puddings was ready to pour in as soon as the fat was very hot; they would be cooked by the time Amy and her son had washed their hands and eaten their chicken soup.

Ciaran did not take long before he was helping his mother get seated at the table and joining her.

'There' a lovely smell in here and I'm more than ready to sample your cooking, Roxie,' he said with a grin.

Roxie was pleased to see they both ate up their soup with relish.

'Mmm, that was really good,' Ciaran said, 'I'll collect up the soup plates.'

So Roxie brought a bowl of apple sauce, followed by a pile of hot plates, and then a large table mat, which she placed in front of Ciaran. On this she set down the roast on the blue-and-white ashet, as Amy called the meat dish.

'Mmm, this looks wonderful.' Ciaran eyed the roast of pork. 'I see you're giving me a job to do, Roxie.' He tapped the top of the pork with the flat blade of the carving knife. It sounded satisfyingly hollow and Roxie gave a sigh of relief when he said, 'The crackling sounds crisp, exactly how I like it.'

Roxie met Amy's eyes and they exchanged a smile as he set about carving the juicy meat onto the plates while Roxie brought the creamed potatoes and a dish of crisp golden roast potatoes, buttered carrots, a smaller dish of Brussels sprouts and another of peas.

'Help yourselves while everything is hot,' she said. 'I'm bringing the gravy and apple sauce, oh, and a dish of stuffing balls. I'm not sure whether either of you like stuffing, but I love sage and onion, especially with pork. We always had it at home for our New Year's dinner.'

'We both like it, Roxie. You have gone to a lot of trouble, my dear.' Amy beamed at Ciaran. 'This was worth waiting for, wasn't it, son?'

'It was indeed.'

'There's still Yorkshire puddings to come. They're best left until the last minute,' Roxie said. 'I didn't put them in the oven until I heard the car turn into the drive.' She retrieved the beautifully risen puddings and swiftly tipped them onto another serving dish, then carried them to the table with a jug of steaming gravy.

'Ah, super! You've made my day, Roxanne Carr. If this lot tastes half as good as it looks and smells, you must be a far better cook than you are a driver.' There was a decided twinkle in his blue eyes and Roxie knew he was baiting her, but it was his mother who protested indignantly.

'How can you talk such nonsense, Ciaran? Roxie is a far safer driver than you are, and she has an advanced driving certificate to prove it, too.'

'Oh, Mum! Roxie knows I was only teasing.'

'I know you're never going to let me forget driving over that big stone on your drive,' Roxie said drily.

'I know you better now so I reckon I'm allowed a little teasing. I have to admit I'm in genuine admiration of your cooking skills, though. Did you qualify as a chef, or something?'

'Nothing like that. I come from a long line of farming families and my grandmother and my mother encouraged me to cook as soon as I could stand on a stool and hold a bowl and spoon.'

'Well, you've certainly made a good job of this. It's delicious. I'm going to have another slice and some more crackling. So, you must have cooked quite a bit, then?'

'After Mum died, and I changed my mind about going to university, I cooked for my father and my brother, Tommy, and all his friends when they came. Dad encouraged me to attend the Young

Farmers' Club too. I had always enjoyed stock-judging and cattle-dressing. He had coached me in those himself, but we had some good coaches for cookery and handicrafts too, so I learned a lot of different ideas from them, and I began to enjoy experimenting. I had a go at most things, even judging the sheep, although we never kept sheep at home. The only thing I didn't seem to have an eye for judging was poultry. I was hopeless at that.'

'You never told me all this, Mum!' Ciaran said, almost crossly. 'You must have known?'

'I didn't know Roxie was such an excellent cook as this. We are getting to know each other as we go along. She was surprised to hear I had been a teacher before I married your father.'

'Mmm, but you knew all about farming before you became a teacher, and you said you always loved country life,' Ciaran said. 'Roxie could have been from the bright lights of the city for all we knew.'

'Ah, for all *you* knew! I did know where her interests lay. I tried to tell you I needed some lively company. I still have an enquiring mind and an interest in what is going on in the world. You must admit, Ciaran, you were convinced I should have one of the older women. That's why I stopped discussing details with you.'

'Donald and Jenny both tried to tell me you'd appreciate someone younger,' Ciaran said in a subdued tone. 'So, what else should I know about you, Miss Roxanne Carr?' he asked with a smile, but she didn't miss the glint of challenge in his blue eyes.

'I don't think there's much else to tell.'

'There must be. You're what, nearly twenty-three or twenty-four years old? Why did you move so far away from home? What did you do for work before you came as chauffeur companion for Mum? Why were you so interested in the Young Farmers?'

Amy had obviously not discussed her background with him.

'If you're both finished, I will clear the plates and bring the pudding,' she said firmly. He sensed his question had irritated her.

'Sorry,' he said. 'I didn't mean to spoil the atmosphere.'

His mother chided him. 'You don't deserve any pudding.'

'I am so full, I don't think I need more than a cup of coffee.'

'Well, I am looking forward to my crème caramel. It is one of my favourites, especially after such a splendid main course.' Amy smiled at Roxie.

'Crème caramel? It's one of my favourites too!' Ciaran said quickly. 'I will clear this lot and stack the dishwasher. If I move around, I shall make room for pudding.' His mother looked from him to Roxie and shook her head with a wry smile.

* * *

When they had finished pudding, Roxie looked at Amy with concern.

'I think your visit to church was a bit tiring,' she said quietly. 'Shall I bring your coffee through to the sitting room?'

'Yes, please, dear, I would like that. It is a raw November day outside and a few people wanted to chat after the service because I haven't seen them for a while.'

'And you are too proud to be seen there with your wheels,' Ciaran said. 'That tires you out as much as anything.'

Roxie smiled at her and offered an arm to help her through to her comfortable chair beside the fire.

A short time later, Ciaran carried his mother's coffee through, but he came straight back and set it down on the kitchen table.

'She is sound asleep already,' he said. 'Shall we have ours in here so we don't disturb her?'

'All right. You help yourself. I like to put everything away and tidy the kitchen before I have mine. Then I can relax.'

Ciaran smiled. 'I'll wash the pans and roasting tin then,' Ciaran volunteered. 'You do the rest then we can both relax.'

'Thank you.' Roxie smiled back. 'I'm not used to someone else helping.'

'I do most of my own cooking these days,' he said. 'I had three years at agricultural college before I joined my father. Four of us shared a flat and we took turns at cooking and clearing up afterwards. We all enjoyed our food.'

'My brother, Tommy, went to college, too, but it seemed to make him think my father's way of farming was old-fashioned. Then he went off to Australia with some of his friends, but he was just as unsettled when he returned. I don't know how he and his wife, Gilda, will be getting on as neither of them know how to cook.'

'So, you're from a farm yourself, then. Mum never mentioned that. But then, she never even told me someone younger had applied.'

'As I told Jenny, my application was at the last minute. It was so soon after my dad died and I was still in shock. Tommy and Gilda were newly married. My life was turned upside down all of a sudden. But your mother telephoned as soon as she received my letter. We had a very long talk and I answered all of her questions openly and honestly.'

'I see . . .' Ciaran finished washing the roasting tin and placed it above the Esse cooker to dry, then wiped down the surfaces next to the sink.

'Thank you.' Roxie smiled. 'You have earned your coffee now.' They exchanged a friendly grin.

They settled themselves at either end of the kitchen table in the two wooden armchairs, each with a crocheted cushion.

'It was an excellent lunch. You could get a job as a cook anywhere. Look, Roxie, I'm sorry for being so sharp, impatient and unwelcoming the day you arrived, especially when I realised what a horrific accident you were caught up in, and how brave you were. I didn't realise you had recently had such a painful upheaval in your own life as well. I'm truly sorry.' Their eyes met in a moment of genuine understanding.

'You couldn't have known,' she said quietly.

'I must admit you do seem to be exactly the sort of person my mother needed,' he continued gently. 'You have no idea how much happier she is since you arrived. I believe Jenny has mentioned my twin sisters. On the way home from the kirk, Mum told me you are the sort of daughter she would have loved my sisters to be if they had grown into young women.'

'That is a lovely compliment. Thank you for telling me.' She heard the warmth in his deep voice and knew she was more affected by Ciaran than she had ever expected, especially after their first encounter. 'My only concern is I don't feel I am doing enough to earn the salary she is paying me, in addition to providing me with lovely accommodation.'

'My mother obviously thinks you are worth every penny. So long as you're happy here, you shouldn't worry about it. She has money of her own. She isn't taking anything out of the farm since my father died. My uncle, her brother, inherited their family farm. Grandfather thought she had had her education, so she didn't get much of a share. Uncle Dan improved the farm over the years and he remained a bachelor so he left it all to Mum when he died. She had been very good to him over the years. He came every week for his Sunday dinner, and at Christmas and other special times. She regularly took baking and stocked up his freezer, so I suppose he felt she deserved it.'

'I don't know anything about all that, but it is not my business anyway. Your mother knows this year is giving me time to sort out my life and decide what I want to do with my future. Tommy will necessarily find his own way with the farm. He will have to get his head around the milking parlour and whether he wishes to change it as he always told Dad he should and . . .'

'Wait a minute. Did you say milking parlour? So! Was it a dairy farm where you were brought up, then?'

'Of course it was. I think it was probably one of the things your mother felt we would have in common — that, and the fact that I am used to living in the country, and it is what I enjoy.'

'I see . . .' He whistled softly and pushed his hands through his hair roughly, and it had been so tidy after being at church. He looked at her intently, almost incredulously. 'No wonder you get on so well together.'

Chapter 6

The month of November had passed more quickly than Roxie had dared to hope when she had set out for her new employment with a heavy heart. It was already the first week in December when Amy approached her with unusual diffidence.

'It will soon be Christmas, Roxie. I know this will be the first year without your father so I do understand if you wish to spend a few days with your own family over the festive season. I don't want you to feel I am a burden. I could go to stay with Ciaran while you are away.' Roxie gasped and shook her head. She was unprepared for the unexpected tears that sprang to her eyes. She blinked them away.

'I don't think you would ever be a burden to anyone. It is kind of you to think of me, though, and you're right — this would be the first Christmas without my father and things can never be the same,' she said huskily. 'It is also the first Christmas my brother and his wife have been married, and for both those reasons I would rather stay here with you, but only if it is convenient?'

'It is more than convenient, my dear.' Amy smiled widely in relief. 'It is what I hoped you would say.'

'What do you usually do at Christmas?'

'After Jenny's mother died, Jenny always joined us at the farm. Last year, when my leg was so painful, Jenny made Christmas dinner at her own home for Ciaran and me. I'm not sure what we shall do this year. Jenny's house is not so convenient in her present condition and with so many stairs between the kitchen and dining room. I don't know whether they will want to spend it with Ciaran.'

'Couldn't we make the Christmas dinner here, for everybody? I don't mind doing the cooking. In fact, I would enjoy doing it. We could have it in the dining room for once. I would set the table the day before as we used t-to d-do at home . . . ?' Her voice quavered.

'That's a very generous offer, Roxie, my dear. I am sure Jenny would appreciate it — this year especially. Ciaran will be glad to get a Christmas dinner anywhere so long as he doesn't need to cook his own. It would certainly make me happy to have it here.'

'All right, that's what we shall do, if you help me arrange things. What do you usually have? Turkey? Goose?'

'We have a free-range turkey. I will phone and order one from the butcher, unless Ciaran has already ordered one in the hope someone will cook it.' She chuckled. 'He loves a Christmas dinner with all the trimmings. I don't usually make soup, but maybe a light starter? I still enjoy a Christmas pudding, with rum sauce or brandy butter, but I will leave the menu entirely in your hands, Roxie. I will help prepare the vegetables, though. I can sit at the kitchen table to do them.'

'I could make something with smoked salmon for a starter or a melon cocktail, which is very light and might be more refreshing?'

'Either sounds delicious. I shall leave it to you, my dear, and thank you for being so considerate and willing to take so much trouble.'

'It will be my pleasure to do it, so long as it doesn't tire you too much.'

'I shall enjoy having young company. I will phone Ciaran and ask him if he has ordered a turkey, then I will let Jenny and Don know what we are planning. It is up to them whether they stay overnight with Ciaran or go home. It is only about eleven miles away, but it may depend on the weather.'

Roxanne felt much happier after their discussion. She had not been looking forward to Christmas. Nothing could be the same without her father. At least she had something to plan for now and her efforts would be appreciated. She would always miss her dad and being away from him and Willowbrook and everything familiar, but she felt more settled than she had believed possible.

Amy was eager to go shopping in spite of the cold weather. She used the shopping trolley as her support, although she always kept her walking stick in it. Roxanne couldn't help but smile when Amy found the greatest pleasure reading the contents on the boxes of crackers and choosing the ones she considered most suitable for their small party, irrespective of the price.

'You will enjoy Christmas even more next year,' Roxie said with a grin. 'Jenny and Donald will have their baby by then and Christmas is such a lovely time for children with all the lights and surprises.' For a fleeting moment, her thoughts went to the baby boy who had survived the car crash. She hoped he was in loving hands somewhere and his dad had survived and recovered well.

'I would enjoy it even more if Ciaran was planning to have a family.' Amy's comment brought Roxie's mind back to her surroundings. 'I wish he would meet a suitable girl who would make him happy and be a good wife.'

'Jenny told me he had lost the girl he loved in a skiing accident,' Roxie said. 'I suppose something like that must take a lot of getting over.'

'I was sorry about the accident because Amanda was such a fun-loving girl. She didn't deserve to die so young. I'm not sure they were ever really in love, though. When I look back, I can't visualise them ever settling down to marriage. They had been friends for some time and the rest of their friends were gradually getting married. They drifted towards being a couple, rather than finding each other irresistible. There was no spark between them and the Baxter men are a passionate breed — both in anger and in love. Ciaran is very like his father, including the red hair. Neither of us felt Amanda would make an ideal wife for a working farmer. She had no love for animals, even a pet cat or dog, and no interest at all in Ciaran's work.'

'I see,' Roxie said quietly, and tactfully enquired what drinks they should buy.

'I must ask Ciaran to bring us a Christmas tree, one which will fit in the hall,' Amy said on the way home. 'Maybe he should take you with him because he always chooses one that is far too large once he gets it home, even for the hall at the farm, and it is far bigger than ours. The decorations are all in the top cupboards in the utility room. Perhaps I should ask him to get them down for us. Do you mind me expecting you to do so much, Roxie?' she asked hesitantly.

'Of course I don't mind. I am pleased. I was dreading Christmas without my father. Now it doesn't seem quite so awful when I have things I can do. I feel I am so lucky that you selected me for your companion.' In answer Amy gently patted her hand.

'I have counted my own blessings several times since you came, my dear, even though I understand how badly you must miss your father, especially when you had been so close and worked together too. Er, there is one more thing I would like you to help me do, Roxie,' her voice was gruff with emotion. 'Ciaran told me you know about my little girls and I know you understand. We never forget those we have loved. I always take a wreath for them, and one for their grandfather. They are buried side by side.' She drew out her handkerchief to wipe away a tear, and Roxie gave her a few moments to steady herself.

* * *

Roxie decided to put on her jeans when Amy told her Ciaran was on his way to collect her in his pickup to choose a Christmas tree. She had not worn them since she arrived in Scotland. Hurriedly, she scrambled into them, wriggling as she went downstairs, trying to fasten them. She joined Amy in the kitchen.

'I must be eating too much and not doing enough exercise,' she said, struggling to fasten the button after tugging the zip up. 'I never had jeans as neat as this before.' She bent over, feeling them tight around her bottom. 'It's a good thing they're supposed to stretch a bit.'

'Mmm, they look very fetching to me.' Ciaran chuckled from where he was leaning against the back doorjamb. Roxie gasped, and spun round to see him with a devilish grin on his face and his eyes dancing with glee. Her cheeks turned rosy red to think he had seen her showing the shape of her backside right in front of him.

'I never heard your vehicle! Where did you spring from?' She cursed the ready colour springing to her fair skin.

'Hello, Ciaran.' Amy greeted him with a smile and a twinkle in her eyes when she saw the admiration in his expression, then his effect on Roxie. 'I am just finishing my coffee. Do you want a cup?'

'No, thanks. I had mine before I left. I drove over the field so the pickup is at the bottom of the garden.'

'So that's why — you crept in the back.' Roxie muttered as she zipped up her red anorak and pulled on the red woolly hat which Amy had recently knitted for her. She was always busy with needles. When the light was best in the afternoons, she had been crocheting an evening stole in one-ply wool, which resembled black lace. It was for Jenny's Christmas present and Roxie had told her it would cost a fortune to buy one as fine and delicate, even if she could find one.

'Right, Red Riding Hood,' Ciaran said teasingly. 'If you're quite dressed, we'll go this way. I see you've a pair of wellingtons waiting at the back door.'

Roxie tried to balance while she folded the leg of her jeans neatly to fit inside her boot. Ciaran supported her, then shepherded her down to the bottom of the garden, through the orchard, or wild area, as Amy called it. When they reached the fence, he vaulted over effortlessly. Roxie stared after him in dismay. It was far too high for her to do the same. He grinned wickedly. He was in a teasing mood today. She could tell.

'Put one foot on that strong rail about halfway up, then the other foot on the top.' He smiled impishly. 'Don't worry, Red Riding Hood, I will catch you.' She had little option but to obey. He almost lifted her bodily over the top and she clung to him automatically. His body was strong and firm, and she felt secure in his arms.

'You can put me down now. Your mother sent me to restrain your enthusiasm — for big trees,' Roxie mumbled. His arms tightened and he grinned wolfishly, bringing the colour back to her cheeks.

'Are you afraid I might turn into the big bad wolf when I get you to the forest?' he asked, putting on a gruff voice. He held her close to his chest with one strong arm while he opened the door of the pickup with the other, then deposited her on the passenger seat, chuckling to himself as he went round to the driver's side. His blue eyes danced with mischief as he glanced at her.

Roxie ignored him. 'I have brought a tape measure. We measured the height of the hall where the tree has to stand. Is that woodland in front of us part of the farm?' Ciaran was silent for a moment as they continued bumping over the grassy field.

'Yes, that stretch of wood is part of Oaklands Farm, but the young trees at the front are not oaks. The trees make a good shelterbelt for the cows when the wind blows from the east. If you look the other way, the land on the other side of the public road is ours and it stretches up to the oak woods near the top of that hill. That is our boundary, but the area of woodland beyond that belongs to the Forestry Commission. We should miss the shelter up there if they ever clear-fell it.'

'My father planted some areas of woodland in various places at Willowbrook. He said the land where he planted was wet and rather poor anyway, and trees would be more benefit as shelter for the cattle.'

'Your father sounds a wise man.'

'Yes, I think he was.' She sighed. 'I'm afraid my brother, Tommy, didn't agree. I hope he will see things differently now he's in charge.' She sighed again, biting her lip and struggling to hold back tears as thoughts of her father sprang into her mind. 'My father made a new will. It was shortly before Tommy got married . . . The trouble is, I suspect Dad changed his will because Tommy and Gilda were determined to get married so quickly. They hadn't had much time to get to know each other.'

'It probably made him anxious if he thought they were rushing things.'

'Oh, he was very anxious. Dad wasn't sure whether Tommy would stick to farming if he and Gilda were on their own, or whether Tommy would knuckle down and make a success.'

'Had he any reason to think that?

'Dad was anxious because he didn't think Gilda would make a farmer's wife, but Tommy had always wanted to farm, even though he never liked milking cows. Dad added a condition that if Tommy sold Willowbrook within ten years, he must pay half the value of the land to me. I'm sure Tommy must resent that. I know Gilda did when she heard the will read, even though she has nothing to contribute herself, not even her help.'

'It seems to me your father was unsure about Tommy's future and he was being very cautious.'

'I'm sure we would all have accepted them being married if it hadn't been so hurried. I think the solicitor was partly responsible for the way things were worded in the will, though, and I realise everything has to be set out in legal terms, but it does stir trouble. We have known him a long time. I think he wanted to make sure I was repaid for looking after my father and working at home, instead of following my intended career as a pharmacist.'

'A pharmacist?' Ciaran sounded astonished. He took his eyes off the rough ground and Roxie fell against him as the pickup tilted.

'Sorry!' Ciaran grinned. 'A pharmacist, you said? I can't imagine you doing that?'

'I thought I would when I was eighteen. I doubt if I would be happy spending all my time indoors now, not after the years I spent working with my father. Anyway, I felt the decision had been made for me. Dad was . . . he was so lost when my mother died.' Her voice wavered. 'Even though we had known it had to happen,' she added gruffly.

'So, you don't regret staying home?'

'Not at all. I think it was the happiest time of my life, helping him with the cows and sharing his interest in breeding and the pedigrees. We got on so well . . .' She was silent for a moment or two, then she said vehemently, 'I suppose the law has to cover all circumstances, but Tommy would never have known about the new will, or Dad's doubts and fears, if only he had not died so soon. He would probably have changed his will several times over the years.'

'I'm afraid legal affairs do sometimes cause trouble when none was intended,' Ciaran said seriously. 'A person can only express his or her wishes as things stand at that time, though. Whoops, sorry,' he said as Roxie bounced against him. 'The ground is a bit rough near this boundary.'

''The ground or the driver?' Roxie quipped with a chuckle.

'Not the driver! You were saying about your sister-in-law?'

'Gilda and her family don't know anything about farming. They don't understand that most of the money is tied up in stock and machinery. That doesn't help Tommy. He wanted me to stay and continue working as I had done with Dad.' She gave a slightly bitter laugh. 'It would never have worked for any of us. I would have been an unpaid herdswoman, cook, housekeeper and general factotum, and I know Gilda didn't want me around.' She hesitated, then said in a rush, 'Tommy has never even called or sent me an email or — or anything.' Her voice was husky with unshed tears.

'Dear Roxie,' Ciaran murmured softly, and put a comforting arm around her shoulders. 'Their loss is certainly our gain. I am as happy as Mum is that you decided to come to us.'

'Th-thank you, Ciaran. I shouldn't have burdened you with my worries. It's just that building up the pedigree herd was my father's life work. He was well known as a breeder. I do hope Tommy doesn't let all the pedigree records lapse. I do worry.'

'He'd never do that. Surely? What was the name of your herd? I'm grading up my own herd to get them all pedigree eventually, so I often study up the sales catalogues and pedigrees. I always read the monthly journal.'

'Do you?' Roxie asked eagerly, turning to look into his face. 'Our herd is called Caldbrook. My father had gradually changed from British Friesian to Holstein for higher yields, but he was careful not to include the extreme Holsteins. I could never have managed the arable and machinery side of Willowbrook, but I loved the cattle. I often went with my father to the sales and to shows.' Her eyes sparkled with enthusiasm and for the first time Ciaran realised the extent of the upheaval she must have been through over the past few months. He stopped the truck near the trees and they both scrambled out.

They measured the circumference of several trees, as well as estimating the height, but Roxie kept insisting they were too big.

'It's a shame to cut a good tree down and then have to saw off a great chunk to get it into the house,' she said. Ciaran grinned at her.

'I can tell Mum has been warning you.'

Eventually they agreed on a tree and Ciaran brought his saw to cut it down, and she helped him load it into the back of the pickup.

'There's still quite a bit hanging over the back,' Roxie said with a glint in her eyes. 'Anything bigger would have been far too tall.'

'All right, boss!' Chuckling, Ciaran saluted her.

* * *

When they arrived back at the bungalow Ciaran helped Roxie plant the tree firmly in the large tub his mother kept especially for the occasion, then he carried it through to the hall and placed it carefully on the big mat Roxie had placed for the purpose.

'That is splendid. It is the perfect size for the space available,' Amy said, clapping her hands.

Ciaran smiled at his mother. 'I know it's not quite lunchtime, but I was hoping I might be invited to stay after all that effort.'

'We expected you would say that. Roxie put in a big rice pudding this morning. As you suggested, Roxie, I have taken out three of the cottage pies you put in the freezer, so that is dinner sorted.'

'Yes, there is a layer of carrots and onions already in the pies, but I'll wash my hands and cook some peas from the freezer.'

'Sounds good to me. It's ages since I had rice pudding. I always loved it.'

'It's so easy to make,' Roxie said. 'You could put one in your own Aga and leave it all morning, so long as you don't put it in the hottest oven, long and slow with a stir or two early on. Don't forget to add a pinch of salt. It brings out the flavour, even though it is a sweet pudding.'

Ciaran nodded. 'Write it down in detail and I'll give it a go. Can you also please remind me to reach the decorations down from the top cupboards after we have eaten?'

'I'm sure I shall manage to reach them with the stepladder,' Roxie said.

'We don't want you falling and breaking a leg too. It's bad enough Billy, my dairyman, being off with one, but at least I can milk my own cows. I wouldn't make a very good job if I had to cook the Christmas dinner. We should probably end up having mince and tatties.' He chuckled.

'Ah, Roxie,' Amy said suddenly. 'I almost forgot! There is a letter for you. I put it on the stairs so you would be sure to see it when you went up.'

'Oh, thank you. Perhaps Tommy and Gilda have sent a Christmas card after all.'

'We-ell, I don't know . . .' Amy said hesitantly. 'It looks a bit official. It has, er, a Darlington post mark.'

'Oh?' Roxie frowned. 'I don't know anyone from Darlington. I'll go and get it right now.' She was tearing open the envelope as she returned to the kitchen, frowning a little as she withdrew a smaller envelope with large loopy writing that was totally unfamiliar.

She gasped. 'Well! I never expected this!' The paper was thin and lined as though taken from a notebook. She began to read and gasped again. 'It's from the grandmother of the little boy we rescued during the car crash. Gosh, I . . . but, oh, I'm so glad to know he is well and loved. She writes, *I want to thank you for taking care of Richie after the crash. I have wanted to write before this, but I could not get an address from the police. Richie's dad, my son, has had several operations on his leg. They thought they would need to amputate but now they are fairly sure it can be saved, although he will have a limp. As soon as he was able, he asked his friend to take him to the police station in person and he explained we wanted to write to you to thank you. They promised to forward a letter if we sent it to them, so I do hope you receive it.*

'My word, I can't believe it!' Roxie said with delight. 'She says, *We can never thank you enough for our dear little Richie who is sitting up now and smiling, and making our hearts so glad. As Christmas draws near, we grieve even more for the loss of his dear mother and my darling granddaughter, Daisy. On behalf of my husband and son, I send you our heartfelt thanks and wish you great happiness in your own life.* Isn't that lovely.' Roxie blinked away tears.

'It is wonderful to know the wee boy is being well cared for. You deserve their thanks, Roxie. It is good you have heard from the family,' Amy said warmly.

'It is. I think we all wondered how things would work out after we saw how awful it was on the news,' Ciaran said.

'I wondered if the driver would even survive. His mother has included her own address, so I shall send a note to let her know I received her letter and thank her,' Roxie said.

Chapter 7

It was Christmas Eve morning and Roxie was doing as much preparing as she could for the Christmas dinner the following day, peeling the vegetables, making stuffing, checking ingredients for bread sauce and gravy. Then she spent time making the starter with finely grated orange and lemon rind, and squeezing the juice into a bowl ready for the neat round melon balls she was making out of the two melons they had bought at the supermarket in town. She was glad Amy already possessed a melon scooper so she could make neat little balls rather than simply dicing the melon into small chunks. Sometimes she wished she had brought some of the kitchen gadgets she'd had at home, especially now she knew she had free rein with cooking. Amy always seemed to appreciate her efforts. Jenny had said her aunt Amy had enjoyed cooking herself when she'd been fit and well, so she appreciated appetising meals. Roxie brushed away a tear as she remembered how her dad had always praised her efforts when she had made one of his special favourites. She wondered whether Gilda would learn to cook for Tommy and if she would make use of the utensils Roxie had bought. It would be even better if Tommy had a go at learning to cook, too.

She sighed as she thought of last Christmas. She swallowed the hard lump in her throat when she thought of her father, and how happy and content they had been. So much had happened since then. She had begun to think she was not even going to receive a Christmas card until one arrived that morning, the very last post before Christmas. It was Tommy's writing on the envelope and a first-class stamp. Inside it said simply, *from Tommy and Gilda*, and, in brackets underneath, in Gilda's tiny writing, *My parents are spending Christmas with us*. Roxie felt it was obvious she had not expected, or wanted, Roxie back at Willowbrook for Christmas. She had wondered about sending Christmas gifts, but was glad now that she had set that thought aside. In her heart she felt Gilda would be happy if she never returned to the home she had known for almost a quarter of a century.

She would need to go back some time to retrieve the rest of her clothes and other possessions, including the painting and the precious smaller items of antique furniture her maternal grand-mother had left her. She had stored everything safely in her bed-room and there were plenty of rooms at Willowbrook so her room would certainly not be needed, except by herself, when she even-tually returned for a visit. If she did decide to go to university next September, she would have enough money to buy a small flat, even though she had only received a third of the money so far. She would clear out her bedroom at Willowbrook then. The strange thing was, she felt so happy and settled here with Amy she couldn't visualise uprooting herself again for a while. She remembered how delightfully warm and secure she had felt in Ciaran's arms when he'd carried her the few steps to the Land Rover. Privately she admitted she was more than a bit attracted to him.

Amy came through to the kitchen, leaning heavily on her wheels. She often came to sit at the table to chat companionably while Roxie worked. Today she had glimpsed Roxie's expres-sion through the open door as she passed on her way from the cloakroom.

'Are the preparations for Christmas bringing back memories and making you feel a bit homesick, lassie?' she asked in her kindly voice.

'I was thinking of last Christmas and how much has changed since then,' Roxie replied. 'But I can't say truthfully that I'm homesick to go back. I would never have believed how much at home I feel here, and in so short a time. I sometimes pinch myself and wonder if I once had another life and lived here then.' She gave a whimsical smile. 'You have made me so welcome.'

'I am glad you feel like that, Roxie, and I know exactly what you mean. I can scarcely believe we didn't know of each other's existence six months ago.' She gave a little shudder.

'One of the women Ciaran selected was a widow in her fifties who had been a French teacher. He thought we should have a lot in common because we'd both been teachers. She had no conversation, no hobbies, she didn't even read a book or a newspaper. She seemed content to watch television the whole day, whatever was on. I was so bored with her company I used to go into the kitchen and do the crossword. She didn't even make her own bed or tidy her room.'

'Surely everyone would expect to do that themselves?'

'Don't you believe it! She expected Iris to do it, so she was not pleased when she discovered Iris didn't come to me every day. I believe she was looking for a free retirement home.' Amy declared this with unusual cynicism. 'Worst of all was her driving. I was petrified even driving as far as the kirk with her. I simply had to tell her she wasn't suitable. She phoned Ciaran because she said he had employed her. Fortunately, he knows I don't complain without reason. He agreed she had to go. He paid her an extra month's wages out of his own pocket, as well as a month in lieu of notice, so there would be no trouble.'

'Gosh! Did she take it?'

'She certainly did. So, you see, my dear, Roxie, I'm sure my guardian angel brought me you. I am so pleased I didn't listen to

Ciaran's other choices. He agrees with me now he sees how well we get on together and how you've cheered me up. I know he had the best of intentions and he genuinely cares about me.'

'Yes, I can see he cares very much,' Roxie said gently.

'At the farm he has made a room downstairs into a bedroom and put a shower in the cloakroom next door to it, so that I can stay there anytime. I have stayed once or twice for various reasons, but he is out working most of the day so I'm better up here where everything is on one level and more compact. Ciaran bought me the wheels to help me get around more safely.'

'I think you manage splendidly. Now, I think I have done all the preparing I can do ready for tomorrow, but I would like to make some mince pies after we have had our lunch, then I will set the dining room table.'

'Is that the melon cocktail you've made? Can I have a wee taste?'

'Of course you can.' Roxie put some into a small dish and passed her a spoon.

'It's delicious — so refreshing. We must get out the small crystal bowls to serve it in. They are in the sideboard in the dining room. They belonged to my mother. They're very pretty and ideal for this starter. You will find a jar of maraschino cherries in the drinks cupboard too if you want to put one on top of each dish tomorrow. It is Christmas!' she added with a happy laugh. 'I think this is going to be the best Christmas I have had in a long time, Roxanne Carr, my dear young friend.'

* * *

Ciaran collected them that evening to go to the carol service. They thought they were in good time, but there were already a lot of cars there so Ciaran dropped them off at the gate into the church and went to park.

'Take your time, but get a seat. I will soon find you.' So, Amy leaned on her stick and Roxie's arm as they made their way slowly inside. The old building looked lovely with the coloured lights of the large Christmas tree. On a small table in front of the altar there was a nativity scene with a beautifully thatched roof to the stable. A small light discreetly hidden inside, illuminated Mary in a blue dress and a tiny baby in a manger with the animals round about. Behind it all, a light, in the form of a star, shone down on three kings making their way towards the stable.

'How lovely it is.' Roxie helped Amy into her chosen seat.

'Sit near the end with a space between us so we can save a place for Ciaran,' Amy whispered, before she looked up with a smile and a nod at two older women. Roxie guessed they had intended sharing their seat, but they smiled back and moved on to another one. 'There is usually a good turnout for the Christmas Eve carol service, but there are always enough seats for everyone, except when there is a big funeral of someone very popular.'

It did not take Ciaran long to find them and Roxie stood up to let him pass, but he shook his head, indicating she should move closer to his mother. With a smile, he eased himself into the seat close to her.

It was a beautiful service and there was only one of the carols Roxie didn't know, and she knew the tune so it was easy enough to fit in the words after listening to the first verse. She could not lay claim to being a talented singer, but she had always enjoyed joining in. She was surprised to hear Ciaran singing in a pleasant tenor voice and enjoying singing the familiar carols as much as everyone else. At the end of the service, he stood in the aisle and held his arm for her to link hers through, then he drew her in close to his side and smiled down at her. His mother edged her way from the pew and linked his other arm with a happy smile. One of the older men grinned at him.

'It looks as though you have your arms full of pretty women tonight, Ciaran. I wish you a merry Christmas, laddie.'

'Thank you, and the same to you, Mr Jamieson, and your family.'

'Merry Christmas, Walter,' Amy said with a smile as they passed. 'He is an elder,' she told Roxie. 'And a very genuine man.'

Later, Ciaran chuckled when he told Roxie Mr Jamieson was indeed a very nice man. 'He is a widower now and there was a spell before Mum had her accident when he came visiting regularly. I expect he was lonely. That was before Mum had her accident, but he visited her several times while she was in hospital.'

'Then he is a genuine sort of man,' Roxie said. 'They're obviously still friends.'

They all made their way slowly into the annex where tea and coffee were being served, along with a selection of mince pies, shortbread and small savouries. Most people were standing around in groups, but Ciaran found a small table and three chairs so that his mother could sit down.

'What would you like, Mum? I will bring it over. There's too much of a crush for you to choose your own.'

'I will have tea, please? Coffee at this time might keep me awake. I would like one of the mince pies with a star on top instead of a lot of pastry. Roxie made them this afternoon. You could bring me a finger of shortbread as well, please. There is always a surplus of food.'

'I think I had better come with you to carry the drinks,' Roxie said, glancing questioningly at Amy.

'Aye, you do that, Roxie. Leave your scarf over one of the chairs and I will put my bag on this one to show they're taken.' Roxie knew what she meant when she turned around and saw Joan Smith heading in Amy's direction. Amy need not have worried. Joan lingered only long enough to thank her for her contribution of mince pies for the teas.

'They are Roxanne's contribution,' Amy told her.

'But you are paying her to do such things.' Joan didn't bother to lower her voice so all those around could hear her.

'No, I didn't,' Amy said. 'She volunteered of her own accord. It is the sort of thing she was used to doing for her own church.'

'You pay for the ingredients, so I am thanking you.'

Ciaran met Roxie's amused glance and winked.

'No wonder the younger members of the congregation don't bother,' he muttered, shaking his head. 'I don't know why some people need to be so pedantic.'

They all enjoyed the hot drink and refreshments, but it was very cold outside after the heat of the small meeting room.

'If you two wait inside, I will bring the car to the gate,' Ciaran said as he headed off.

Amy, of course, refused to wait. She pulled up her collar, so Roxie buttoned the top button of her own coat and took Amy's arm, seeing the determined glint in her eye. 'I'm quite capable,' Amy said. 'As you well know. We'll walk to meet him.'

Roxie hoped Ciaran would not be too annoyed at her for ignoring his instructions, but Amy was a strong-minded woman and also her employer. As it turned out, they arrived at a convenient place as Ciaran brought the car round and he simply shook his head.

'I should know better than to expect either of you to listen to me.'

'Of course you should.' Amy chuckled.

* * *

Roxie was up in good time on Christmas morning, even though she had little to do except prepare the turkey for roasting. After their late night she had offered to give Amy breakfast in bed, but she had refused, as Roxie suspected she would.

They were both surprised when Jenny arrived by mid-morning with her arms full of packages to put under the Christmas tree, including something resembling a giant-sized Christmas card in a black-and-gold envelope. She was full of good cheer and gave them both a warm hug as she wished them happy Christmas.

'I have dropped Don off at Ciaran's. They will come together about twelve o'clock, or so Ciaran said, but he knows lunch is not until one so I expect the pair of them will get involved in some job, or preparing ahead for milking this afternoon. Ciaran says it's his turn to do it this year, so he will have to leave around four.'

'Yes, Ciaran was off at Christmas last year, so it's Billy's turn to be off this year,' Amy said.

'Billy doesn't deserve to be off for Christmas after being off so long with a broken leg,' Jenny said.

'It's custom to take turns. Somebody has to milk cows and feed animals, just as nurses and doctors have to work,' Amy said. 'Ciaran will be off at New Year so Billy will milk then.'

'Oh, yes! That's more important this year,' Jenny said quickly. Roxanne learned later why Jenny considered the New Year so important this year.

* * *

The vegetables were almost cooked when Donald and Ciaran arrived, laughing together. Roxie happened to be crossing the hall from the dining room to the kitchen.

'Dinner is almost ready,' she told them. 'Your mother and Jenny are in the living room, Ciaran. There's a tray of drinks for you to help yourselves.'

'Hey, not so fast, my fair Roxie!' Donald chuckled, holding a sprig of mistletoe above her head. He kissed her cheek wishing her happy Christmas. Colour flooded Roxie's cheeks as she escaped to the kitchen. She heard Don giving Amy a hug and a kiss — under that mistletoe — and telling her she was his favourite lady. She was putting the sprouts into a hot dish so she didn't hear Ciaran follow her into the kitchen holding the piece of mistletoe. He was close behind her when she turned. She could feel herself blushing . . . And that was before she noticed the mistletoe he held above their heads. 'Well?' he said quietly, with a raised eyebrow.

Roxie didn't know what to say. She intended to opt for a dodge and get on with the vegetables. But then he said, with a grin, 'I dare you. Didn't you always say you rise to a challenge . . .'

'That's not playing fair,' she said.

'It's Christmas and it's tradition and . . .'

'Fine, fine, get it over with so I can get on with th—'

He pulled her into an embrace and his kiss . . . was longer than a sprig of mistletoe merited.

'You blush so delightfully, I am tempted to do it again,' he said gently. 'You didn't think I would let you get away without a Christmas kiss, did you?'

'I-I d-didn't think about mistletoe.'

'You look so Christmassy in your red outfit, and far too lovely to escape when I have a good excuse.' She saw the wicked glint in his blue eyes and lowered her own gaze to his broad, manly chest, remembering the beat of his heart and how good it had felt when he'd held her close the day they'd got the Christmas tree.

'You and Donald haven't been at the whisky before you came, have you?' Roxie knew her cheeks were far too pink, even before Jenny burst in on them to enquire if she could help.

Once everything was ready, Roxie removed the large white apron she had been wearing to cook. She wore a red skirt and waistcoat, and a snow-white shirt.

When she and Jenny went through to the dining room, Amy said, 'Ciaran has just been remarking how lovely you look in your outfit. He's right, Roxie. Now I see you without your white apron, you look beautiful and so Christmassy.' The white shirt had three-quarter sleeves with deep, turned-back cuffs. 'Are they gold cufflinks I see sparkling in your sleeves?' She drew Roxie closer to her chair to peer at them. 'They are lovely, so dainty, and I see they have your initials engraved on them. What a splendid idea.'

'They were a twenty-first birthday present from my friend with the twins,' Roxie told her with a smile. 'I wear them whenever I have a suitable blouse to go with them.'

* * *

'That was a delicious starter,' Jenny said. 'And so right for the huge dinner to follow — thank you! I will gather the dishes while you see to the next course.'

'That's really helpful. Those crystal bowls mustn't go in the dishwasher, though. I will wash them by hand later. Ciaran, shall I bring the turkey in here for you to carve or would you rather do it at the kitchen table where there's more room? I have a smaller meat dish already warmed.'

'I'll come through and do it in the kitchen,' Ciaran said.

'Well, no more dallying with the mistletoe,' Jenny called with a laugh. Neither Roxie nor Ciaran heard Amy murmur, 'I would be delighted to see Ciaran dallying a lot more in this case. It is ages since Amanda died, but he has never been serious about anyone else.'

'I don't think Ciaran was all that serious about Amanda,' Donald said. 'I mean they were good friends, but Amanda wasn't cut out to be a farmer's wife. She was forever playing one sport or another. Ciaran is not short of girlfriends when he is out with us, is he, Jenny?'

'No, but none of them ever manage to interest him for more than a few dates.'

'I suspect he's already smitten with Roxie whether he admits it yet or not.' Donald grinned. 'She's perfect for him.'

In the kitchen, Ciaran grinned wickedly at Roxie.

'You'd better get to work,' Roxie urged, placing the turkey in front of him. He looked anxious.

'I've never carved a whole turkey before. My father used to do it. Mum always took away the legs and these bits,' he said, pointing at the wings, 'before bringing me the breast to carve.'

'Oh, I see. My father always did the carving at our house, but I know he removed the leg and the wing on a bird before he set about the breast.' She came to stand close to Ciaran. He couldn't resist slipping an arm around her waist as she took the carving knife from him. She tapped his hand away, but smiled. 'You're supposed to concentrate on the carving. Look, you feel for the joint with the knife, as close as you can to the breast, then cut through.' She did that for the wing. 'Now, you do the same for the leg.' Ciaran did as she instructed, then grinned triumphantly.

'Now I see! That leaves the breast free.'

'Yes. I do hope it has stayed moist. Don't carve too thin so as to keep the slices juicy. If you think Don, or anyone else, prefers the dark meat, or fancies a joint, you could carve a few pieces off the leg and put it on the serving platter with the breast. My father always said it had more flavour so he had a bit of both. I will leave you to it while I load the hostess trolley with the vegetables, potatoes, stuffing and the bread sauce. I will come back to carry that hot plate through with the turkey slices if you will carry the gravy — without spilling any, mind.'

'Okay, boss.' Ciaran grinned and gave a mock salute. Roxie was still smiling when she pushed the laden cabinet through to the dining room.

'Oh my, Roxie, you have been busy,' Jenny said. 'Is that stuffing balls as well as a loaf of stuffing? Lovely. Don and I enjoy the trimmings as much as the turkey, don't we, darling? If you leave me the cloth, I will lift the hot dishes to the table.'

'All right, thanks. Have we enough table mats for all of them?'

'They will be all right, lassie,' Amy said. 'You have done us proud. I never expected to get anyone so capable, or so caring.' Her voice was husky with emotion.

In the kitchen, Ciaran had carved a plateful of turkey slices onto the hot meat platter so Roxie grabbed another oven cloth to carry it through.

'I like everything to be piping hot,' she said. 'Can you manage the gravy? The boats are hot, but the bases they sit on are all right.'

'I think I would rather take the turkey. I'm not sure I could manage the gravy without spilling some.' Roxie loved his boyish grin when he was less than his usual confident self. She passed him the oven cloth. 'That dish is very hot. I would double the oven cloth when you have such tender hands.' She gave him a teasing grin.

They went through to the dining room, both smiling happily.

* * *

It was Donald and Ciaran who flamed the Christmas pudding with hot brandy and brought it through.

Afterwards, Amy and Jenny both declared they were too full to finish with coffee and mince pies.

'Maybe we could have them before Ciaran has to leave to do the milking?' Jenny said.

Amy nodded. 'Yes, that would be best. I think we should open our gifts now if Ciaran and Don will bring them through to the room. What did you used to do after Christmas dinner back in Derbyshire, Roxie?'

'Much the same as Ciaran does, I suppose. When Tommy and I were young, and Mum was in good health, she usually took us for a walk to "shake our huge dinners down", or so she said, but I think it was to let Dad have a nap and a bit of peace before he went to milk the cows. Later, when I was tall enough to reach in the milking parlour, I helped him with the milking. It was quicker with both of us and we had more cows by then too.'

'Did you genuinely milk cows, even on Christmas Day?' Donald asked in surprise.

'Of course. Someone had to do it, whatever day it was. Dad enjoyed a bit of company as well so we did it together.' Roxie smiled at Don's expression.

'Oh, oh,' Ciaran said. 'In that case, Miss Roxanne Carr, you can come and help me. We shall leave Jenny and Don to tidy the kitchen.'

'You're not serious, Ciaran!' Jenny said. 'I mean, Don and I will tidy up anyway after Roxie has worked so hard for us, but you surely don't expect her to milk cows?'

'Oh, I don't know.' He pondered. 'A bit of help is worth a lot of pity. Would you like to come, Roxie? It is always a help even if you only chivvy along the stragglers or feed the youngest calves?'

'I wouldn't mind helping you but . . .' She looked at Amy, eyebrows raised in question.

'Yes, you go, dear,' Amy said. 'So long as you're sure it's what you would like to do. It might make you feel like home, when that was your custom. Jenny and Don will keep me company and we shall have the trifle and Christmas cake for tea, as well as all those savouries you prepared. We'll set it out for when you both return. You will have worked up an appetite again by then. Now, Donald, where are those parcels?'

Roxie had not been sure what do about Christmas presents until she'd realised Donald and Jenny had always come for Christmas since they'd been married, and opening gifts had become a ritual Jenny and Amy both enjoyed. She had done her best to get something suitable for everyone. She had bought a pink silk scarf for Amy because she noticed how often she liked to add a scarf if she had on a blouse or dress that didn't button to the neck now the days were colder. She suited pink with her silvery hair and pink cheeks. Even better, Roxie had spied a small silver scarf ring in a scuffed leather box in the window of a small antiques shop next to the photographer's. It was marked Edinburgh silver and was in the form of two sprigs of heather entwined to make the ring for threading a thin scarf through. Amy seemed delighted with both scarf and ring.

Roxie had bought a white silk blouse for Jenny after they discovered they were the same size. To make it more personal, and a bit special, she had embroidered a small sprig of forget-me-nots on the collar and on the placket down the front. Amy had seen her embroidering it and expressed genuine admiration for her skill with the embroidery silks.

'Jenny will love that. She does like clothes that are a bit different to everybody else. That will be unique. She was bemoaning the fact that her clothes are getting too tight at the waist. She will be able to wear a blouse loose with a skirt or trousers.'

It had not been so easy to choose something for Don but in the end she had bought three pony prints which she thought might be suitable for his waiting room and make some of the nervous children smile, or maybe for the nursery when their own baby arrived. Ciaran had been her biggest problem because she didn't want to resort to something impersonal. When she realised he was genuinely interested in pedigrees and was grading up his dairy herd until they could all be registered pedigree, she knew exactly what to do, except there was not much time left. On her laptop she had photographs of her father's best cows, which had won at various shows. She selected one of her favourites and emailed it to the small photographer Jenny had unwittingly recommended.

He had promised to enlarge it and mount it in an oak frame — plain but smart. On the back, she had written *Caldbrook Duchess 3rd, Champion of Champions*, with the name and year of the show. She had also bought him a small box of liqueur chocolates in case he wasn't impressed by a cow that someone else had bred. She need not have worried. He barely looked at the chocolates when he saw the photograph. He was full of questions about her breeding and Roxie knew she had made a good choice when he asked if she could add the full pedigree to put on the back.

She had already seen the beautiful, fine black evening stole Amy had crocheted for Jenny, but she had never expected anything like that herself. She was overwhelmed when she opened the squashy parcel to find the same lacy stole in ivory instead of black.

'I-I don't know how to thank you,' she said huskily, and to her dismay her eyes filled with tears and she had to blink furiously to prevent them falling. 'I know better than anyone how much time and effort it took to make Jenny's. How did you manage to make two without me seeing you?'

'The black is more difficult to work on in electric light,' Amy said with a smile. 'So it suited me to do it during the afternoons. It was easier doing the second one to the same pattern and I could work on the creamy colour anytime — in the mornings while you were busy in the kitchen or in the evenings when you had gone to bed with a book, or to watch your own programme on TV. You're worth every stitch, both of you.'

'Come on, Roxie,' Jenny said. 'You haven't opened your present from us yet.' She thrust the giant-sized envelope at Roxie and collapsed onto the sofa beside her.

'I think you're more excited than I am, Jenny. Is this some of your own artwork?'

'Only a little bit — the calligraphy inside. Open it and see.' Laughing, Roxie did as she was told. On the front of the huge

Christmas card was a large photograph of Oaklands View taken in the summer with the garden in full bloom.

'How lovely it is.' Roxie looked closely at the flower borders then beyond the garden to the green of the fields and the darker green of the trees, and then at the range of low hills behind, with a beautiful blue sky and fluffy white clouds. She could almost see them floating. 'It's a beautiful photograph,' she said. 'Whoever took it must be an expert photographer to compose such a background and yet show the beauty of the summer garden. I shall have it framed and treasure it.'

'Never mind the photograph,' Jenny said impatiently. 'Look inside.'

'At your stylish calligraphy?' Roxie asked with a grin at the bright-eyed young woman beside her.

'Jenny is always as excited as a five-year-old at Christmastime,' Don said teasingly. Roxie opened the card and read the Christmas greetings so carefully written, but there was also an envelope fixed to the top of the card.

'Open it, Roxie,' Jenny said. Roxie looked at her with affectionate curiosity, then did as she was asked. She gasped aloud, her eyes wide with shock. She put a hand to her mouth, lost for words for a moment.

'I-I could never accept all that!' she said in a choked voice. 'It is far too much and . . . and . . .'

'It is from all three of us, Roxie,' Jenny said. 'We all think you're worth twice that, the way you have brought Aunt Amy back to the lively woman we all knew.'

'That is true, Roxie,' Ciaran said seriously. 'I take back every reproach I uttered.'

'We do have an ulterior motive in giving you a gift token, and making it from all three of us,' Jenny said, ignoring Ciaran and unaware of Roxie's blushes.

Roxie protested softly. 'No motive could cost so much.'

'Remember I asked if you had brought an evening dress with you?' Jenny asked.

'Ye-es, I think you did.'

'You said you had left most of your clothes at home for that sort of entertainment.'

'That's true. I left a wardrobe full of clothes until I knew what the job entailed. Remember, I had no idea what to expect.'

'I know, but, you see, Don and Ciaran have tickets for the four of us for the New Year dinner dance. I was shopping for a new dress for myself as mine are all too tight. I saw this lovely dress in deep-blue satin and it is in our size — well, your size now. I asked the shop assistant if she would reserve it until after Christmas so that I could take you in to try it on. We have to go the day after Boxing Day in case you prefer a different one and she needs to put the blue one back on display.'

'B-but . . . it's truly kind and generous of you all but — but I can't accept so much. In any case I couldn't possibly go to a dinner dance and leave Amy here on her own for the whole evening—'

'Of course you can, my dear child,' Amy said. 'You have never even had a day all to yourself, even less a weekend off since you arrived. Jenny and Ciaran both asked for my opinion before they got the tickets. If you make me my meal and set it on the table beside my chair in the room, I promise not to stir all evening until I go to bed. You can even put my electric blanket on at low so that I simply need to get into my nightdress and into bed. I will leave the night light on and you can look in to make sure I'm asleep if that will stop you worrying. Everything is planned. I want you to go with Jenny and buy yourself whichever dress you like. Then I want you to enjoy the dinner dance and see that Ciaran enjoys it too before he becomes a crusty old bachelor.' She chuckled at Ciaran's indignant expression.

'It is true, we certainly do want you to come with us,' Donald said. 'It will be far more fun if there are four of us.'

'He's right there.' Ciaran nodded in agreement. 'I'm not going to play gooseberry to this pair if you refuse to come.'

* * *

Roxie had changed into the jeans she had brought with her, but Ciaran insisted she wear one of the new waterproof smocks he always kept in the dairy cupboard at the milking parlour.

'This parlour is not so very different to the one at home,' she told him as she looked around. 'I see the feeding is done by the computer reading the cow numbers as they come into the stalls. That makes things easier, especially for a stranger, quicker too. I have sprayed and dried their udders. Can I have a go at putting the clusters on down this side?'

'You certainly can,' Ciaran said instantly. It was not long before Roxie got used to the slight differences in the milking machines and she was as quick at doing her side of the parlour as Ciaran was with his, but it didn't stop her taking in details of the cows.

'This is the kind of cow I like,' she said, as she put the clusters on one. 'We used to have beautifully square British Friesians and it took me a long time to learn to like the big bones of the Holsteins, even though they do give more milk.'

'I know what you mean. That is one of my favourites too. I am grading up her progeny to pedigree, also this one at the end.'

'I can almost tell which ones are already pedigree Holsteins,' Roxie said with a laugh.

'I know.' Ciaran smiled ruefully. 'It took me a while to make up my mind to change. I don't think my father would have approved, but he would understand me needing to move with the times and get as much milk, as economically, as I can.'

'That is exactly what my father would say,' Roxie said with a sigh.

'You miss him badly, eh?' he said sympathetically.

'I do, but I have been so lucky in finding a person as kind and generous as your mother.'

'I reckon the feeling is mutual.'

They chatted easily as they got on with the milking, with Ciaran telling her a bit about his own father and how he missed his advice on many aspects of the arable side of the farming. By the time young Vic, the general worker, arrived to start hosing down the concrete in the gathering area, he couldn't believe they were already finished milking, or that Ciaran had a young woman and she was actually helping him. Vic couldn't wait to tell Billy, who believed he was the only one capable of milking cows.

* * *

Roxie genuinely felt the combined gift of an evening dress was far too much, but she went with Jenny to the shop as arranged. The one Jenny had asked to be set aside was a perfect fit and she loved the colour. Jenny insisted she cast an eye over the remaining dresses to make sure it was the one she would have chosen herself, but there was nothing she liked as much. She bought herself a pair of navy patent court shoes with higher heels than she normally wore and she already had a small matching handbag that was adequate for evening. She could now look forward to the New Year's dinner dance with a lighter heart than she had had since the fateful day of Tommy's wedding and her father's accident.

Chapter 8

When Ciaran called to collect Roxie for the dinner dance, he came in to see his mother before they left.

Amy greeted him drily. 'I know you've come in to check up on me, Ciaran, but Roxie has made sure I have everything I could possibly need. You're looking very well tonight. Go and enjoy yourself for once. I don't believe you've had a good night out since Donald and Jenny were married, and that's nearly two years ago.' She broke off as Roxie came into the room. 'Aah.' She caught her breath. 'You look wonderful, my dear!'

Ciaran turned to look at Roxie. His eyes widened, then darkened in admiration. 'You do look lovely, Roxie. I can see I shall have a job fighting off the competition tonight,' he said, unusually serious.

'You leave me breathless, Ciaran Baxter. I was not expecting a handsome man in a kilt as my partner tonight,' Roxie murmured demurely.

'There will be quite a few in kilts tonight.' Ciaran laughed. 'It is Hogmanay, remember.'

'The pair of you make a lovely picture.' Amy sighed. 'Could you fetch me my camera, please, Roxie?'

'Now there's an idea.' Roxie retrieved it from the sideboard. 'I need a picture of you in your kilt, Ciaran,' she said gleefully.

'I shall send one to my friend, Lucy. She keeps asking if I have met any men in kilts yet.'

'But I would like one of you together,' Amy said.

Ciaran grinned happily and clasped Roxie around the waist, drawing her close while his mother clicked several pictures on her small camera.

'Now, away you go, the pair of you. Have an evening to remember and welcome in the new year.' Amy sounded a little husky and Roxie glimpsed the sheen of tears in her blue eyes. On impulse, she bent and kissed the elderly woman's cheek.

'I shall look in on you later,' she said softly.

Ciaran helped Roxie into the passenger seat. He tucked the material of her dress in carefully.

'That colour does suit you, Roxie. Are you pleased now that Jenny organised it all?'

'I love the dress and the colour, and I know it was kind of you all to buy it for me, but I feel a fraud accepting so much.'

'As far as I'm concerned, you are worth every penny. I'm proud that you agreed to be my partner for tonight,' he said as their eyes met and held for a moment. 'Why should you feel a fraud?'

'We-ell, I would never have expected any of you to make me so welcome so soon, even less pay as much as you did for a Christmas present. You have only known me for a few months.'

'The way you fit in so well, we feel as though we have always known you,'

'I feel a bit like that too, but if Jenny had told me about the dinner dance I would have considered payment of my ticket was a generous gift in itself. You see, apart from earning a generous wage from your mother, I do have some money of my own since m-my f-father died. I ought to have paid for the dress myself. I know you want to spend any spare cash on grading up your herd and my father would have approved of that wholeheartedly. Then Jenny and Donald will have their baby this year and it costs a lot by the time they've bought all the equipment and baby clothes. So . . .'

Ciaran took one hand off the steering wheel and clasped hers for a moment. 'We all know you are not a fraud, Roxie,' he said quietly.

'Will it repay you a tiny bit if I offer to drive us home tonight? Presumably everyone enjoys a few drinks when it's New Year's Eve.'

'That's true. Hogmanay has always been a great time to celebrate up here. Surely you will enjoy a drink or two yourself, though?'

'Jenny will not be drinking on account of the baby so she will drive Donald home. If I have a small glass of white wine with my dinner, I don't think that will do me any harm by the time we've danced the night away, do you?'

'No, but we all have a drink at midnight to welcome in the New Year, as well as several as the evening goes on. I wasn't going to drink so I didn't book a taxi for us.'

'There's no need as I am happy to drive us home. I will have something non-alcoholic for the toast. So, are we agreed?'

'You're a wee gem. I didn't expect you to chauffeur me. I was prepared to abstain for this Hogmanay so long as you agreed to be my partner. There will be lots of fellows wanting to claim you for a dance, but I hope you will save at least the first and last dances for me.' Roxie was sure his blue eyes darkened with desire in the dim street lights as they passed through one of the villages.

'Of course I will, if that's what you want, Ciaran. Anyway, you forget I shall not know anyone else except you and Donald.'

Ciaran gave a crow of laughter. 'Looking as gorgeous as you do, most of the fellows will be queuing for a dance regardless.' Roxie blushed. Ciaran chuckled. 'I do love that delightful flush.' Returning his eyes to the road, he asked, 'Did you have a serious boyfriend down in Derbyshire?'

'How serious is "serious"?'

'Someone you considered as a husband, seriously considered, I mean?'

'No, not seriously. I knew lots of pleasant men, but . . .' She frowned. 'Sometimes, in retrospect, I think I was subconsciously looking for someone modelled on my father.'

'From what you have told me about him, I don't think that's a bad thing, is it?'

'Maybe not, but not many men are as dedicated as he was to his farming and his animals, and I found I shared his interests. He was devoted to his family too. He missed my mother dreadfully when she died. Fortunately sharing his interest meant we were never lost for things to discuss, or to plan.'

'I reckon that's the best kind of relationship to have. Too many young folks disparage their parents, especially if they can't get their own way. I was lucky with mine. They truly cared about each other and they cared about me. I know my mother must have grieved terribly over my sisters, but she never made me feel I was less loved. They always welcomed my friends. Jenny is actually my second cousin, but Mum has always treated her like her own well-loved niece. Jenny's father and mine were cousins. Ah, we're here already. Now to search for a parking space . . .' It was a large car park, but there were a lot of people already there. They circled slowly down one side and back up another.

'There's one over there, beside that wall, under the trees.' Roxie pointed.

'It's a bit dark over there. Are you sure you don't mind?'

'Of course not. That's probably why there's a space and it looks fairly wide so I shouldn't have too much trouble getting out to come home.' She gave a little cough. 'Ahem, especially if you're drunk as a lord and can't remember where we parked!'

'I shall remember that cheeky remark — expect comeback before the night is over,' Ciaran said with a chuckle. 'I will reverse in while there is plenty of room, though. That will make it easier to get away.'

Ciaran came round to the passenger door to help her out, then tucked her into his side, holding her close, not that Roxie minded. She felt warm and safe. She knew she was getting far too aware of Ciaran's charms.

'Are you still sure you don't mind driving us home?' he asked, so close his breath tickled her ear.

'I'm quite sure. I feel honoured to be here at all, and my ticket paid too.'

Ciaran switched on the torch on his phone so they could see where they were putting their feet. 'It's a long while since I've been out and about, so I haven't seen most of the old crowd for a bit. I hope I don't get offered too many drinks to make up for lost time, even though I know I can rely on you to get me safely home, Roxie.'

'Presumably you had your reasons for not socialising?' she murmured thoughtfully, wondering if it was due to losing Amanda.

'Not really. I have known them all well enough for years, but it was not the same after Don got married. I suppose he was always more sociable than I was. He made arrangements and I usually went along with them, the same as he bought the tickets for tonight. We've been friends since we were at the academy — school — together. We joined the Young Farmers' when we were old enough and went to most events. That was until I invited Don to stay at Oaklands for a weekend when he was home from university. Jenny happened to be staying too. The rest is history, but they do seem happy together.'

'They're a lovely couple. You can't regret bringing them together?'

'No, I don't, not a bit. We're still good friends.'

As they emerged from the shadows into the lights from the hotel, Ciaran switched off the torch and put his phone away.

Someone called his name and he half turned, but kept her firmly at his side. They were surrounded by a group of laughing people around Ciaran's age, all wanting to know where he had been for the past year or more. Three persistent young men, all in kilts and already a little merry, wanted to know the name of the lovely lady and why he was keeping her so close.

Laughing good-naturedly, Ciaran parried their questions but told them nothing about his partner, except to keep their hands off.

The dinner was delicious and the company lively, with a great deal of repartee. A few couples and several single men swapped tables between the courses, often confusing the smiling servers. It was obvious to Roxanne that both Donald and Ciaran were popular, and that their company at some of the gatherings had been missed. Jenny knew a lot of people, but not all of them because she had been away at university and a member of a different Young Farmers' Club before she'd met Donald.

Eventually the band started tuning up in the ballroom and people began to drift through for the dancing. There were banquettes around the large room, with small drinks tables and odd chairs here and there along both sides. As soon as the dancing began, Ciaran claimed her for his partner and Donald drew Jenny to her feet.

Although Ciaran was tall and broad-shouldered, he was surprisingly light on his feet. Roxie enjoyed dancing and she remarked on his expertise.

'Don and I were members of the Scottish country dancing team for a couple of years in our early teens,' he said with a grin. 'Do you know any Scottish reels?'

'No, I don't. I shall enjoy sitting down to watch you all in your kilts demonstrating the various moves.'

'Don't you believe it.' He laughed. 'You will not get the chance to sit out, but don't worry — there are plenty of fellows only too eager to show you the moves, and don't be surprised if one or two tuck you under their arm and lift you sometimes if the moves are complicated.'

'I doubt if any of them would manage that. I'm neither small nor skinny.'

'You wait and see.' Ciaran grinned. 'Do you know how to do the Gay Gordons?'

'I don't think so, although I have heard of it.'

'Save that for me. I will teach you the steps. One of my favourites is the Pride of Erin Waltz so if you hear it being announced, say you're booked for that and I shall find you wherever you are.'

'If Jenny wants to rest a bit between dances, I think I should keep her company. After all, it is due to Jenny that I'm here at all.'

'We'll see. She usually enjoys the dancing, but I suppose she might tire a bit now.'

The evening seemed to speed by and Roxie never lacked for partners. She was astonished to find herself tucked under someone's arm more than once though, in line with Ciaran's prediction. He was as good as his word and made sure he claimed her for both the dances he had mentioned and one or two besides.

'I see Ciaran is keeping his eye on you,' one of her partners said with a chuckle. 'How about saving the last dance for me instead?'

'I can't do that.' Roxie smiled. 'I pr—'

'Promised Ciaran! I should have known. Well, I can't grudge him having the prettiest girl in the room. He has not had the easiest of times in recent years between his father being ill and then dying when they thought he was on the mend. Then his mother had a nasty accident and Ciaran has always cared deeply for his parents.'

'That is a quality I admire in anyone,' Roxie said quietly.

'Yes, I guess you're right, but it's more of a responsibility being an only one. Now me, I have a twin brother and three sisters. Sometimes I could see them all far enough.' He grinned.

'Ah, I thought I had seen another blond-haired man very like you. Are you identical twins?'

'We are, and I can see my shadow coming this way now, determined to claim you for the next dance.' He gave a theatrical sigh. 'Some things I would rather not need to share.'

All too soon the evening was coming to an end and people were getting their last drinks ready to welcome in the New Year. Roxie looked across to the table that Jenny and Donald had more or less claimed as theirs for the evening. Ciaran was moving in that direction, too, and he held up a glass for her with a smile and a nod. She nodded and made her way to join him the moment the dance ended.

'It is only tonic water — is that all right?' Ciaran asked anxiously, handing her her glass. She grinned happily and took the glass as midnight chimed. There were cheers and laughter, hugs and kisses, and Roxie knew she had never expected to feel so happy after the shock and grief of her father's death. Ciaran wrapped his arms around her and tilted her face to his. Their eyes locked. She could see his intention. She smiled and nodded happily. It was no fleeting kiss. He held her tenderly as his mouth claimed hers in a lingering exploration. Roxie found herself responding in a way she had never done with any other man. She was sorry when someone she had danced with earlier interrupted them.

'Give another man a chance, Ciaran, old boy.' Ciaran grimaced at the man, but he had no option but to release her. Then Donald came and rescued her with a hug, and a kiss on the cheek.

'It's been a wonderful evening, Roxie. Jenny and I are both so pleased you agreed to come with us.'

'I have thoroughly enjoyed it. Thank you both for making it possible.'

'We're going to get away now if we can. Jenny is feeling tired, but we shall see you all tomorrow for dinner mid-afternoon?'

'That's right. Happy New Year, Jenny!' She gave her new friend a warm hug and kissed her cheek. 'Thanks for everything,' she said softly. Jenny smiled and nodded. Ciaran had not moved far from Roxie's side and he asked if she was ready to leave as well. His words were very slightly slurred and Roxie smiled. She had heard a lot of his friends pressing drinks on him, although he had declined several. She wondered if he would remember the way he had kissed her by tomorrow. She suspected he would have no recollection, but she knew she would not forget. It concerned her a bit that she had never felt like responding to any man as she had to Ciaran tonight. Perhaps it was the atmosphere and the season of goodwill, but in her heart she knew it was more than that.

Chapter 9

The celebrations were over and the weather had turned bitterly cold. Amy was less inclined to venture out when the pavements were slippery with ice or after snow, but Roxie continued to enjoy a brisk walk each afternoon, dressed in the woollen hat and matching mittens that Amy had knitted for her. She sometimes regretted leaving so many of her possessions behind in her bedroom at home, but was glad she'd brought her thicker trousers and her padded anorak to keep out the cold wind.

Even in the depths of winter the garden never looked stark or bare, with the golden leaves of the privet, the variegated holly and the euonymus, as well as the darker green of rhododendrons. A few of the winter heathers were in bloom and the first snowdrops nodded their dainty white heads.

She had felt a little self-conscious with Ciaran after the intimate kiss they had exchanged at Hogmanay, and she wondered if he remembered it quite as clearly as she did. Sometimes she caught him watching her with a puzzled look. He had taken to calling most days unless he was at the market or had other business to attend. It was usually around midday when he appeared, so Roxie got into the habit of making sure there was plenty of soup or pudding and whatever they were having for meat. Amy was always happy to see him and encouraged Roxie to prepare extra food. She was always generous, especially regarding money spent on food. She had explained that she kept a credit card specially for household expenses. When the weather was uncertain, she gave Roxie the card and told her to keep the supplies well stocked in case of snowstorms.

'I have never grudged the money spent on good food so if you don't mind the extra cooking, it will please me if Ciaran wants to join us every day for his midday meal.'

Roxie had been used to keeping a good stock of food for her father so was happy to continue doing the same for Amy, but she was meticulous about presenting the itemised bills. She had done the same with her father, even though he had never looked at them.

Gradually she had got to know Sam Green, the butcher in Thornielee, quite well, after Amy introduced her. He chattered all the time as he cut and weighed, wrapped and priced. He always told her if he had a particularly good joint of meat or some well-hung beef. He remembered Amy's particular preferences well. Sometimes he butchered one of Ciaran's own lambs or pigs for the freezer as a favour.

'Amy was always a good customer with my father,' he told Roxie. 'We like to look after the folks who look after us, and don't buy everything from the supermarket for the sake of a few pennies.'

One morning when she had gone in to buy bacon and some liver, he told her he had some good lamb chops if she was interested. He gave her a quizzical look, then remarked with a grin, 'I hear Ciaran has his dinner at the bungalow most days since his mother got a pretty young housekeeper who cooks like an angel.' Roxie knew she was blushing and cursed her fair skin.

'I doubt if angels do much cooking,' she mumbled. Sam winked at her.

'Maybe not, but it's true what they say, the way to a man's heart is his stomach. Ciaran is a grand fellow. He would make a good husband for a lassie like yourself.' Roxie didn't know what to say in reply. 'Iris told us,' Sam went on conversationally. 'Ciaran told her what a grand cook ye are. She's glad about that. She never cooks for herself and Joe, except bacon and sausages. Joe enjoys our steak pies, aye, and a Scotch pie on Saturdays. Cooked roast beef or ham on Sundays in the summer.' Roxie wondered if he knew the favourite meals of all his customers. Iris and Joe were a pleasant middle-aged couple and had both welcomed Roxie warmly.

Whatever their diet they both kept fit, healthy and active, and Iris had made no secret that she was relieved to know Roxie had taken over the cooking, and brought such cheer to the mistress, as she always referred to Amy.

* * *

It was dark and very cold when the main telephone rang early one Sunday morning at the beginning of February. Roxie always slept with her door ajar in case Amy should need her during the night, so the phone in the hall wakened her immediately. She looked at her little alarm clock. It was not five o'clock yet. She knew Amy had an extension beside her bed, but why would anyone be phoning so early unless there was something wrong? Could it be Jenny? The baby? She pulled on her dressing gown and shoved her feet into her slippers to hurry down the stairs. Amy always left her bedroom door slightly open. She was speaking, but she sounded sleepy and a bit irritable. Roxie tapped on the door and pushed it wider.

'Is anything wrong?' she asked softly.

'Ciaran, Roxie is right here in my bedroom. The phone must have woken her too,' she said crossly. Ciaran must have spoken again so Roxie waited.

Amy protested. 'But Ciaran, you can't ask her to do all that! Especially on her own, and on a cold winter's morning. But — but Roxie is in my care. What about the relief man you got when

Billy broke his leg?' Amy listened again, then heaved a huge sigh of exasperation. She looked at Roxie.

'Ciaran wants you to do him a big favour. A huge favour, I call it. Refuse if you want, lassie. I would not blame you. He was at a pedigree-cattle sale yesterday. He bought chicken on a roll from the refreshment van. He was late and he got the last one they had. He thinks it must have been off. He is ill with food poisoning, spent the whole night at the toilet, he says. It is Billy's weekend off so he is away with his pals on their motorbikes. Their football team was playing up north somewhere. He will not be back until later today. The man who helped before is doing relief milking for a week over at Glenluce . . .'

'Does he want me to do the milking?' Roxie asked and moved closer to the bed. Amy handed her the phone with a resigned sigh. She listened to Ciaran.

'All right, I'll get dressed and be there as soon as I can. At least it's winter so the cows are all indoors. I don't need to gather them in from the field. That will save time. I'll phone you on my mobile once I get there and have made a start. You shouldn't have used the main phone. You have given your mother a shock,' she said severely.

Ciaran began to speak, but she interrupted sharply.

'No, stay where you are! Don't dare come outside. I don't want to bring any stomach bugs back here to your mother. Oh, and my grandma swore by boiled milk with a good swig of brandy in it, no sugar. Try that, but the milk must come to the boil to dry you up.' She put the phone down, knowing she had been a bit abrupt, especially when Ciaran was probably feeling rotten after being up all night. He must feel awful or he would never have asked for her help, even as a last resort. She looked at Amy with some concern.

'You will promise to stay in bed until I can get back, won't you?' she asked anxiously. 'Shall I make you a hot drink before I leave?'

'A drink of the fresh orange juice and some plain biscuits would be very nice, dear. You must eat something yourself before you go.'

'I will bring yours now and get the same for myself. I can eat while I get dressed, or on my way down to the farm.' Roxie hurried away. She knew it was imperative to get the cows milked and the milk cooled to a sufficiently low temperature in the bulk milk tank before the lorry arrived to collect it at seven forty-five. Everything had to be clean and cold, otherwise the creamery could refuse to accept it and that would be a week's profits gone. She understood such things well enough and hoped Tommy had not had to find out the hard way. She felt a little pang of longing for her father. Tommy had never been good at getting up early and he had never found any fulfilment in milking, as she and her father had done.

Roxie knew Ciaran would be listening for the milking-machine engine to start so that he knew she had arrived. The noise also alerted the cows in their cubicle shed and let them know it was time for milking. They were more intelligent than many people believed and the leaders would start coming into the milking parlour of their own accord. They had their own order of precedence at coming in for milking, often the high yielders coming first to have their swollen udders relieved of the weight of milk they had produced overnight, as well as to get their ration of tasty cattle cake that automatically poured into each trough according to the cow's number on the computer. That way they munched contentedly while the vacuum machine relieved them of their milk. Roxie had always found the milking routine satisfying, but she hated when things had to be rushed. She waited until she had fixed the teat clusters onto each animal down both sides of the milking parlour, then she took out her phone and dialled Ciaran as she had promised.

'I didn't have your mobile number, Roxie. Is Mum all right after I disturbed her?'

'Yes, she says she will read if she can't get back to sleep.'

'I shall have your number now, but I'm truly sorry to ask you to do this. I will repay you somehow.'

'Oh, Ciaran, people don't think about repayment when it's an emergency. I must keep going, though. I don't want to be late for the milk tanker.'

'I phoned the company. The driver is going to make a detour and pick up two neighbouring farms first. That should give you about three quarters of an hour extra time.'

'Oh, thanks. That's a relief. While you're on the phone, there are two cows with red tapes around their tails. Is that significant?'

'Oh, gosh! I'll say it is. The ones marked red have been treated with antibiotics for mastitis. On no account let the milk go in with the rest. The creamery makes cheese and antibiotics prevent the starter from working properly. I would get a big penalty if that happened.'

'Fine. I have seen one with a blue tape so . . .'

'There will be two. They are newly calved so I keep the colostrum separate for feeding their young calves. I'll wait until about six thirty, then phone young Vic. He will come and do the cleaning and hosing down, and feed the older calves. Do you think you could manage to feed the young ones? I'm dreadfully sorry to ask so much of you, Roxie, but . . .'

'Don't worry about it. I'm glad I had seen the parlour at Christmas so it's not so strange. I must get on. Try to get some sleep, but don't come near the milk today. It's not safe if you have picked up a bug. I will come back for the afternoon milking unless Billy has returned from his football match.'

'Thanks. I will let you know as soon as I get hold of him. I think he will be home before afternoon milking. Oh, I meant to say, I bought an in-calf pedigree heifer and a younger one at the sale. They're in the small loose box if you wouldn't mind checking on them?'

All went well, and both Roxie and Vic beamed with pleasure when the tanker driver arrived and complimented them both on getting everything done and cleaned up. In typical country fashion, he also spread the news at the remaining farms he visited, telling everyone Ciaran had got himself a capable young woman to do the milking for him, and a pretty one at that. Fortunately, Roxie knew nothing of the gossip, but it was not long before his neighbours were pestering Ciaran with questions and giving him advice about choosing a good wife. Worse still were the ones who teased Billy, the Oaklands' stockman, telling him Ciaran had got a young woman who could do his job as well as he could. They didn't intend to cause the festering resentment that began to eat at Billy, but he had already heard from Vic that a young woman had helped Ciaran with the milking on Christmas Day.

Chapter 10

Ciaran was not sure whether Roxie's grandma's recipe had helped or whether the stomach upset had run its course, but after a good night's sleep he felt more like himself again. Even so, he did not go near Oaklands View for five days to make sure he didn't spread any infection to his mother or Roxie. They both thought he seemed subdued when he did arrive for his lunch again.

Roxanne knew there were several cows due to calve and it was Ciaran who always attended to them, partly because Billy's house was a distance away from the farm and he needed to be up early in the mornings to get the milking done so could not be expected to be up during the night as well if a cow needed help, as so often seemed to happen. It was true, Ciaran had had several disturbed nights, but he was pleased he'd not lost any calves and the cows were all producing well. What really troubled him was Billy's moodiness, almost as though he resented someone else doing his job, even though he had not been available himself. He didn't realise that Billy detested the thought that a mere woman could do what he did, and he did not take kindly to the leg-pulling from the tanker driver and several other locals.

It was about two weeks later when Ciaran asked Roxie if she would like to go with him to the little theatre in Dumfries. He seemed unusually diffident about asking her.

'It is a very small theatre, you know. The performers are not professionals as you would see in Edinburgh or Glasgow.'

'I would be happy to give it a try so long as your mother doesn't mind me leaving her on her own for the evening.'

'I'm sure she will think you deserve a night out,' Ciaran said. 'We'll ask her.'

'Ask me what?' Amy was making her way into the kitchen.

'If Roxie can go with me to the theatre in Dumfries.' Ciaran grinned.

'Of course she can go! You don't need my permission, Roxie, if I know you are going out. It's a lovely little theatre, the oldest in Scotland. I believe Robert Burns, Scotland's famous bard, is supposed to have been a regular visitor, as well as the man who wrote *Peter Pan*, or so they tell us.'

'J. M. Barrie went there? I loved *Peter Pan* when I was a little girl.' Roxie smiled at the memory. 'If it was good enough for such illustrious people, then it is good enough for me. Are Donald and Jenny coming too?'

'No.' Ciaran frowned. 'I didn't ask them. Do you mind us going on our own?'

'Of course not. I'm flattered you asked me.'

'You might not be if the performance isn't as good as you're expecting. We shall need to have an early tea so I'll pick you up about six thirty.'

* * *

Ciaran was a little late, but Roxie was waiting and hurried out to the car. He was still eating the remains of a sandwich.

'Had a bit of a delay,' he mumbled. 'A cow with milk fever. I didn't want to leave her until I saw she was going to be all right. I think the calcium has done the trick.'

Although it was a cold night, the sky was clear with the stars shining brightly. Roxie wished she'd brought her smart winter coat with her instead of her anorak. In the end, she had opted for her blue tweed suit. She'd managed to get her anorak on top, but it was warm in the car.

She was fascinated with the small theatre. It seemed warm and friendly, and nothing like the big impersonal theatres often shown on television. She had only been to a London theatre once and that had been while she was still at school.

'That man has a lovely voice,' she whispered close to Ciaran's ear during the applause for a particularly good performance. It was a light musical and the costumes were colourful and seemed to suit the characters. There was an enjoyable duet between another tenor and quite a good soprano, but Roxie was pleased when her favourite performer of the evening came on again for the finale.

As they made their way back to the car, Roxie repeated how much she had enjoyed the performance, and especially the male soloist.

'Yes, we-ell, he was always a good singer even when he was a choirboy and he was always in the school concerts. He enjoyed performing.'

'You know him? You were at school together?'

'Yes, that's partly why I bought the tickets, but I hoped you would enjoy it.'

'Oh, I did, I really did.'

'These days, Daniel is a bank manager.'

'Really? In my humble opinion he is a lot better singer than many we hear on television.'

'I agree, but I imagine acting could be an uncertain profession. Daniel always worked hard at school and he did well, too. His parents were not all that wealthy and he has two brothers, so I expect he opted for a more secure occupation and kept the theatre for a hobby he enjoys.'

'Mmm, a wise man then, and his talents made the evening for me.'

'So,' Ciaran said hesitantly. 'If I hear they are putting on another evening show around Easter, will you come again?'

'I would love to, so long as you enjoy it too,' she said shyly.

'I do, especially with good company.' He gave her a warm smile. 'Er, I didn't get much tea. Do you mind if we stop for fish and chips?'

'Of course I don't mind. We passed a fish-and-chip shop on the way here, didn't we?'

'Yes. It's the best one, if I can get stopped there.'

'I will run in and get what you want if you find a place to wait. What do you like? Fish and chips, salt? Vinegar?'

'Everything, and mushy peas as well if they have them. What are you having?'

'I'll just ask for a small portion for myself to keep you company. Shall I bring you a drink?'

'Yes, please. Anything will do, so long as it's wet.' He looked at her with a faint smile. 'You know, I did wonder if you were disappointed I had not asked Jenny and Don tonight. I'm never sure where I stand with you. Sometimes I think we get on well together on our own, but I don't know how you feel.'

'I think I'm always the same, but I do feel your mother's care must be my priority. Now we have discovered we have some interests in common, like the farm and breeding cattle, we always have things to talk about.'

'Yes, we do, but there are other more pers . . . Ah, here we are.'

Roxie wondered what else he had been going to say.

'Looks like you'll have to double park. I'll run in and get them if you wait in the car, ready to move if needed.' Without waiting for an answer, Roxie jumped out.

The service was fairly fast as fresh batches of fish and chips were being lifted out as she entered the shop, and there was still plenty left when it came to her turn. The smell had made her hungry too, but she knew she would never eat a whole fish supper herself.

'Mmm, the smell makes me famished,' Ciaran said as she climbed back into the car. 'I will drive a bit further along the road. I know a turnoff where it will be less busy.' He soon found the turning he wanted and parked on the grass verge beneath some trees. They both tucked in with relish, but, after eating the fish, Roxie knew she could never finish all the chips, even though she had asked for a small portion. She hated wasting food.

'Want me to help you?' Ciaran asked with a grin.

'Yes, if you can?' She moved closer to him, but instead of putting the chip in his own mouth he fed it to her with a chuckle, before eating a couple himself.

'They were extra good or I was extra hungry,' Ciaran said as he started the car again.

'A bit of both, I think.' Roxie smiled. 'If you had told me you hadn't had any tea, I would have brought you something to eat while I drove us here.' They chatted in a friendly manner all the way back until Ciaran drew the car to a halt outside her door.

'That was a lovely evening,' Roxie said with a sigh. 'Thank you for taking me.' He turned towards her.

'So, do I get a goodnight kiss?' he asked. Roxie leaned closer, expecting him to kiss her cheek, but he cupped her chin and turned her face to his. He kissed her tenderly on her mouth.

'I'm pleased you came,' he said softly when he released her. 'I wanted to repay you for milking all the cows for me. I don't believe I ever thanked you properly.'

'Oh,' Roxie said flatly. 'I would help any friend in an emergency. Good night.'

Ciaran knew by her tone, and the brisk way she got out of the car and slammed the door, that he had said or done something that had not pleased her.

Roxie chewed her lower lip as she unlocked the door and let herself in. She was not a weepy person, but, for some reason, she felt her eyes filling with tears. She tried to blink them away when she heard Amy call from the sitting room.

'I'm ready for bed, Roxie, but I thought I would wait to hear how you enjoyed your first visit to our little theatre.'

'I enjoyed it very much,' Roxie replied and wished she didn't need to see Amy face-to-face for once.

'Come on in, dear and tell me about it. Was it a good performance? Some of them are very talented, although they all have other jobs to do.'

'Yes, they were good. One man was especially good. Ciaran seemed to know him.'

'That would be Daniel. I remember him in the school concerts. He is a talented young man. He often won at the music festivals when he was younger. So, what bit didn't you enjoy?' Amy asked shrewdly.

'I-I enjoyed it all. Ciaran was famished so we stopped for fish and chips. He demolished them in no time. He'd had to skip tea due to a cow with milk fever.' Roxie knew she was babbling.

'I see. But, Roxie, my dear, I can see by your expression that something has upset you.'

Roxie couldn't stop herself from blurting it out. 'I'm not upset. I thought he enjoyed my company, but he only took me to repay me for doing the milking for him! Friends don't need repaying for helping out. I wouldn't have gone if I'd known he was only doing it for that reason.'

'I am sure Ciaran did want your company, my dear. I know him well enough to know he would not spend an evening with you if he didn't enjoy being with you. He would have bought a big box of chocolates or a bottle of perfume to repay you.'

'I . . . I think I'll go to bed now. Would you like me to make you a hot drink first?'

'No, thanks, my dear. I'm ready for my bed too. I do hope you sleep well.'

* * *

The following day, Ciaran arrived at midday for his dinner, which had become a daily occurrence unless he was working in one of the more distant fields, when he carried a flask and sandwiches to save time travelling home with the tractor. As soon as she heard the pickup, Amy tapped on the window and beckoned him into her sitting room so he kicked off his boots and went in at the front door.

'What did you say to upset Roxie yesterday evening?' Amy asked in a low voice.

'And a good day to you too, Mum.' Ciaran mocked his mother irritably.

'Roxie is not someone who resorts to tears, but I am sure she had a struggle to hold them back when she came home last night.'

'I thought she had enjoyed the evening as much as I did.' His colour heightened as he remembered their goodnight kiss. He frowned. He really wasn't sure what he had said or done to spoil things.

'Ciaran, I know Roxanne Carr is different to the giggly girls you and Don used to take out. She is more mature, capable and competent at everything I have seen her undertake so far, but you have to remember she has had a lot of upsets in recent times, losing her father so suddenly, leaving the only home and work she had ever known. I know how much she appreciates the emails from her friends, especially news and photographs from the girl who has the twins, her best friend, Lucy, but she never hears anything from her brother or his new wife. That is bound to hurt.'

'I had no intention of hurting her!' Ciaran said crossly.

'Then what did you say?'

'I don't know, damn it! Everything was fine until she got out of the car. Oh, I said I wanted to repay her for doing the milking for me . . .' He frowned. 'She said goodnight and slammed the door.'

'Don't you see?' His mother shook her head. 'She wanted you to take her because you enjoy her company, not to *repay* her for anything.'

'I do enjoy her company!' Ciaran said. 'I'm never sure if she enjoys mine, though.'

'Of course she enjoys your company or she wouldn't have gone with you. Why shouldn't she enjoy your company? You're an eligible young man and a hard worker. I expect I'm prejudiced, but you're quite handsome when you're scrubbed up. You can be charming, too, when it suits — in fact, you have a pleasant manner when you don't lose your temper.'

'You're definitely prejudiced,' Ciaran said drily. 'Now, I'm hungry and ready for some dinner.'

'Maybe you are, but let me tell you this, son. If I could have had a girl tailor-made to be your wife, I couldn't have chosen one more suited than Roxanne. She even shares your interest and knowledge of breeding cattle. Amanda never showed any interest in your work.'

'Mum, I was genuinely sad when Amanda was killed. We were good friends, but I know we would never have got as far as marriage, even if we had got round to getting engaged to please you when you were so keen to get Dad moved out of the farm.'

'I see . . . One more thing though, Ciaran. You are the only child I have so it's important to me that I like the girl you marry, although I would always try not to interfere if I did disapprove. I think I have got to know Roxie very well in the time she has been here and she is almost like a daughter.' For a moment her face clouded, remembering the two small daughters of her own, now buried in the churchyard.

'Mother, we all know how you feel, but I can't make a girl love me to suit you, however much I might want her.' Ciaran sighed. 'Let's have our dinner now.'

* * *

It was impossible for Roxie to stay aloof with Ciaran, and deep down she felt they were good friends. If only she was not so unsure of herself. They were easy in each other's company. She enjoyed their witty exchanges and his teasing, but deep down she knew she wanted more. Her heart always beat faster whenever he was near, and especially when he kissed her.

* * *

Roxie got a shock when she read the latest email from Lucy. Usually, she was full of the twins' latest achievements and news of mutual friends. This email concerned only Tommy and Gilda.

> *I expect Tommy will have telephoned to tell you they had a baby son on the tenth of February, 'supposedly' two months premature, according to Gilda, but he must be a decent weight when they have already been discharged from hospital. They are staying with her parents.*
>
> *Steve says people are speculating about things. I expect he means because Tommy only returned home from Australia in July. Gilda and her family had moved down here from Glasgow while he was away, so he had never met her until he returned home. Steve thinks they met for the first time when his old gang took him to the club that had opened during his absence. My cousin, Celia, thinks there may be other reasons for speculation, but she didn't say what. It is more than her job is worth to gossip.*

There was a little more general news and the usual good wishes.

'You look pale,' Amy said when she came into the kitchen and saw Roxie putting her phone into her trouser pocket.

'I have had an email from Lucy, my friend.'

'She usually cheers you up with news of your little god-daughters. I hope they are both well?'

'Yes. She thought I would have heard from Tommy, my brother. He and Gilda have got a baby boy. Gilda says he is two months premature, but they have already left the hospital. Why hasn't Tommy let me know? I can never get him on his mobile and he never gets in touch. We were always the best of friends. He sent me lots of emails when he was abroad and phoned a couple of times. He had not been home long when he met Gilda. Nothing seems to have been the same since. My father urged him to wait a while before getting married — in fact they quarrelled over it.'

'I see. I supposed he had known his wife before he went away and . . .'

'No, he only met Gilda after he came home from Australia. That's what troubled my father. He was so concerned that he changed his will just before their wedding.'

'Would you like to take a few days' holiday and go to visit them, Roxie? I could stay with Ciaran until you return.'

'I think if they had wanted me to know, they would have sent word. Anyway, Gilda and the baby are staying with her parents.'

'I have knitted one small jacket for Jenny's baby. Would you like to send it to them with a card? Maybe it will let them know you wish them well?'

'It's very kind of you. Will you let me buy it from you?'

'Of course not, dear. Or if you thought it wouldn't be your gift if you didn't pay, you can buy me the wool to make another for Jenny's baby. I do enjoy the knitting. It helps me pass the time while I am not so active.'

'Yes, I will do that. I will drive into Thornielee and buy a card. I can replace the wool at the shop where we went before.'

Roxie bought some pretty blue paper and wrapped up the lovely little garment with a baby card.

Amy never asked if she had received a thank-you letter from Tommy or Gilda. She would probably have seen a letter if one had arrived, and she knew Roxie would have told her if they had phoned to acknowledge her gift, but there was nothing.

* * *

It was the beginning of May before Ciaran asked Roxie if she would like to go with him to the theatre again.

'It's their version of *The Sound of Music*. It will not be anything like the film, of course, but I thought you might enjoy the music. Daniel will be in it again.'

'I would love to go, if you're sure you want my company?'

'Oh, Roxie, of course I want your company!'

Surely she must realise how much I miss her if I don't see her for a day? he thought with a frown. Even half a day and he was looking for an excuse. He missed her smile. He missed her teasing. Oh, God, she had really got under his skin. He grasped her shoulders and turned her to look at him.

'I wouldn't ask you if I didn't enjoy your company, Roxie. I thought you must know that. Or would you be fishing for compliments?' he asked with a hesitant smile.

It was indeed another lovely evening with just the two of them. The performance was excellent, including the children's singing. Both Roxie and Ciaran sang with enthusiasm when the audience was invited to join in.

'I don't need fish and chips this time,' Ciaran said on the way home. 'But I will stop for some if you're peckish.'

'No, thanks. I'm not hungry. We have had a lovely evening without the chips.'

'I'm glad you enjoyed it. They must put in a lot of work rehearsing.'

When he drew the car to a halt, Ciaran simply turned to her and drew her gently into his arms. Roxie found herself winding her arms around his neck and responding with a passion that seemed to affect her whole body, in places she had never considered before.

'It has been a wonderful evening, Roxie,' he murmured softly as he nibbled her ear, before his mouth found hers again, and again . . . Reluctantly they drew apart. Ciaran sighed. 'I expect Mum will have heard the car. She will be wondering why I'm keeping you out.' Roxie opened the car door to climb out but she laughed softly.

'Your mother is a wise woman and she was young herself once. I expect she knows the sort of things her son gets up to.'

'I suppose you're right, but I don't want to let you go.'

'I know.' Roxie smiled and her eyes sparkled.

'Is there any chance you might feel the same, Roxie?'

'There's always a chance,' Roxie replied lightly as she gently closed the car door.

* * *

Amy was pleased to see Roxie still smiling when she entered her sitting room. She looked happy.

Chapter 11

One lovely morning in May, Amy was at home, but Roxie had driven to Dumfries on her own to do some shopping, both for herself and for Amy, including household goods. Jenny's baby had been born a few days ago, a little earlier than the due date, but he was a fine, healthy boy. The beautiful shawl Amy had been knitting on and off for months was almost finished and she was determined to complete it today so that she could get Roxie to pin out all the delicate lacy points onto a bedsheet on the floor. Once everything was absolutely in perfect shape, they could give it a light press with a cool iron. It was a delicate work of art. The fine one-ply wool had taken a lot of effort, but Amy knew it had been worth it. She was sure Jenny would appreciate it and maybe use it for the christening along with the beautiful christening robe Roxie had made and embroidered with white silk thread. They might even become a family heirloom.

Roxie had made no further mention to Amy of what she planned to do with her life, except to say she knew she didn't want to spend several years studying at university. Amy was seriously considering having another operation and if she was going to do it, she wanted to have it done while Roxie was still around to look after her. She had seen a surgeon privately recently. He told her frankly there was always a risk, but he could almost guarantee she would walk without pain, and hopefully without a limp, if it was the success he anticipated. It would involve re-breaking the femur and setting it in line with her hip joint, instead of the way it had knitted together at a slight angle. She would have the whole of her leg in plaster for several weeks until it was completely healed.

Amy was debating what she should do when the telephone rang on the small table beside her chair. It took her a few moments to realise that the caller was Roxie's brother, Tommy. He was speaking quickly, obviously agitated. His accent made it more difficult to understand quite what was so urgent. She interrupted Tommy to tell him Roxie was not available at present.

'She has gone into town, but she should be back by twelve o'clock. Can I give her a message?'

'I need her help! I am selling off the dairy herd. All of it!' Amy could hear a desperation in his voice. 'The . . . the sale is fixed for two weeks on M-Monday. Roxanne has always known more about the cows than I ever did. My father showed her how to prepare them for sale. How to trim them to look their best. She knew all the pedigrees. S-some of the records have g-got in a muddle, and—'

'Just a minute, young man.' Tommy was obviously upset, he was almost gabbling and Amy was having difficulty understanding him. He sounded young and distraught. 'So, it is nothing wrong with the baby, then? You want me to tell Roxie you need her help sorting out all the pedigrees of your dairy herd so a catalogue can be printed. Have I got that correct?'

'Yes, but I need her to come! I really need her to help me! Please tell her I need her badly to prepare the cows for sale. I know I don't deserve her help. B-but please, please ask her if she will come for our father's sake, if not for mine. He deserved better than I can do. Tell her — tell her he was right about — about everything.'

'When do you want Roxie to come?'

'She will need at least ten days before the sale . . . She was always good at organising. She often won the cattle-dressing competitions. The auctioneer hopes she will be here before the sale.'

'I'm sure Roxie will do her best. I shall ask her to telephone you.'

'Ask her to use the landline. I don't have a mobile now. I will wait in the house to hear from her.'

Amy put the phone down. He certainly sounded overwrought.

Amy rarely phoned Ciaran during his work, but she called his mobile now. She explained about Tommy's phone call.

'I just want to warn you not to get angry if you are here when I tell Roxie about her brother's plea for help. She must go and help him, Ciaran. He is her brother — her only brother. Family is important and he is all she has. I know how hurt Roxie has been by their silence. He admits he doesn't deserve her help. I could stay with you for ten days while she is away.'

'What if she decides to stay there?' Ciaran asked tensely.

'I am certain Roxie would give me some warning if she did feel she must go back, but why should she go back if her brother is selling the dairy herd? That was her main interest, that, and looking after her father.'

'I hope you're right,' Ciaran said. Amy heard the dejection in his voice. She prayed she was right and that Roxie would return to them. She was almost certain Roxie and Ciaran were meant for each other.

Amy telephoned Jenny next. The phone rang a long time, but eventually Jenny picked up and Amy wondered if she'd been crying. Young babies could make a mother very tired, especially if the birth had taken a lot out of her.

After the preliminary greetings, Amy said, 'I was phoning to say I am going to stay with Ciaran for ten days next week. Roxie is out shopping so she doesn't know yet, but her brother phoned this morning. He wants her to go down to Derbyshire to help him organise the sale of their father's pedigree dairy herd. I promised to tell her when she returns. He is all the family she has, even if they have not treated her very kindly. She will have to go. I'm afraid Ciaran is not too happy about it.'

'Is that because he thinks she might not come back? Or is he worried about you staying at the farm if he will be working at the silage during the day?'

'Both, I think. But we don't own Roxie and she never takes time off. Besides I got the impression her brother genuinely needs her.'

'Oh, Aunt Amy, I don't think I'm a very good mother,' Jenny said tearfully. 'I never know why Peter is crying and whether I should feed him, rock him or change him. I know I wouldn't be much help to you, but if you want company at the farm I'd love to come. I'm sure you could advise me about Peter. I know Don wouldn't mind travelling to work from there for ten days or so.'

'By the sound of things, Jenny, the change will do you good, too. I was half-hoping you might suggest coming to keep me company. I'm not much use, but I can still nurse a baby or rock the pram and I would love to spend time with you and wee Peter.'

'I'm so glad you said that, Aunt Amy. I was feeling at the end of my tether. There's no one else I can ask for advice.'

* * *

Roxie had had a good morning shopping and she drove home in high spirits. She was surprised to see Ciaran's pickup already parked at the side of the house. She glanced at her watch, but it was still only quarter to twelve and it was usually after midday before he came. It was a regular arrangement now and they usually waited for him if he was a bit late. She hurried in at the back door with her grocery bags and was surprised to hear both Amy and Ciaran talking in the kitchen.

'I'm not late, am I?' She quickly pushed the pan of soup onto the hot plate, then washed her hands. Without stopping to take off her jacket, she dashed back through to the utility room to grab the garlic batons she had bought and thrust them in the oven.

'The soup will soon be ready. I made ham-and-cheese sandwiches ready for toasting before I went out, but I need to put the freezer shopping away first.'

'There's no hurry, lassie,' Amy said calmly. 'Ciaran was here early and we were only talking things over. Relax and take your coat off.'

Ciaran volunteered to toast the sandwiches while Roxie put the shopping away.

'The soup smells good,' Ciaran said. 'You must have been up early to be so organised.'

They all ate with relish, but Roxie had a feeling something was bothering Ciaran. He kept glancing in her direction and frowning. As the meal progressed, she sensed Amy was a little tense too and wondered what they had been discussing when she'd arrived.

'If you're still hungry, Ciaran, we have ice cream, or cheese and oatcakes.'

'No, thanks. That was good. A cup of coffee and one of your shortbread biscuits would be nice, though.'

'We'll all have that. Come and sit back down at the table, Roxie, when you have made it. I want to talk to you,' Amy said.

'Have you heard a date for your operation?'

'Nothing new, but I've made up my mind to go, so long as I know you will go to Glasgow and stay with me until I am allowed home again. I think I told you I can take one relative and they will provide accommodation.'

'So they should at the fees they'll be charging,' Ciaran muttered.

'Do you think I shouldn't pay to have it done privately, Ciaran?' Amy asked in troubled tones.

'Oh, Mum, you know I think you should have the very best we can afford and you're worth every penny if they can give you back your independence. I only meant they will charge anyway, so if Roxie is willing to go and stay, then that's the best solution.'

'Of course I'm willing to stay, if it will help. It would be easier to stay than to drive up there every day to visit.'

'Thank you, dear,' Amy said. 'Now sit down and drink your coffee because I have some news for you. I had a telephone call meant for you about twenty minutes after you left this morning.'

'Oh? A call for me? I don't think they tried to get me on my mobile.'

'It was from your brother, Tommy. I promised you would telephone him after dinner, when you returned.'

'Tommy? He phoned here? Is there something the matter with the baby?'

'No, no. He didn't mention the baby. He is selling the dairy herd. He needs your help to check the pedigrees for the sale catalogue and to do the cattle-dressing for the sale.'

'I can't possibly go! How could he even ask? I have never heard a word since I left.'

'He says you were always better at cattle-dressing than he is. I think he really needs you, Roxie. He sounded quite desperate.'

'He did ask me to stay with them and carry on working, but he didn't seem unduly worried when I was leaving. Anyway, I would never go now you are going to have your operation. He will have to postpone the sale. *Maybe* then, I might consider helping, once I see you properly healed and back on your feet.'

'Family must come first, Roxie,' Amy said quietly. 'The sale date is fixed for two weeks next Monday. He says you will need at least ten days to help him organise everything. He sounded quite frantic.'

'Then why is he selling Father's precious herd? He hasn't given himself a chance to like dairying . . .' Her voice cracked, but she swallowed her tears and went on. 'He can't be short of money. I know Father had more than enough capital set aside to build the new house for him and his wife. The solicitor was keeping it invested until everything is settled. If only they could have waited . . .' She gulped and Ciaran realised she was very near to tears. 'They don't deserve any help. You have been far kinder to me than they ever were and I came to you as a stranger.'

'You are no longer a stranger to any of us,' Amy said quietly. 'You have made a place in all our hearts and you will be back here before you know it, lassie. I have not booked a date for the operation yet so I will wait until the week after you return. That will give us time to prepare for our stay in Glasgow.'

'You truly do feel I ought to go?'

'Yes, I do. Your brother admits he doesn't deserve your help, but he hopes you will go for your father's sake after all the years he put into building up the herd. I agree with that. I believe you would regret it if you didn't give it your best effort, don't you agree, Ciaran?'

Roxie turned to look at Ciaran.

'You don't want me to go and leave your mother at this time, do you?'

'No, but it's true what Mum says. Maybe you would regret it if you didn't help to make the sale a success,' he said reluctantly. 'Mum will be fine for ten days or so, but whether or not you return depends where your heart is. Are you sure you will not want to stay down there when you see all your old friends again?'

'My heart is more here than it is back there now,' Roxie muttered. 'It isn't truly my home any longer and soon even the cows will have gone.' She turned back to Amy. 'You know I would never let you down after you have made me feel so welcome, don't you?'

'I do know that,' Amy said firmly and gave Ciaran a speaking glance. He shrugged.

'Mum will stay with me until you return.'

'And Jenny is keen to come to keep me company and advise her about the baby.'

'Oh. All right. I had better phone Tommy, then.' She sighed and took out her mobile. 'I will phone from my room.'

'Your brother asked you to phone his landline. He says he does not have a mobile phone.'

'No mobile? But he . . . Oh, I almost forgot . . .' Her eyes brightened as she looked at Amy. 'I got an email while I was in town from my friend, Lucy — the friend who has the twins. She and Steve are planning to book a holiday cottage up here about the end of August or beginning of September, so they can visit me. I'm sure you will like them. The twins are adorable. Lucy wonders if there is any particular letting agency you can recommend.'

'Jenny might know,' Ciaran said, sounding more cooperative, although she still sensed he didn't want her to go home to Derbyshire.

* * *

Although Amy had told her she had arranged for Jenny, Donald and their baby son to stay at the farm with her, Roxie knew Jenny would not have much time or energy for cooking meals for them all, and she still had a niggling feeling of guilt about leaving Amy at this time. During the days that followed, she baked and cooked to stock up Ciaran's freezer for the time she was away. After he had eaten his lunch each day, she had a box or a tray of food for him to take to his freezer — fruit pies, savoury dishes, cakes and puddings. One of his favourite puddings was steamed syrup sponge and custard, so she had made several individual ones.

She had spoken to Tommy on the telephone and been surprised to find her heart aching for him. He sounded young, and unhappy, and strangely defeated, not at all like a proud new daddy. He told her he couldn't cope with the dairy and he must sell now before their father's reputation as a breeder, and all his hard work, were lost.

'I shall make sure the solicitor pays you the remainder of your share according to our father's will, without more delay. I realise now how hard you must have worked. You have earned it more than I have, Sissy.' He had not called her that since they were young.

'How will you make the farm pay without the monthly milk cheque?'

'I am going to buy some commercial beef cattle and I would like to try breeding some pedigree Suffolk sheep. I am interested in breeding better stock, but not dairy cows. I detest being tied to milking twice a day every day of the year. You know I always liked the arable side of farming, so I shall plough more land and grow more cereals.'

'I wish you every success, Tommy, whatever you decide to do,' Roxie said sincerely.

She felt better after they had discussed things openly. She could understand that not everyone shared her interest, or her father's commitment to the dairy herd. Even so, she had to try hard not to feel a bit bitter that Tommy had never been in touch until he needed her help. He had never mentioned Gilda or their baby son, and he had not even thanked her for the beautiful little jacket she had sent. Instinct told her there was more than the sale of the dairy herd troubling Tommy.

Roxie felt too tired to drive the two hundred plus miles on her own.

'All that cooking and baking you have done for our benefit has exhausted you, Roxie,' Amy said. 'I think you should travel by train.'

'I thought if I took the car, I could bring back some of my own items of furniture, like my precious sewing table, but it is an awful thought to drive so far on my own, especially after that awful crash.'

Ciaran was finishing his lunch. He immediately volunteered to drive her to the station in Dumfries the following morning. While she was clearing the table, Ciaran studied his phone.

'According to this, you would have to change at least once so I will drive you to Carlisle to save you one change there. You will still need to change further down the line though, I think.'

'Thank you, kind sir.' Roxie gave him a dimpled smile. 'I accept your offer.'

The next morning, Ciaran arrived in good time to collect her. 'Is this all the luggage you're taking?' he asked in surprise, loading it in the back.

'Yes,' said Roxie, climbing in the front seat. 'I had no idea when I was coming here what sort of accommodation I would have, or even if I would need to share a room. Remember your mother and I had never met. I left at least half of my clothes hanging in my wardrobe. Everything is still in my own room so I am not cluttering up the house with my belongings. I intend to fill my big suitcase and bring some of my things back with me, so the less I take now the easier it will be, especially as I shall be on the train.'

'I see. Will you have wellingtons and other work clothes?'

'Yes, of course. I didn't need them to be a chauffeur companion! I bought a new pair of wellingtons after I came here, when I realised I would be living in the country.'

They chatted on in their usual friendly fashion, commenting on the fields and animals they passed until they drew nearer to Carlisle. The road was busy. As they drew nearer the station Roxie murmured reluctantly, 'We're in good time. You can drop me at the door if it will save you looking for a parking space.'

Ciaran patted her hand where it lay on her knee. 'I shall never hear the end of it if I don't see you safely on the train. You know my mother has adopted you like a mother hen with a new chick.'

He drew into a parking spot without too much searching and insisted on carrying her backpack for her. Once she had her ticket and had located the platform, Ciaran bought them a cup of coffee and a huge fruity biscuit each, individually wrapped. They sat side by side on one of the benches.

'When I return, I could catch the sprinter train up to Dumfries from Carlisle, if that would be easier for you. Shall I send you a text to tell you what time I hope to arrive?' She thought he hesitated, but then he smiled.

'You can do that if necessary. More importantly, phone to let me know when you arrive. I'm going to miss you, Roxie,' he added, more urgently, as the train approached. He still held her bag as the carriage doors began to open. To Roxie's delight, he wrapped his arm tightly around her, holding her close. He kissed her mouth firmly, very firmly indeed, and felt her response. His eyes met hers in a lingering look she found impossible to interpret, but knew she would never forget.

'Be safe,' he said softly, handing her bag up to her as she climbed aboard.

'Thank you, for everything,' she whispered huskily over a sudden lump in her throat. In that moment, she wished she had not agreed to go, even though it was for Tommy's sake and in her father's memory. The train was already pulling away. Ciaran was still standing watching. All too soon he and the station were left behind.

Chapter 12

Roxie had changed trains and was settling down with a seat to herself for the last leg of her journey when she received a call on her mobile from Lucy.

'Hello, Roxie? Did you catch the connection?'

'Yes, no problem.'

'That's good because Steve has arranged his calls for today so that he can meet you at Derby and bring you here for tea.'

'But Tommy is—'

'I phoned Tommy and told him there was no need for him to meet you. I will drive you to Willowbrook later. I am looking forward to seeing you so much and this may be the only opportunity we shall have. From what Steve tells me, it sounds as though you will have a lot of work getting ready for the sale.'

'Yes, I expect we shall,' Roxie said with a sigh.

'Steve has told some of our old crowd that you're coming back to help Tommy get the cows clipped and shampooed. I think some of them will volunteer to help out. The Davies twins and Gerry Green are definitely intending to help.'

'That's a relief. Tommy didn't sound very optimistic when we spoke on the phone last night and he hasn't allowed a lot of time when he arranged the sale date.'

'No . . .' Lucy hesitated. 'I don't think his life is very easy just now. Tommy was always a straight, honest and kindly lad, as I remember him, and I've known him since he was twelve, when I used to come and stay with you at Willowbrook. According to the grapevine, Gilda is living at her mother's. She will not be doing anything to help at the sale apparently.'

'Why is she still staying with her parents? Not that I'm sorry if she will not be at Willowbrook, but even Gilda must realise it's to her own advantage to put in some effort to make the sale of the herd a success. I can't make the food and work with the cows as well.'

'Don't worry about the food, Roxie. Beth Corby will help out. She and her mother are making a great success of the tearooms they started, and she does cater for small functions occasionally now. She provides sandwiches and rolls for the morning-shift workers to take away, as well as the light lunches and the afternoon teas they did when they started off with the tearoom. They employ two women now and a Saturday girl. You do remember Beth from school, don't you? She was two years below us.'

'Of course I remember Beth,' Roxie said with a light laugh. 'She was always a hard worker. She travelled on the same school bus as us. She hero-worshipped Tommy. I helped her with her maths homework on the way home sometimes. I remember she did well in all her exams. I'm glad the tearooms are a success.'

Roxie had thoroughly enjoyed her chat with Steve on the drive from the station. They had many old friends in common from their days as Young Farmers. He had worked for the same firm of seed merchants since he'd left college and had done well enough to be made a junior partner in the firm now they were expanding. In many ways it felt as though she had been away from the area for years instead of months, but it was a sheer delight to see the twins again, both toddling around the house now.

Lucy had made a delicious salmon mousse and salad for tea, followed by freshly baked scones, rhubarb pie and Roxie's favourite lemon cake.

'I didn't think I was hungry until I saw the lovely spread you've made, Lucy. I see the twins have not stopped you cooking.'

'No, we all love our food too much for that. I can ignore a bit of dust if necessary, but I enjoy cooking.'

When they had finished their meal and chatted for a while, Lucy asked if Roxie was ready for the drive to Willowbrook.

'I know you said you didn't want to be too late?'

'Yes, please, if you can take me now, Lucy. I know it's early and I am reluctant to leave such a happy atmosphere, but Tommy wants me to check through the sale catalogue as soon as possible in case any of the pedigrees are incorrect and the auctioneers need to print supplementary pages. We don't want buyers claiming compensation for clerical errors with the wrong sire or dam in the pedigree.'

'We'll leave now, then. Steve can put the twins to bed later on. Do you remember before you went away to Scotland, you were going to give me your grey dress? Maybe you can show it to me, if you're still sure you will never wear it yourself?'

'I am quite sure I shall not wear it. I hadn't thought I would be leaving the area when I bought it to wear for a mourning period, but Dad would never have expected me to go round wearing drab, dull colours anyway. He knew, and I know, what I feel in here.' She tapped her chest. 'I remember how beautifully you can transform clothes. You said you had a red blouse to make a collar and cuffs so that should brighten up the grey.'

'It will, and I shall add some red stitching at the front, I think. I would still like to pay you for it, though. I know it was expensive.'

'I don't want anything. I was in shock when I bought it, but the past months in Scotland have been more like a period of relaxation than paid employment.'

'I must admit you're looking well — much better than I thought you might.'

'Yes, if I had known I should have such a lovely place to stay I could have taken some of the smaller pieces of furniture Grandma Horne left me, as well as the rest of my clothes. I'm almost wishing that I had driven down now, but I felt so tired last night.'

'Doesn't it depend on what you decide to do longer term?'

'I haven't made up my mind yet, but if Amy's operation is a success and she doesn't need me, I think I might buy a small house of my own in the area. I could set up as a farm secretarial agency. I have done enough farm records and book-keeping during the past six years to be familiar with all the different records required.'

'Roxie, that would be a great idea!' Steve spoke up with enthusiasm. 'I can't tell you the number of farms I visit who could do with that sort of service. Record-keeping gets more instead of less, even for my job, with things we supply for treating the crops and diseases. The farmers are supposed to keep a record of them too, as well as all the vet medicines used.'

'I suppose it is a good idea,' Lucy said slowly. 'But why not buy a house and set up in business down here?' She looked sharply at her old friend. 'Or . . . or is there some other attraction north of the Border?' she asked with sudden enlightenment.

'I had better help Tommy get the sale over, and see Amy through her operation, before I make any plans of my own,' Roxie said noncommittally, gathering up her things ready to leave, but she knew by the look in Lucy's bright eyes that her friend would persist, and she also knew her own heart now belonged to Ciaran, although she had tried to keep herself aloof as his mother's employee. Whether he guessed or not, she truly longed for him.

As soon as they were alone in the car, Lucy returned to the subject.

'You know how much I would love you to settle down here, Roxie. Not only me either. You have such a lot of friends.'

'I know, but nothing is the same since Dad died and Tommy got married. I know Willowbrook has been my home all my life, and Tommy didn't want me to leave, but I got the impression Gilda didn't expect me to return at all, even to visit.'

'It's not only that though, is it?' Lucy asked. 'After all, you could have a house of your own anywhere.'

'I suppose I could,' Roxie said doubtfully.

'Roxanne Carr!' Lucy chuckled. 'You can't fool me. We have been friends since our first day at grammar school. You've fallen in love with some man up there, haven't you? Half the men in the Young Farmers' Club wanted to marry you and you never encouraged one of them. You escape to Scotland for five minutes and wham! What happened? Was it one of those men in lovely sexy kilts at Hogmanay?' She glanced at Roxie who could feel the delicate colour mounting in her cheeks as Lucy glanced at her. She was remembering the parting kiss Ciaran had given her at the station. Surely it had meant something to him too?

'Is it the man you almost quarrelled with the day you arrived?' Lucy asked gently, no longer teasing. 'Isn't he your employer's son?'

'Yes, he is.'

'Yes, he is your employer's son, or, yes, he is the man you have fallen in love with?'

'Both,' Roxie said softly.

'Ah, I see. Does he return your feelings?'

'I don't know. Sometimes I think he does, then again . . .'

'You seem to have a lot in common whenever you mention him in your emails?'

'We have. I have never met anyone else who shared so many of my own interests, but I don't know how he feels if it comes to a serious relationship, and marriage is a serious business. Tommy sounded dreadfully unhappy after making a hasty marriage,' she said anxiously.

'Don't measure any relationship according to Gilda and Tommy!' Lucy said sharply. 'Steve reckons most of Tommy's old friends believe Gilda trapped him into marriage. You know she had been going out regularly with the son of the couple who own the Chinese restaurant in town?'

'No. I didn't know that. But I didn't know Gilda until Tommy brought her home to meet Dad and tell him they wanted to get married.'

'Well, the boy was younger than Gilda. He was ready to start university. Rumour has it that his parents sent him back to China for his further education, but a few have wondered if they sent him away to escape Gilda's clutches.'

'I see . . . Here we are.' Roxie sighed and wished her spirits had risen at the sight of her old home, but she was thinking of the quarrel between her father and Tommy. Her father had pondered whether Gilda and her family had set a marriage trap for Tommy, but her brother had been either too besotted, or too angry to listen to reason, or even to agree to postpone the wedding for six months until the new house was taking shape. She had a feeling Lucy knew more than she was saying.

They were both surprised to see Gilda hurrying out of the door at Willowbrook carrying a cardboard box as they arrived. She was clearly startled at the sight of them. It was obvious she was not expecting to see Roxanne.

'You! Why have you come? I didn't believe you would ever return!' Gilda seemed more alarmed than annoyed. 'I'm just going . . .' She still stood blocking the door.

'Aren't you going to let us in?' Roxie asked, summoning a smile with an effort. There was not a vestige of warmth from Gilda, but maybe married life, and being a new mother, was not easy for her either.

She stepped back to allow them to pass.

'Come in, Lucy. I'll not be a minute. I'll take my bag up to my room and bring the dress to let you see if you still want it.'

'There's no hurry.' Lucy turned to Gilda, whose blue eyes seemed to be darting everywhere like a frightened rabbit. 'How are you enjoying married life, Gilda, and living in the country?' she asked pleasantly. 'It must be a big change for you. Is your baby, Liam isn't it, a good sleeper? I remember how I struggled with my two for the first six months, and more.'

Before she could answer, Roxie came running down the stairs calling Gilda's name. Gilda ran across the kitchen, grabbed some keys from the table and darted past Lucy and out to her car. One glance told Roxie her sister-in-law was intending to escape. Roxie ran after her, her face white as a sheet and her green eyes blazing. Bemused, Lucy followed slowly. Before Gilda could get the key in the ignition, Roxie wrenched the door open.

'Where are all my things?'

'Your clothes are still in the wardrobe where you left them,' Gilda replied sullenly. She tried to shut the car door.

'I didn't mean clothes! Where is my sewing table? My little desk? My other small pieces of furniture? What have you done with them?' Roxanne knew her voice was rising, but she couldn't help it. Gilda glared back.

'It was only furniture,' she muttered. 'I wanted some cash. I don't like dark-coloured stuff,' she added.

'They were all in my room. You didn't need to look at them. Where have you put them? You — you haven't painted them for a nursery for the baby?' Roxanne asked faintly.

'Let me shut the door!' Gilda jabbed the car key at the ignition but it wouldn't fit. She realised she had grabbed the key for Tommy's car in her hurry. She hadn't thought Tommy would send for Roxanne, or that she would ever come back. She had destroyed his mobile phone, making sure he had lost Roxanne's number so he couldn't contact her, unless he used her employer's landline phone and she knew he wouldn't want to do that. Before that, she had, accidentally on purpose, deleted most of the email addresses from the computer. Tommy had been angry over that because she hadn't realised a lot of them were business email addresses, as well as friends' and Roxie's.

'Where are my antique pieces?' Roxanne asked again, holding the car door open.

'I sold them. So there!'

'S-sold them! You sold my antique table? I can't believe this. Who to? When?'

None of them noticed Tommy coming across the yard towards them.

'What's going on? You!' He stared at Gilda with contempt. 'What are you stealing this time?' he asked icily.

'Who bought them?' Roxanne demanded sharply. Gilda was a captive in the car. She had no option but to answer.

'A man in a white van,' she muttered.

'Surely not those people who travel round the countryside looking for bargains?' Roxanne gasped in dismay.

'That's right,' she said jubilantly. 'He hadn't room for the bigger stuff from your room, but he paid me for it,' she added exultantly, casting a defiant glance at Tommy. 'He's collecting it next week, except the wardrobe. He said that was too big to go with the things he plans to send to America.' Roxanne was leaning against the car, white-faced and shaking, before becoming aware of Tommy, who was staring at them both.

'How could you let her sell my precious sewing table?' Roxanne asked in a shaking voice. 'You knew it belonged to our great-grand-mother. Grandma Horne left it especially to me in her will, and my little desk, and . . . and . . .' The woman's voice almost broke in her distress and she was clearly struggling to hold back her tears.

Gilda had never believed Miss Roxanne Carr of Willowbrook could get emotional. Even at her father's funeral she had been pale-faced, but composed. She had acted with dignity, greeting many in the crowd of folk who had packed the church. Later that night, Gilda had sneered to herself when they had heard her sobbing in the privacy of her bedroom, but Roxanne had been up the next morning as usual to milk the bloody cows.

* * *

'What are you talking about, Roxie?' Tommy asked. It was Lucy who told him what had upset Roxie so badly.

'You can't have sold Roxie's things! All her treasured pieces were in her own room!' he said, staring incredulously at Gilda.

'You promised we would have a new house with modern furniture, not an old barn of a place.'

'Don't speak to me about promises!' Tommy said through gritted teeth. 'What did you need the money for? When did you sell them?' He knew how much his sister had cherished the family heirlooms from their grandmother. He had inherited his grandfather's gold hunter watch and chain. The memory of his father came back as though he was standing beside them.

'It is worth a lot of money, but it is unlikely you will wear it unless such things come back into fashion. I will take it to the bank. It will be safe there in case you do need it sometime. I wouldn't like to think that girl's father might get his hands on it and sell it for beer money.'

Tommy remembered how furious he had been at the time, not because he'd wanted the watch, but because he'd known his father had had no respect, and no trust either, for Gilda or her family.

He had learned several hard lessons since then. How he wished he had listened to his father. He sighed heavily and looked unhappily at Roxie.

''We shall never be able to trace him to get my things back,' she said dejectedly. 'I can never replace them. It's the sentimental value as much as . . .' She broke off, biting back a sob.

'Wait a minute,' Lucy said. 'Didn't you say he had paid for some bigger items, Gilda? If he is coming back to collect them, he must have left some sort of invoice or receipt? Maybe that will have his name?'

'It's nothing to do with you!' Gilda screamed at Lucy hysterically.

'You're right, Lucy,' Tommy said. 'He must have given you an invoice and kept a copy himself to claim the other items. When were you here? Did you arrange to meet him? Did he come the day I was at the auction mart making arrangements for the sale? That is the only time I have been far away from the farm recently, at least long enough for a van to come in and take things away. Show me the receipt.'

'Don't know where it is.'

'You must know. How else can he prove he paid for the rest? Gilda, I want that receipt.'

When she refused to answer, Tommy frowned. 'Perhaps we should get the police here and tell them you have sold some rare antiques that did not belong to you?' he said, his voice ominously quiet. He saw Gilda turn pale and her eyes widen in shock. Her father had been to prison. It was the reason they had moved down here.

'You wouldn't do that! I'm — I'm still your wife . . .'

Tommy bit back a sharp retort, remembering the solicitor's advice not to antagonise her until they decided how to proceed. He pulled the car door wide and took her arm in a firm grip.

'Let me go! All right, he did have a white van. It belonged to Mr Jacobs, the antique dealer in town. He said it was a sin to leave them in a house where nobody appreciated them and I was doing the right thing to sell them.'

'I appreciated them!' Roxie said. 'Anyone would appreciate the beautifully inlaid design on the top of my little sewing table, not to mention the Devonport desk.'

'Well, I didn't!'

'You should not have been in that room!' Tommy knew Gilda had resented Roxanne from the beginning, and more so since Mr Robson, their solicitor, had read his father's will, leaving Roxie with money of her own. 'The solicitor! Of course! He will know what to do, Roxie. Mr Robson and Jacobs are both in the Rotary Club, I think, or the Round Table, one of the men's clubs in town anyway. They are bound to know each other. Jacobs will not want to be known for handling stolen property — and that's what it is, Gilda.' He glared with contempt at the girl he had married. 'He can't have disposed of your things yet, Roxie. I promise I will do my best to get them back for you.' He looked at Gilda. 'You understand he will want his money back.'

'I hope you're right, Tommy,' Roxie said wearily. 'I know Mr Robson will help if he can. He was a good friend of our father.'

'His son has joined him in the law firm now and he is very on the ball.' Tommy's expression was grim. 'He often works late at the office. I'll telephone him right away and see if I can catch him.'

* * *

As soon as Tommy went into the house, Roxie watched as Gilda ran in for her own keys and back to her car. She drove away fast, scattering pebbles as she went.

'I'm so sorry you had to witness all that aggro, Lucy,' Roxie said tiredly. 'I don't know what I have done to cause so much — so much resentment.'

'You look exhausted,' Lucy said gently. 'Forget her. Gilda is simply one of those people who is jealous of her own shadow, and everyone who possesses anything worthwhile.'

'It's the tension. I feel so depressed to think I have lost the things I cherished, things my grandmother, and my mother, treasured. I am glad Gilda will not be here for the sale. I can't understand why she should envy anyone. It doesn't sound as though things are happy between her and Tommy either. Did you hear him say she was stealing things? She is his wife.'

'Even happily married couples disagree sometimes,' Lucy said. 'But you're right. I believe trouble appears to be brewing big time and I feel sorry for Tommy. I know he rushed into things, and maybe he has himself to blame in a way. I suppose the old saying may be true, marry in haste repent at leisure.'

When Lucy had driven away, Tommy told Roxie that Mr Robson, the son, had promised to look into the missing furniture urgently, maybe even this evening.

'Will you take a walk with me, going round the cows in the field? They have been milked. They're grazing in the field near the house.' Tommy looked thoroughly dejected and weary, but Roxie heard the pleading in his voice.

Although she was tired, Roxie knew the walk and fresh air would probably help her sleep, and seeing the cows again was like seeing old friends to her.

'I could never have kept the herd up to the standard you and Dad kept it, Roxie,' Tommy said. 'You have to be dedicated to make a first-class job.'

'I think Dad would understand, Tommy, and at least you are having the sale now, and not waiting until the herd has deteriorated. Most of the breeders will remember Dad and the Caldbrook herd. I am sure there will be a good attendance, and if we can present the cows and heifers at their best, it will help the prices.'

'Er . . . yes. Did Lucy have much to say? Well . . . I mean, did she tell you anything about the baby?'

'Your baby?' She turned to look at her brother. 'No, she didn't. Is there something wrong with him? Is he ill?'

'Nothing like that. The poor wee soul.' Tommy scuffed the grass with his boot and looked even more miserable. 'I'm surprised Lucy didn't tell you. There are plenty of rumours going round. Everybody must think I was a stupid sucker to be taken in so easily. I was so unsettled when I came back from Australia, but I was a conceited fool to be taken in so easily by her looks and her flattery.'

'Gilda is a very attractive girl.'

'Maybe on the outside she is,' Tommy said bitterly. 'She is as sly and greedy as her father when you get to know the real person. If only I had listened to Dad, but it's too late for me to tell him now.' His voice sounded choked. 'When the Davies twins come, they'll give you the gossip.'

'What about?' Roxie asked with a puzzled frown.

'I'm not the baby's father, Roxie,' he said bitterly. 'He was not premature. Both the doctor and the nurse in charge said he was full term. Gilda still tries to deny it and worm her way out. She still insists she is not to blame,' he added derisively. 'I got a real shock when I saw him. I told the staff nurse she had shown me the wrong baby.'

'What do you mean?' Roxie asked tensely.

'Liam was born with a lot of jet-black hair, and his skin is yellowish. His eyes are not at all like Gilda's or mine. Gilda and her father are still trying to bluff their way out and insist he is my child, but I asked for a DNA test and Mr Robson Junior has arranged it.'

'I see,' Roxie said slowly.

'Gilda's mother is a decent sort of person and she sits silent, looking uncomfortable and miserable. I don't think she really knew the truth either until she saw the baby for herself.'

'Oh, Tommy, no wonder you are so unhappy.'

'I was a gullible, headstrong fool. I know that now. Looking back, I think Dad must have suspected, or heard something, or maybe he was wiser than we knew. He tried to persuade me to postpone the wedding until the baby was born, then either agree to support Gilda and her child, or marry her if I still felt the same. I thought I was doing the honourable thing. To tell the truth, I didn't really want to get married so soon, but I was amazed at our father suggesting such a plan. I flew into a temper. I had enjoyed my time in Australia so much. I didn't know how I was going to settle down to milking cows and the sort of life Dad expected.'

'Oh, Tommy, I'm so sorry things are this bad. I wish you had told me what was bothering you. You had never wanted to do anything else but farm, even though you didn't want to milk cows every day.'

'It was because of all this mess that I met Mr Robson's son. He is more knowledgeable about divorce and things than his father. He has advised me not to aggravate Gilda, if I can help it, until we can see how I stand over the baby. But, Roxie — I can't go on living with her. Truly I can't. Even before we came back from honeymoon, I knew she didn't love me. She thought she had married money because we owned a farm.'

'A lot of people have that impression.' Roxie nodded. 'They don't understand that most of the money is tied up in land and stock and machinery.'

'Mr Robson says the DNA proves I am not the father. I don't know what happens now. He says the circumstances are unusual. I suppose what he really means is I was every kind of a fool not to suspect. He'd be right, too. I was too conceited to wonder why she favoured me instead of all the men she already knew at that club.'

'You did seem to be instantly attracted,' Roxie admitted. 'But Gilda is a lovely blonde, and she's so dainty too.'

'Yes, well I know now you can't judge by appearances. Gilda invited me for a meal when I hadn't known her long. When I arrived at her house, her mother had prepared the meal, but her parents were ready to go out for the evening. Her father plonked a bottle of whisky on the table and told us to enjoy ourselves.'

'I thought you didn't like whisky.'

'I don't. I only had one small drink and it was well watered. Gilda had two or three. She was either drunk or pretending to be. She got undressed. She wanted me to stay the night with her.'

'And did you?'

'Of course not! I hadn't known her that long. I had never been in favour of one-night stands. Anyway, I expected her parents would be returning. B-but I er . . . She got into bed. I stayed a while . . . too long obviously.' His face had a guilty flush and he looked young and unhappy, almost bewildered. Roxie's heart went out to him.

'I suppose Gilda got in a panic when she knew she was having a child and the father had disappeared to China,' Roxie said. 'It must have taken a lot of nerve, though, to go through with everything as she has done. I'm sorry I made such a fuss about my furniture. You have far worse problems.'

'That is only one of several deceitful things she has done, and continues to do.' He groaned audibly. 'Her father is sly and he's not above cheating if he can get away with it. Gilda knows I don't want either her or her baby living in the house anymore. I pay her an allowance for her and the baby until we can get things sorted out legally, but whenever she is short of money she slips into the house when she thinks I'm at the milking, or working in the fields. She is always taking food. She was hopeless at budgeting.'

'I'm so sorry, Tommy. Why didn't you tell me? I longed to hear from you.'

'I couldn't confess what a mess I'd made of my life, but I did hanker for a talk with you several times. I lost my mobile and I couldn't remember your number without it. I bought another recently. I have your number now, since you phoned me. I hope your employer didn't mind me phoning her on her landline?'

'Of course she didn't. In fact, she insisted I must come to help you with the sale.'

'Gilda deleted all the email addresses. She said she had done it accidentally. That was early on and I didn't think much about it at the time. It was very inconvenient because a lot of them were business contacts. I have wondered since if she wanted to cut me off from everyone I knew.'

'It sounds as though Gilda might take after her father,' Roxie said slowly.

'She needn't have worried because I have felt too stupid to keep in touch with any of our friends, but, when they heard about the sale, the Davies twins and one or two others have said they will come to help. I hope they do, but I can't blame them if they don't.'

'I'm sure they will. We both had such a lot of friends in the Young Farmers' Club and Dad did a lot for the club too with coaching and holding stock-judging classes for them to come and practise.'

'He did. Anyway, Roxie, if you're not too tired, I had hoped you might have a glance through the catalogue tonight and then check it properly tomorrow evening for any errors.' They walked slowly round the cows, then returned to the house both deep in thought.

Tommy telephoned Beth Corby to arrange about the food for those coming to help with the cattle-dressing in the morning, while Roxie had a look through the catalogue, surprised how much she remembered about each of the cows, but she had reared many of them from birth and she had loved her work. She yawned and set it aside. She was on her way upstairs when Tommy shouted to say there was a phone call for her.

'Someone called Ciaran Baxter.'

'Oh, thanks.' Her spirits lifted at the mere mention of Ciaran, in spite of all the troubles she had found waiting. 'I promised to phone when I got here, but so much has happened. Tell him I will phone him from my mobile in a few minutes. I'd left it in my bedroom. I'm going to the bathroom first. See you in the morning, Tommy.'

Ciaran answered as soon as her phone connected.

'Hello, Roxie. Are you all right? Your brother says you have had a stressful day. Was it a bad journey?'

'Oh, Ciaran, I am so very pleased to hear your voice.'

'Really?'

'Yes, truly. I am. I'm so sorry I didn't phone earlier. The journey was fine. Steve, Lucy's husband, met me at Derby, which saved some time.' She went on to tell him about Lucy and the twins, then she hesitated.

'But?' Ciaran asked seriously. 'Have you quarrelled with your brother? He sounds pleasant enough on the phone.'

'We haven't quarrelled at all. I feel so sorry and sick at heart for Tommy, but he is trying hard to be as normal as possible. He has troubles of his own. Serious troubles. I understand now why he didn't get in touch and confide in me. It was nothing to do with Father's will, or money.'

'Is that what is upsetting you, Roxie?'

'Partly, but I got upset when I arrived and came up to my old room. All the pieces of antique furniture my grandmother left me have disappeared. You probably think it silly of me to care so much about old bits of wood.' She gulped, still distressed, although she tried to make light of the situation.

'I don't think it's silly, Roxie. I have never heard you make a drama about anything, however important. Besides if they are antiques, presumably they will be worth something.'

'They were, but it is not the money so much as the sentimental value. One of them belonged to my great-grandmother so it was . . . Oh, Ciaran, this is ridiculous going on about things, but I c-can't forgive Gilda for selling my possessions. I think she hoped I would never return.'

'She sold them? Even though she knew they were yours?'

'Tommy has contacted Dad's solicitor. He thinks he associates with the antique dealer who bought them, so we may manage to get them back. Anyway, I'm sure you must be bored with my moans. Don't tell your mother. She worries about people. Give her my love, and Jenny too.'

'What about me? Don't I get any?' Ciaran asked, and she could hear the smile in his voice.

'I'm so pleased to hear you, you can have all my love. Thank you for being so understanding.' It was easier to admit how much she cared on the phone and she was trying hard to respond to his lighter manner.

'I hope you mean that, Roxie. I can be a very demanding man,' Ciaran said. 'I sent for a catalogue of the sale and it arrived in today's post. I thought they weren't published yet?'

'They are. The auction firm wanted to get them out in good time, to let people know the sale was being held because it's not a lot of notice. I am hoping I shall not find many errors. If there are any, they are going to publish supplementary pages and hand them out at the sale. What did you think of the breeding?' she asked.

'I'm impressed. I fear they will be beyond my price range. I noticed your father has used the Sunwick bull a lot. That surprised me. I have had three of my cows inseminated by that bull. I think he is one of the best breeding bulls presently available. How did your father get so much of him?'

'My father owned him,' she said quietly.

'He *owned* him? My goodness, Roxie, and you never boasted or even breathed a word.'

'He bought the bull's mother as an in-calf cow. She calved at the farm when we were about to load her in the trailer to bring her home. Old Mr Lister, who owned her, said he would like to register the calf with his own herd prefix because it would be the last calf he would ever have to register. As the bull calf began to mature, my father thought he was a fine specimen, plus his mother was milking well and she had a lovely calm temperament. So, he kept him for a stock bull. He used him more than he would normally have done. The buyer for one of the artificial insemination companies saw his progeny and asked if he could bring one of the directors to see him with a view to buying him. So that's the history.'

'Quite a history, I'd say.' Ciaran whistled. 'I expect you're ready for a good sleep now. I'm missing you, Roxie. I might phone tomorrow night to see how you're getting on, if that's all right?'

'Oh, yes. I would like that.'

'That's good. Night, night, and sweet dreams.' Roxie thought she heard him blow a kiss down the phone and she smiled happily, greatly cheered at the end of an awful day.

Chapter 13

Roxie was up early the following morning to help Tommy with the milking and to refresh her memory regarding the individual cows, their breeding and their present yields. The cows were ambling into the gathering area ready for milking when she entered the parlour. There was a young man standing in the pit ready to wash the udders of the first cows in the stalls before putting on the milking machines.

'Good morning.' Roxie greeted him with a smile.

'Good morning. I'm Harry. Tommy said you would probably be here before we finished the milking. I don't think he expected you would be out before we had begun,' he added with a grin.

'The sooner I get into a routine, the better,' Roxie said. 'We shall have a busy ten days ahead of us if we're to show all the animals at their best on sale day.'

'Yes, Tommy says you're very good at cattle-dressing and trimming them into shape. I have never done any of that, but I'm keen to learn. I have been trying to learn about the pedigrees and how the cows are bred, so I'm disappointed Tommy has decided to sell them.'

'Not all young men take such an interest in their animals. Are you staying on here to help with the beef cattle when Tommy gets some?'

'No. Tommy gave me a good reference and I've got a job as assistant dairyman in a big herd about twenty miles away in the next county. They're not pedigree, though. The owner is a dealer.' He gave a little shudder. 'There are all sort of breeds, depending what he picks up at the markets. It's not what I would have liked, but I shall be able to stay with my mother now I have bought a motorbike. She is not keeping well so the company, as well as the money, should help her a lot.'

What a pleasant, genuine sort of young man he is, Roxie thought. He would have been a great asset to Tommy if he had wanted to carry on dairying. As they worked together, she was surprised how many of the cows he already recognised and knew by name and number.

Tommy ushered the last of the stragglers into the gathering area to await their turn, then he joined them in the pit of the parlour.

'I see none of the cows have had their udders clipped,' Roxie said. 'They will all need to be done and it would be easier to do them in the parlour. I know it would hold up the milking a bit, but if there are two of you to milk do you think I could clip a few of the worst during the afternoon milkings?'

'All right. We could start a bit earlier,' Tommy agreed and grinned at Harry. 'In case this handsome lad has a heavy date tonight.'

'He knows I haven't,' Harry said. 'I'm never in a hurry to get away, especially now the evenings are lighter. I often come back for a walk round the fields, and to see the heifers. I have lodgings with an old lady in the village, so there's not much to do there.'

'I'm pleased you told me that, Harry,' Roxie said. 'Because I would like to get as many of the heifers roughly clipped as soon as possible, ready for shampooing, then we can make them as smart as possible when they're clean. Most of the helpers can make a good enough job of washing the heifers, but they do need to be clipped into shape to emphasise their good points and hopefully disguise any poorer ones.'

'I'm looking forward to it all,' Harry said. 'It's a new experience for me so tell me what I can do to help whatever the time.'

'Harry usually comes in for some breakfast with me. He leaves the house too early in the mornings for his landlady to make him any.'

'Speaking of breakfast, Tommy,' Roxie said. 'There are only two eggs and some milk in the fridge. I will go round the hen houses and see if any of the hens have laid before I go in. If you're lucky you can have a choice of scrambled eggs or omelette. There was half a loaf of bread in the freezer so I have taken that out for toasting.'

'You can't have looked properly, Roxie,' Tommy said. 'I got two packs of bacon and a fresh loaf from Beth Corby yesterday, as well as several other things.'

She smiled. 'That must have been in your dreams. The fridge is empty.' Tommy's eyes narrowed and his mouth tightened.

'No prizes for guessing who stole them yesterday afternoon,' he muttered angrily. 'This is not the first time it's happened.'

'Never mind,' Roxie said more gently. 'We need to do some shopping for ourselves, apart from Beth coming to cater for the extra workers. There's very little in the freezer and no food in the pantry, not even the jam or pickles and chutneys I'd made before I went away. It is needing a good scrub out too. I'm surprised Maggie has let it get so smelly.'

'Maggie hasn't been for ages. Gilda said she was ill. Her mother came to clean a bit before the baby was born.' Tommy's expression was grim. He looked older and thinner. His green eyes, so like Roxie's, held a look of bleak despair.

Roxie went to collect the eggs, some of them so newly laid they were still warm, but when she went back to the house, Beth Corby's van was already there and she was unloading trays of filled rolls for later, along with freshly baked scones and two tins containing homemade biscuits. She had brought six hot bacon rolls as well and set them on top of the Aga to keep warm.

'Hello, Roxie. It is lovely to see you again. We have missed you terribly around the village.'

'It's good to see you too, Beth, especially as you come bearing food. You must have been up very early to get this lot ready.'

'We always start early, Mum and me. We catch the trade of the early-shift workers. We have two helpers who come in about eight thirty. Tommy phoned to say the bacon he got yesterday had disappeared. I'll bet Gilda was here scrounging again. She doesn't seem to care who suffers or even understand she is stealing. I don't know why Tommy doesn't change the locks. My brother says that is what he would do.'

'I don't know much about what's going on yet. Tommy hadn't been in touch until he phoned to ask for help with the sale. I would not have known the baby had been born if Lucy hadn't kept me informed, and I only arrived yesterday afternoon and . . . well, I got upset over other things Gilda had done.'

'Things like sacking Maggie for no reason, you mean?'

'What? Maggie? Our Maggie? Tommy says she is ill.'

'Maggie has never been ill! She's desperate to work and not only for the money. She needs to be busy, a bit like my mum. She came to ask if we had a little job for her, but we already have two regulars and a Saturday girl.'

'I can't believe this! Tommy obviously doesn't know.'

'Men are so gullible sometimes.' Beth sighed.

'Tommy and Harry will not be so gullible when they see your van here already. They will be in for their breakfasts. I must tell Tommy about Maggie. I'll bet the whole house is ready for a good clean. I told him the pantry needs a scrub. That's when he said he hadn't seen Maggie for ages. We shall need to feed the auctioneers and their clerks in the dining room, I think. They might expect a cooked meal. This household has nothing to do with me now, but I'm sure Tommy will be pleased to welcome Maggie back.'

'She will jump at the chance, especially now Gilda isn't here. At least Maggie would cook Tommy a hot dinner every day instead of him having to come for a filled roll from us, and quiche or a pizza for his tea. He has an account with us now. I send him a bill once a month and he always pays the next day so I'm not grumbling, but it seems so unfair on him. I get most of his groceries for him too, now. I don't mind because I have a delivery man twice a week, so if you want to make a list I could get them for you if it would save time going into the supermarket?'

'It would! That's a real help, Beth. Thanks. I will make a list tonight.'

'I got the bacon, so I knew he should have had plenty for today. By the way, Roxie, add a fried egg to the rolls if you want, now you have plenty.'

'Yes, I'll do that. I'm famished myself and I know Harry and Tommy will be. Harry seems a very pleasant young man and he is a keen stockman.'

'He's a lovely young fellow. He didn't want to leave here he told me, but I'm sure his mother will be pleased to have him home.'

'I expect you hear all the gossip now you live in the middle of the village, Beth?' Roxie laughed.

'Oh, we do. Sometimes more than we want. I am glad we have a big garden and the orchard at the back. It's a relief to escape on Sundays and on summer evenings.'

'I suppose you miss the farm, too?'

'We do, sometimes, but it wouldn't be the same without Dad. You must feel the same. We are lucky. Mum and I get on well with Elsie. She's a warm-hearted lass and a hard worker. She makes my brother Derek a good wife. Mum says that's a lot to be thankful for.'

'I'm sure she's right. Ah, here come Tommy and Harry. The eggs are almost ready and I will make a big pot of tea. Will you have a cup with us, Beth?'

'No, thanks. If you don't mind, I would like to get back now I have delivered this lot. I will cover everything and come back with the tea urn around ten o'clock, if that's all right?'

'That will be ideal, but will you wait a minute?' Roxie asked urgently. She turned to her brother. 'Beth tells me Maggie West has never been ill, Tommy. Gilda had told her not to come back. She is keen to work, and I have a feeling both you and the house are needing her. Can Beth call at her cottage and ask her to start as soon as possible? She might help with serving the food and teas as well. I don't want to stop work with the cattle, if I can help it. Once I start on the clipping I need to keep going.'

'Maggie is not ill? I can't believe it! Please do ask her if she will come back, Beth. Tell her I will welcome her with open arms.'

Beth giggled. 'Like you used to do when you were five years old and running home from school?' she said teasingly. 'Maggie has told me several times about that. She thinks the world of you two. She will be overjoyed when I tell her you want her back to work at Willowbrook.'

* * *

Later that evening when they were alone and Roxie was writing out a long shopping list for Beth to get from her delivery man, she raised with Tommy the risks of stocking up the cupboards and freezer.

'I'm planning on filling up the freezer too, but is the food safe? I'm thinking frozen vegetables and some convenience foods for you to cook, as well as rump steak, mince, chicken and chops, things I know Maggie can cook during the time she is here cleaning, and you enjoy that sort of thing. It is not worth running the freezer with so little in it anyway — a couple of joints of beef and one of lamb. It's a waste of electricity.'

'Neither Gilda nor her mother, have ever cooked a roast. That's why they're still there,' he said drily.

'You could put a lock on the pantry door, I suppose, but we always keep a lot of food in the kitchen cupboards too.'

'James Robson advised me to change the locks on all the doors,' Tommy said. 'He didn't even know she has been pilfering food and Lord knows what else. He suggested the locks because Gilda tried to stay overnight a couple of times. I nearly lost my temper, but I made it clear I didn't want her, or her baby, in the house. I believe she thought she could entice me with her feminine wiles, if she got back into my bed.'

'Oh, Tommy.'

'Don't worry, Sissy. I'm not as naive and foolish, or as conceited, as I was when I first met her,' he said bitterly. 'She knew I had recently returned from Australia so she thought I had loads of money, and I knew nothing about her previous activities. I didn't know much about her, or her family. I am wiser now. Beth's cousin is a joiner. Maybe I will give him a ring and ask him to change all the locks.'

'If you do that you must give Maggie a key of her own to come and go when she needs, but warn her not to leave it lying around in case Gilda comes when she is here on her own.'

'I shall tell her not to let Gilda in and keep her own key in her pocket. I closed my petrol account at the garage in the village. She had been filling her father's car with petrol, as well as her own, and putting it all on my account. They can both pay for their own petrol from now on.'

'It makes me wonder why anyone ever gets married if there is so much deceit and unhappiness.'

'Most people manage to make a go of things. Your friend Lucy looks very happy.'

'She is, but they are a lovely couple.'

'They love each other, that's the difference. I didn't know Gilda long enough to learn to love her, or to hate her. I was presented with a dilemma. I can't believe I was so bloody stupid.'

'I don't remember you ever being angry or bitter, Tommy. You seem so dejected now.'

'Sometimes I think I should sell up everything and return to Australia.'

'Oh, surely you wouldn't do that! Willowbrook is your heritage. Our grandfather came here as a baby with his parents. Dad was born here, and so were we.'

'I know. Even when we knew Mum was not going to get well again it was still a happy home, but I don't find it very happy now.'

'You will feel a lot better when you have Maggie back. She will get things shipshape again, as she used to do. She will enjoy cooking your favourite meals and mothering you.'

'We shall see. Part of me had hoped you might decide to stay here once you knew I was on my own. Then the bitch was the first person you saw! I still can't believe she sold your furniture. I sincerely hope old man Robson will get everything back. He knows they are yours and that you're here for the sale. He said he might call in to see you.'

'I hope he doesn't come during the day while I'm working. There's such a lot to do, Tommy. We're going to struggle to get every animal looking its best. Harry is a grand worker, though. Dad would have made a fine herdsman of him.'

* * *

The atmosphere in the house seemed very different with Maggie arriving every morning, wafting away cobwebs with her feather duster, humming softly as she scrubbed, cleaned and polished. The scent of lavender greeted all comers once more and the windows sparkled in the sunlight. The only cloud on Roxie's horizon was they had heard nothing more from old Mr Robson, and Jacobs, the antique dealer, had failed to return her beloved sewing table and the other pieces of furniture she had cherished.

Beth arrived every morning, always bright and cheerful and armed with great trays of filled rolls and buttered scones. The rolls were generously filled with ham, cheese, beef or fish. In addition, Beth provided dishes of chutney and bowls of fresh salad for anyone who wanted to help themselves. Maggie seemed to enjoy breaking off from her own work in the house to help Beth serve, and to greet the people she knew personally. She had lived in the village all her life.

Roxie felt they had been luckier than she had dared to hope when so many of their neighbours had come to help with the washing and grooming of the cattle, especially on the final two days before the sale. She wondered if some of them had come for her father's sake, although all but two older men were her own age, men she and Tommy had known from when they'd been in the Young Farmers' Club. None of them dallied over their refreshments, although everyone ate heartily. Tommy and Roxie ate along with their helpers at midday, both knowing there was still a lot more work to do.

Maggie stayed all day, every day, and she prepared a hot dinner ready for Roxie and Tommy to eat for their evening meal. Roxie appreciated her thoughtfulness immensely because she was working hard. Every evening she was glad to flop exhausted into an armchair. The high point of her day was Ciaran's phone calls. He had made a point of telephoning every night to hear how things were progressing. He liked to discuss some of the pedigrees in the catalogue with her, asking her if they looked as good in reality as they did on paper. He had selected six so far that he said were the best in his opinion. She agreed with four of his choices, but said she would not have chosen the other two.

'It is different for me. I suppose I'm prejudiced because I know them and I can see them. You only have the catalogue to look at,' she said.

'Tell me which numbers you would prefer so that I can study them. Maybe we can enjoy a little debate about them,' he said, chuckling.

One evening she was extra pleased when he said, 'Roxie, I could love you for your syrup sponges alone.' He sounded half serious, half joking, but every evening he told her everyone was missing her. Then, on the second last night before the sale, he said he would not be able to phone again but he hoped everything would go well on sale day. Roxie was shaken at how disappointed she felt at missing their evening chat, even though they had never been in the habit of speaking to each other in the evenings when she was at Oaklands. She told herself she was being ridiculous.

Chapter 14

Everyone, volunteers as well as employees, had worked tremendously hard all week to get the Caldbrook herd ready for a good sale and Roxie was proud of them, and honoured to have been her father's daughter. She hoped she would be able to keep her tears in check when she saw some of her favourite cows being sold to strangers. She didn't blame Tommy for selling them when they were not his interest, but she wished she had been born a boy, then her father would have left the dairy herd to her.

On the eve of the sale, Roxie told Harry he need not come in early for milking the next day; she would be starting before four in the morning to get the cows milked and settled down again before buyers started to come looking round. 'Serious buyers always come early before a sale begins, so they can have a good look and take time to examine some of the animals they fancy from the catalogue.

'It will be your job, Harry, to keep going round them to pull away any dirty bedding and giving an extra brush or wipe down if any get in a mess.'

'Isn't four in the morning a bit early to start milking?' he asked, puzzled.

'They wouldn't look so good if they were newly milked and with floppy, empty udders, but we couldn't leave them until after the sale or they would start streaming milk in the sale ring if their udders were too full. We need to relieve them to prevent that, but if we do it early enough, they will have begun to fill up again by mid-morning when the sale begins. We want them to show themselves at their very best. I know some people don't milk them at all before a sale, but experienced dairymen can tell if they have been deliberately hefted and for high yielders it is rather cruel. It might cause mastitis too.'

'I see. I never thought of all that.'

* * *

Harry wanted to be there for the last milking and made sure he arrived early the next morning, as Tommy was bringing in the cows and Roxie was starting to milk.

'I've brought a pair of clean overalls in case these get in a mess,' he said.'

'My word, Harry, you're very conscientious. Dad would have approved of you,' Roxie told him. 'You may have to milk some of the cows this afternoon before they are loaded, if their new owners live a long way away. I think some of them will have travelled a fair distance because my father was fairly well known in various parts of the country. It is better for the cows if they are milked before they leave here to start a long journey. It prevents their udders getting too full before they reach their destination. I doubt if I shall be free to help you at that time of day. I know several of the buyers will be grateful for your help, and your consideration for the animals, so most of them will reward you, a few of them quite generously. My father always did. Accept whatever they offer and thank them. You will have deserved it by the time this day is over.'

As soon as the milking was finished, Roxie sent Harry for a big breakfast.

'We don't know when we shall get another decent meal, but Beth will have rolls and tea going all day today. Grab what you can when the opportunity arises. Don't wait for Tommy or me to tell you.' Harry had seen Beth's van arriving earlier. 'While you're eating, I will check through the animals in all the different groups, then you can come and take my place, constantly checking to keep them clean and bedded. I will go for my breakfast and shower, and change when you come back from yours.' Harry nodded and grinned. He liked the way Roxie gave clear instructions. He had learned a lot from her in the past week.

After his breakfast, Harry was returning to the cattle sheds to take over from Roxie when he met a man he hadn't seen around before.

'Can you tell me where I can find Roxanne Carr, please?'

'I will get her for you,' Harry said. 'She is in one of the sheds. She will be needing her breakfast, though. She has been milking since before four o'clock. You're early for the sale.'

'Yes, I had a better journey than I expected.'

'Someone to see you, Roxie,' Harry called when he glimpsed her about to disappear into another shed. She turned and came towards them. Her eyes widened in astonishment.

'Ciaran!'

* * *

Ciaran smiled as she ran the last few yards towards him, her arms wide.

'Can it really be you? Here?' She hugged him tightly. Ciaran was delighted and relieved by her greeting. It was spontaneous and warm. He lowered his head and kissed her parted lips longingly, returning her hug. She laughed happily.

'It's good to see you, Roxie,' he said honestly.

'Anyone would think I'd been away for a month.' She chuckled warmly.

'It has felt like it to me,' he said seriously.

'I never dreamed of you coming all this way, but I am so, so pleased you have come, and you will get to see my father's cows before they are dispersed to the four winds.'

'I would like to buy four of them myself, if I can afford them.'

'Buy them? Truly? I know you are interested in their breeding, but I never thought . . . Oh, Ciaran, it would be wonderful if you do buy even one of my father's cows.'

'Maybe you will come and see her every evening.' He grinned. 'And then I shall see you too.'

'I shall not want to keep away, that's for sure.' Roxie nodded. 'You'll be sick of me,' she added with a dreamy look.

'You must know I shall never be that, Roxie. As a matter of fact, I have marked the eight dairy cows I think are the best on paper, as well as two in-calf heifers, but I need to see them in the flesh before I decide, and it depends how much money they make, but the lad I saw told me you were going for your breakfast. Can you spare a few minutes to show me where to look?'

'Oh, Ciaran, of course I can spare you as much time as you want — well, not as much as I would like, I suppose. How did you get here so early? You must be ready for something to eat yourself.'

* * *

Roxie forgot about her hunger and the hours she had already worked as she showed Ciaran proudly through the groups of animals, pointing out the ones he had marked for particular inspection before he saw them in the sale ring.

'Do you agree with my choice?' Ciaran asked.

'More or less. I'm prejudiced, but everybody has their favourites, haven't they?'

'Probably. Which one is your favourite?'

'It would be difficult to pick one. I like three of the ones you have marked. I would choose any of them. If I could only choose one, I would have number eighty-four. She is a daughter of the Sunwick bull you admire so much.'

'Yes, I've seen one or two sired by him, but some of them are getting old.'

'One of the heifers you have marked is a granddaughter.'

'I'll give that one an extra star, then. I'll buy them especially for you, if I can afford them. Now, I'd better let you get some breakfast. You will have things to do and people to see, but I know now where to look for the ones I'm interested in buying. Roxie . . .' He turned to face her. 'I was hoping you might travel back with me tonight? You'll be tired, but I didn't get much sleep myself as I travelled through the night to get here early. It will be a slower journey home if I have cows in the lorry, and I hope I shall. We could stop half way and have a couple of hours sleep for safety's sake. What do you think?'

'I didn't know you had your own lorry. I have never seen it. But if there's room and if I've finished everything I need to do here, I would very much like to come back with you. I've packed a big suitcase with a lot of my clothes to take back and I wasn't looking forward to dragging it on the trains.'

So, it was arranged. Roxie took Ciaran in for some breakfast and coffee.

'Beth and Maggie will look after you,' she said. 'I would like a quick shower and I'll eat mine in my bedroom while I dress, if you don't mind? Look after him for me, Beth. His name is Ciaran and he's special. He is going to buy my favourite cow to take to Scotland and he's giving me a lift back tonight.'

'Oh, in that case we'll certainly take good care of him.' Beth and Maggie chorused together as they gave Ciaran a more careful inspection.

'Oh, Roxie, I nearly forgot to tell you.' Maggie called out to her. 'That Mr Jacobs has been and brought back your antique furniture. He has put everything in the little room next to the office for now.'

'Oh, that's wonderful!' She turned to Ciaran with the happiest of smiles. 'These are the things I told you Gilda had sold. I had given up hope of ever seeing my treasures again!'

'Jacobs wasn't happy at having to return them. He says you have some lovely pieces. Mr Robson had told him he would be accepting stolen property. He says he runs a reputable business so he couldn't keep them.'

Ciaran was standing close to her, and he turned and hugged her. 'I'm really glad you've got them back, Roxie. I know it was their sentimental value that meant so much.'

'It was. I couldn't have replaced them. I feel like dancing now.' Roxie grinned. 'But I'd better get a quick shower or I shall smell of cows when I have to stand next to the auctioneers . . . The young one is quite an attractive guy.' She winked at Beth and then promptly shot out the room.

* * *

As soon as Roxie had disappeared upstairs, Beth poured Ciaran a cup of coffee and sat him at the kitchen table with a freshly made bacon-and-egg roll. She grinned at him.

'So how special, is special?'

'I don't know.' He gave Beth a smile. 'How attractive is the auctioneer?'

'You needn't worry about him. Roxie could have had her pick of half the men around here, but she has never been serious about any of them. I've never heard her say any of them were special either,' she added, giving him a cheeky grin. 'Are you going to marry her?'

'If she'll have me.' Ciaran grinned, suddenly feeling full of joy and thankful he had made the long journey. 'It is wonderful that Roxie has got her furniture back. She was so upset.'

'Indeed, she was,' Beth said.

'I wonder if we should take it back with us while I have the lorry here.'

'I don't know.' Beth pondered. 'Would you have room for it in your lorry if you buy some cows? Has Roxie room for it where she stays?'

'I have plenty of room in my lorry, and in my house,' Ciaran said. 'I'll ask Roxie.'

'If you decide to take all her furniture, let me know. My cousin is a joiner and he can come and show you how to take the big wardrobe into three sections. He'd help you load too, if you want. He knows what he's doing for that kind of work.'

* * *

Showered, changed and still eating her breakfast, Roxie returned to the kitchen to find Ciaran at ease and laughing with Maggie and Beth. She poured herself another cup of coffee and offered Ciaran some.

'No, thanks. I see some people have started to arrive and a man is showing them where to park. My lorry is well out of the way, though.'

'Shall we go for a proper look through the rest of the cattle now, then?' Roxie asked, standing up as she quickly drank her coffee. 'I didn't show you where the heifers are, or the young stock. We tried to keep them well spread out so as not to get dirty again.'

Outside they were just crossing the farm yard when they met a smartly dressed man. Roxie stopped suddenly, recognising him. His appearance jolted her memory.

'It may be worth introducing you to this man,' she said in a low voice. 'It is his artificial insemination company who bought Sunwick Best Boy from Dad. I've just remembered something . . .'

'Good morning, Roxanne.' The man greeted her cheerfully. 'I heard you'd moved to Scotland, but I wondered if you would be here for the sale. Selling the Caldbrook herd was a surprise to a lot of us.'

'I know, but dairying is not Tommy's favourite type of farming. I'm pleased he's not waited any longer to dispose of Dad's lifetime's work. I've been here all week helping. Seeing you reminded me your firm has twenty-five straws of semen from the Sunwick bull. My father reserved them in case he wanted to use him again later.'

'Yes, we have.' He grinned exultantly. 'But your brother will have no use for them now.' Roxie reached for Ciaran's hand and squeezed hard, shooting him a look that seemed to him half pleading, and yet excited. Whatever it meant, he gently pressed her fingers in response. 'Tommy doesn't need them, but my fiancé does.' To Ciaran's amazement, she drew him forward. His heart soared. 'He's here to buy some of the Caldbrook stock. He's grading up his own herd.' Roxie knew she was talking too fast, but she felt Ciaran's firm clasp around her fingers and she knew he understood her silent message. He didn't seem to mind her claiming him as her fiancé.

'There was me thinking we could sell the semen for twice the price,' the man said, looking disappointed.

'It's already twice the price it was early on,' Roxie said. 'You bought five straws, didn't you, Ciaran? I couldn't believe they cost so much.'

'Have you used them yet?' the man asked with genuine interest.

'Yes, I've three in calf and two straws in reserve,' Ciaran answered readily.

'What's the name of your herd? Maybe I could call on you when I'm up in Scotland, perhaps at the Highland Show time.'

'I'm still grading up so only half the herd is fully pedigree. The herd name is Oaklands.'

'You'll not be long before you have them all pedigree when you have Roxanne for your wife. Her father always said she could pick out a good animal as well as he could. Well, well, that is a piece of good news. I am only here to have a look how the progeny of the Sunwick bull has done and to see whether there is anything else we should be keeping an eye on. I am on my way south, so I need to get away promptly.'

'We shall leave you to look, then,' Roxanne said, drawing Ciaran away while chewing on her lower lip in the anxious way he had come to recognise. She lowered her voice. 'I'm sorry if I've complicated things, claiming you as my fiancé. I never thought he might want to visit you at home in Scotland. You will have to invent an excuse for b-breaking a phoney engagement, but I thought you might as well benefit from the free semen, if possible. His firm have made a fortune out of that bull already.'

'Roxie, stop talking a moment,' Ciaran said softly, pausing and turning her to face him. 'If I had my way there is nothing, absolutely nothing, I want more than for us to be truly engaged and planning our wedding. You must know by now how much I want you. I love you. The question is could you ever learn to love me? Love me enough to be my wife, I mean, on days when I'm a bad-tempered bugger, the way I was the first time we met?' He was pleading with her boyishly. 'As well as the good days?'

'Ciaran! Are you saying that to make me feel better about telling fibs?'

'I'm saying it because it's true! Much as I appreciate you procuring some valuable semen for me, I would be the happiest man alive if I thought you would marry me.'

Roxie stared up at him. The anxious look in her eyes was replaced by pure joy.

'I do love you, Ciaran,' she said softly and he couldn't doubt her sincerity. 'I don't know why, when we argue, or how you can arouse such longing in me when no one else has ever made me want more than a brief kiss, but — but somehow . . .'

'Dearest Roxie, do you truly mean that? Do you love me enough to be my wife? Could you live with me and love me for a lifetime?' He looked deep into her eyes and she couldn't doubt the earnestness she saw there.

'Oh, Ciaran, it would be a dream come true,' she whispered huskily. He didn't care if they were in a cowshed where anyone could come in, he lifted her off her feet and kissed her passionately. When he glanced up, he saw the man from the AI company standing at the end of the shed grinning. He gave them a thumbs-up, then turned on his heel.

* * *

The sale went extremely well. Ciaran was successful in buying six of the cows he had marked, including Roxie's favourite. He had also bought an older cow on a whim after a remark Harry had made in his youthful wisdom. As the young man had predicted, she was a low price, due to her age, but she was in calf to a well-bred bull, and she had a fine pedigree as well as good milk records, so the calf alone could prove valuable in time. He went on to buy the two in-calf heifers. He was well pleased with his day's purchases, even though he had spent considerably more money than he had intended.

It had been an incredible day in so many ways — and there she was. Roxie. He'd managed to catch her on her own. Resisting the urge to pull her into his arms, he grinned at her instead, with no doubt a very goofy smile on his face. He asked if she'd like him to take her furniture back with them while he had the lorry.

'You would never have room. I've been worrying how you'll manage to transport so many animals home.'

'I was drunk with love, my darling. If I could, I would have bought them all for you. Harry says there are four young calves, still unregistered. I bought the mother of one of them. He said the other day you told him you would take them all with you if you'd had anywhere to keep them, so if we can fit them in comfortably we will take them too.'

'What size is your lorry? It must be huge!'

'It is. It is far too big. To tell the truth, this is only the second time I've driven it with the container on. I bought it second-hand to use as a flatbed truck for carting straw at harvest time. I buy straw from Kelso and North Yorkshire. We never have enough for bedding in our area. I have a man who drives for me if I'm too busy to go myself. Normally the transport costs more than the straw, so it's a help to have my own lorry. The elderly man who sold it to me included the container for free. It had been his son's enterprise until he was killed in a motorbike accident. It broke his father's heart.'

'That's tragic . . .'

'I know, but that's the reason I have such a big lorry. So shall we load your furniture first, then I can put the partition up to protect it from the cows?'

'If you're certain we can get everything in.'

'I can. Maggie said I was to tell you she's cooked us a proper dinner, which we must eat before we set off for home. There is no hurry because Harry is going to milk the cows and the roads will be quieter in the evening.' Resisting no longer, he drew her close and gave her a hug and a lingering kiss. 'I can't tell you how happy you have made me, my darling Roxie.'

* * *

Much later, Roxie was amazed how little room her furniture took, with Beth's cousin helping to carry the larger pieces and carefully pack everything with sheets and blankets for protection. Harry waited to help load the cows safely, then tuck up the four young calves in a small pen well bedded with straw at the very back of the lorry. Roxie had a feeling Harry was near to tears as he saw them all loaded. She wondered if Ciaran thought so too because he said, 'Keep in touch with us, laddie. Call to see us if you're up our way. If ever I need a herdsman, I'll let you know in case you happen to be looking for a change of job. Isn't that right, Roxie?'

'If you say so. Good luck, Harry, in whatever you do, and thank you for being such a willing helper.'

Roxie felt near to tears herself now almost all the sheds were echoing and empty, the last remnants of her father's working life were gone. Tommy sensed her feelings. He felt empty himself now that his father's beloved herd had been scattered to various parts of the country. He turned to hug Roxie and whispered huskily, 'He would have understood, and forgiven me, I hope. He would have been so proud of all you have done to make such a successful sale, Sissy. You made it a fine conclusion to his life's work and achievement.'

Roxie nodded, blinking back her tears but too full of emotion to speak.

Tommy cleared his throat and urged Harry towards the kitchen, telling him dinner was waiting for them, before he turned one last time to give Roxie another hug, almost reluctant to see her leave Willowbrook again, but he promised to keep in touch regularly from now on and wished her well for the future. He shook hands with Ciaran, promising to travel up to Scotland for their wedding.

* * *

Darkness was falling as Ciaran drove the large lorry steadily up the motorway. He and Roxie discussed the sale, the events of the day, and the people Ciaran had met and looked forward to meeting again when they came up to Scotland for their wedding.

'I can hardly believe we shall be planning a wedding so soon,' Roxie said a little breathlessly. 'I hardly dared believe you would ever want to marry me, Ciaran.'

'My darling Roxie, you got under my skin the first day you arrived, even if I was a bad-tempered brute. Every day since, I've wanted more and more of you. I can hardly believe it. Even now, I can't believe how lucky I am. And I like your brother. I think he's had a rotten deal, even though he does say it was his own fault.'

'Oh, I'm so glad you think you can be friends. It will take him a long while to get over this episode, I think.'

'I suspect that lovely lassie, Beth, might help him put his past behind him,' Ciaran said shrewdly. 'Your friend, Maggie, was overjoyed when she heard we were getting married. They think a lot of you, those two women.'

'I have known Maggie most of my life and she couldn't have been kinder or more helpful when Mum took ill. She never let us down.' In spite of the excitement, gradually they both began to yawn as the engine purred steadily along.

'I think we should stop and have a rest,' Roxie said, knowing Ciaran must be even more tired than she was herself.

'I agree. We'll look for the next road services. I don't want to stop in a layby in case some scoundrel opens the doors to let the cows out for sheer devilment.'

'I never thought of that.'

It was not many miles further before they came to a suitable service station with plenty of space for large transports. They went to the toilets before they settled down. Although there were lights on all night, Ciaran clasped her hand all the way to the door. He was waiting outside to escort her back and he couldn't resist giving her a quick kiss the moment she appeared.

As they got back to the lorry, he said a little diffidently, 'I'll lay two blankets on the fold-down bed and open up my sleeping bag so it will act as a quilt to cover us. We shall have enough room if we cuddle up close.' He gave her a tender kiss. 'I'm too tired to do anything but sleep, so don't worry, my darling.'

'I'm not worried, Ciaran. I trust you completely,' Roxie said simply.

They slept soundly, curled together, secure and warm in their love. It was a good two hours later before either of them stirred.

'What do you think your mother will say to our news,' Roxie asked sleepily when she realised Ciaran was also awake.

'It's her birthday tomorrow. Oh, no, it's today now! Our news will be the best birthday present we could have given my mother. She loves you like a daughter already, Roxie. Sometimes I think fate brought you to us, and yet it is as though she has had you made to order and sent by special delivery.'

'I do hope you're right that she will be pleased with our news, because she has been as kind to me as any mother could be.'

The second half of the journey passed more quickly than the first, with the roads less busy as they travelled north. Dawn was beginning to break on another May morning as they drew into the farmyard at Oakfield.

Chapter 15

'Here we are, home again,' Ciaran said with a broad smile. 'Don't get out until I turn on the outside lights, Roxie. Billy will not be here for nearly an hour yet even if he gets here promptly at five o'clock.'

'We seem to have made good time so we might have time to put the six milking cows through the parlour before he comes?'

'We?' Ciaran laughed. 'I thought you would be heading for the house and a few hours' proper sleep now.'

'I'd never leave you to unload them on your own. Everything will be strange to them. We'll get them out together. Then, if you agree, I'll help you milk them.'

Ciaran leaned across and drew her close to give her a lingering kiss.

'I feel I'm the luckiest man in the world, Roxie,' he said softly before he climbed down from the lorry. A few minutes later, he opened her door and held out his arms. She slipped into them as though she did it every day. He held her close while he kissed her again.

Neither of them dreamed of the news and shock awaiting them.

* * *

'We shall have to unload the four young calves first. They're at the back,' Ciaran said. 'I phoned Billy yesterday evening before he went home, and asked him and Vic to bed one of the calf boxes for the four calves and a large clean pen for the older animals so everything should be ready.' He frowned. 'Billy is not the obliging fellow he used to be. He sounded rather disgruntled to hear I'd bought more milk cows.'

'I expect they might make a bit of a mess when they see a strange place and a different parlour. He will be even less pleased at that unless we can wash things down before he arrives,' Roxie said.

'The sound of the milking machine and getting cake in their troughs will help them feel familiar and we'll soon clear up. Once they're milked, they can have the rest of the day to eat and sleep in comfort in a well-bedded pen.'

It was easier than either of them had expected and they were finishing milking the six new cows when Billy arrived.

'I'll take some of this warm milk and feed the four calves we brought,' Roxie said, leaving Ciaran to discuss the new animals with his dairyman.

She had finished feeding the calves and checking they were well bedded in clean straw and had a supply of water, when she saw a car drawing up beside the house. She was surprised when Donald got out. Ciaran was also crossing the yard, after helping Billy wash down the parlour after the six strange cows had left a trail of mess in their nervousness at being in new surroundings. They restarted the engine to start the main milking, a quarter of an hour later than usual, but Billy should still be finished before the milk tanker arrived around seven thirty to eight o'clock. They went together to see why Donald was out and about so early in the morning. They stared in dismay when they saw how pale and strained he looked.

'What's wrong?' Roxie asked urgently. 'Is it the baby?'

'No, no, he's fine. Oh, Ciaran, it -it's your m-mother. She — she fell in the kitchen during the night. I-I have just come back from the hospital.'

Ciaran stared at him in concern. 'Fell?'

'H-h-hospital?' Roxie stammered.

Donald pushed his fingers through his tousled hair and looked as though he might faint with exhaustion.

'We had better go inside,' Roxie said. 'Then you can sit down and tell us what happened. I knew I should not have gone away, especially for so long. H-how is Amy now? Can we see her?' She glanced at Ciaran. She knew how tired he was after the long drive, but now his face was white and drawn.

'Oh, God,' he said. 'I'm the one who should have been here for her.'

Roxie was blaming herself, and near to tears as she ushered them both into the kitchen and sat them down.

'What happened?' she asked Donald as she automatically pushed the kettle onto the hot plate of the Aga to boil.

'You will not be able to visit for a while. The hospital said you could phone in a couple of hours, but the paramedics gave her an injection for the pain when they got here. Then at the hospital they gave her two tablets. They reckoned that was the best thing until the surgeon arrived. I had to admit I'm not her next of kin, but I told them she had been intending to have an operation privately with a surgeon from Glasgow. They seemed to pay more attention when they heard that, but the last thing Amy had said to me was, "Mr Whittaker's card . . . front pocket of handbag. Tell him." So I searched for it.'

'Did you find it?' Ciaran asked.

'Yes, Jenny did anyway, before I followed the ambulance to the hospital. Jenny packed her toiletries and things she might need.' He drew a white printed card from his inside pocket and held it out to

Ciaran. 'I didn't really know what to do. When they knew I'm not her next of kin and I had mentioned the surgeon from Glasgow, they almost showed me the door.'

'Oh, Ciaran, they must surely let you in to see her when you are her only son,' Roxie said. 'Surely they can't operate or anything without your consent. I will drive you there. You're so tired and — and sh-shocked.' Her voice shook and she brushed away tears.

'You're just as tired and shocked as I am, Roxie.'

'I'm sure they'll not be in a hurry to operate,' Donald said. 'I was a bit miffed at the way they seemed to think it was not any of my business. I phoned the surgeon, Mr Whittaker, on my mobile, as soon as I reached my car. I apologised for disturbing him at five o' clock in the morning, then explained what had happened. He said I had done the right thing and he would phone the hospital right away, and tell them he was coming down and they had not to do anything except an X-ray until he arrived, and he had spoken with the chief surgeon here.'

'Thank God you phoned him, Don,' Ciaran said, almost under his breath. 'Thank you.' They heard Jenny padding down in her dressing gown and slippers.

'He said he could be down here in two hours at this time of day.'

'Who are you talking about?' Jenny asked. 'I couldn't go back to sleep. How is Aunt Amy and can we see her?'

While Roxie made them all a cup of strong tea and put some slices of bread in the toaster, Donald filled Jenny in with the details. Looking round them all, Roxie decided they were all tired out and needed at least a couple of hours sleep until about eight o'clock, before driving anywhere.

'I should never have gone away before she had had her operation,' she muttered, as much to herself as to the other three.

'It was pure accident,' Jenny said. 'Aunt Amy came through to the kitchen for a drink of water. She forgot her stick. She meant to grab the table for support, but missed and grabbed a chair. It crashed to the floor and Aunt Amy fell over it. It's a good thing I was feeding Peter or I might not have heard the clatter. When I saw what had happened, I yelled for Don. He was very good and knew what to do. We dared not move her when she was in such pain, but he covered her straight away and kept her warm while I phoned for the ambulance.' She shuddered. 'If I hadn't heard the crash, Aunt Amy would have been frozen by the time we came down for breakfast and found her lying there.'

'That doesn't bear thinking about, and me miles away,' Ciaran said with bitter regret.

'Listen, Ciaran,' Jenny said firmly. 'Billy brought the can of milk for the house to the back door before he went home last night. He told us you had phoned and had bought some cows. He also said you would be setting off home in half an hour and Roxie was travelling back with you in the lorry. I can't tell you how pleased and happy that made Aunt Amy. So don't go blaming yourselves — either of you — for anything.'

'That's true,' Donald said. 'She seemed almost excited. I don't know why because she knew you had gone fully intending to buy at least two cows.'

'I think you should go to bed for a couple of hours at least, Ciaran,' Roxie said. 'There's nothing you can do until your mother wakes up or until Mr Whittaker gets there. Was he going straight to the hospital?' she asked Donald.

'Yes, he said he would. Ciaran, old fellow, we're all exhausted.'

'All right.' Ciaran sighed wearily. 'But I will phone the hospital now and tell them I'm home and available, and I am her next of kin. I will insist they let me know if there's any change, or when she wakes up.'

168

They all nodded agreement. Ciaran caught Roxie's hand as she went to pass him.

'I'd rather you rest here, Roxie, either on the big settee in the sitting room or you can have my bed. I don't want you to go back to the bungalow yet. I would like you to come with me to the hospital. Please?'

He looked up at her with tired eyes, and she longed to take him in her arms and comfort him. Meanwhile they needed to be discreet and hide their secret feelings until Amy was well enough to hear their news.

'Okay. You go to your own bed, Ciaran. I'll rest on the settee.' She was sure there was no way she could sleep. Her conscience was troubling her. What if the new damage to Amy's leg had made the operation impossible? Ciaran followed her into the sitting room and turned on the electric fire before he drew her into his arms and kissed her tenderly.

'Jenny is bringing you the big duvet to cuddle up in. You have had as little sleep as I have so we should both try to sleep while we can.' He sighed. 'We don't know what lies ahead.'

Roxie took off her shoes and undid the button on the waistband of her trousers, before she pulled the duvet around her. Between the warmth, and her weariness, she was asleep before she had time to feel her guilt, or to consider the problems that could lay ahead.

* * *

The ringing of the telephone woke them all a couple of hours later. Ciaran picked up immediately. It was the hospital. He listened as they told him that Amy was awake, but drowsy and a bit confused, possibly due to the medication.

Roxie hurried through to the kitchen and shoved the kettle on to the Aga, as usual. She knew Ciaran would want to get to the hospital without delay, but he ought to have a hot drink and something to eat before he went. She could hear Peter crying for his early morning feed and she knew Jenny would attend to him as a priority. She put some rashers of bacon in the pan and whisked some eggs for a large omelette, hoping Ciaran would take time to eat something. By the time he appeared, the food was ready and the table set. Roxie poured him a cup of tea. He'd had a quick shower and his hair was still damp.

'Mum was asking for you, Roxie. You can freshen up in the downstairs shower if you like, then we can go together.'

'My clothes are still in my suitcase in the lorry.'

'I'll bring it in. A shower helped wake me up. I expect you feel just as groggy as I did. The hospital said that Mr Whittaker has arrived from Glasgow. He spoke to Mum, but needs to speak with me before making a decision. Meanwhile they're taking her for an X-ray to give the surgeons a clearer idea of the effects of the fall.'

'Okay. I'll get myself sorted straight away. Some fresh clothes would be welcome, though, if you wouldn't mind.'

A short time later Ciaran tapped on the door.

'I have your big suitcase here, Roxy.'

'Just a second.' She hastily wrapped herself in a large bath towel and opened the door.

'Ah, what a golden opportunity.' Ciaran's eyes gleamed with mischief, and something like desire. 'Pity this isn't the right time.'

'Good job we have no time to spare,' she replied. 'Can you put my suitcase inside so I can close the door?' she added in a hasty whisper. 'Donald is coming down the stairs.'

Ciaran grinned ruefully as he pushed her suitcase inside the small washroom.

* * *

'Are you sure we shall be allowed in this early in the morning?' Roxie asked as they arrived at the hospital a short time later. 'I can wait in the car until you've seen your mother if you like?'

'I don't like. I need you beside me, my darling girl. Anyway, the nurse who phoned said Mum has asked for you by name.'

When they were shown into the small side room where Amy was, it was obvious from her pale face that she was in severe pain. The Baxters were sincere in their loving warmth, but they were not normally a demonstrative, kissing family in public. This morning, Ciaran bent and kissed his mother's cheek and his voice was gruff with emotion.

'No use asking how you feel, Mum, I can see you are suffering a lot of pain.'

'Yes, but Mr Whittaker has come all the way from Glasgow to see what can be done. And Roxie, lassie—' she lifted a hand feebly in greeting — 'I knew you would come back to me. I am so very pleased to see you.'

'Of course I've come back. I promised,' Roxie murmured softly, her voice quavering a little. She had never seen Amy looking so small and vulnerable as she did in the white hospital bed.

'You will know what I need and where to find everything. Depending what the X-ray shows, Mr Whittaker is going to try to make arrangements to operate here, along with the chief surgeon, if they can arrange to get a theatre.'

'Is it the same surgeon who did your operation before?' Ciaran asked anxiously.

'Oh, no. I think he retired. He is not here now anyway.'

Minutes later two men entered the room together. Ciaran and Roxie quickly stood up, prepared to leave, but Amy made a protesting gasp and beckoned them closer.

'This is my son, Ciaran, and—'

'And my fiancée,' Ciaran said swiftly. Amy's eyes flew to Roxie's face, her eyes wide and suddenly bright. Roxy smiled and gave an imperceptible nod.

'Roxie is the best friend an old woman like me could have,' Amy told Mr Whittaker. 'If you can only set me on the right path, Roxie will give me all the care I need.' Her voice was warm and sincere, if rather weak. Roxie breathed a sigh of relief, but Ciaran doubted if his mother had fully taken in their own news.

The surgeon looked directly at Roxie, his eyebrows raised questioningly.

'I am not a nurse, but I live with Amy and she knows I shall do my very best to look after her, and get her well again and on her feet.'

'Now that will be a great help. It deals in part with what Mr Morgan and I were going to ask,' Mr Whittaker said with satisfaction. 'Mr Baxter, you are next of kin, I presume?'

'Yes, that's right.' Ciaran nodded.

'You would be aware that your mother had agreed to have the operation done privately in Glasgow in about a fortnight's time?'

'Yes, she was looking forward to you being able to take away the pain, and hopefully make her walk more easily.'

'And you were agreeable to paying?'

'Of course. In any case, my mother was intending to pay herself. She is a very independent person,' he said with an affectionate smile.

'Unfortunately, the pain is too severe to move her to Glasgow now. The fall has complicated things. She was admitted here as an emergency. While they cannot take private patients, Mr Morgan, the orthopaedic surgeon in charge here, is willing to let me per form the operation as an emergency, with him acting as my assistant, if Mrs Baxter will agree to have it done immediately? And if you also agree?' He smiled down at his patient and his expression was gentle and understanding, Roxie thought. 'By immediately we mean right now, so that we may use the theatre before the usual rota for the day begins. I am afraid we shall almost certainly need to insert a metal plate. This second break is not as clean and simple as I would have liked. It has made things slightly worse than they were on the X-ray a month ago.'

'Does that mean the pain will be just as bad?' Amy asked wearily.

'No, it does not. We can almost — almost I say — guarantee you will have no pain so long as you are patient and do exactly as we tell you. It means you will be in plaster for several weeks and you must not try to walk or put any weight on it. You cannot live alone.'

'I shall be there every minute of the day and night,' Roxie said quickly, giving Amy's hand an affectionate squeeze.

'That is reassuring.' Mr Whittaker nodded. 'I am pleased to hear that. You will need to be in a wheelchair to begin with, Mrs Baxter, and you will need visits to the physiotherapist once the plaster comes off. You must follow his, or her, advice and do the exercises recommended.' He turned to Roxie. 'Do you think you'll be able to supervise this?' he asked with a smile.

'I shall certainly do my best, and both Amy and I shall be encouraged if we know there will be no pain at the end of it all.'

'You're right there, lassie,' Amy said, reaching for her hand again. 'So stupid of me to land myself in here before you got back.'

'The main priority for all of us right now is to get you fit and well again,' Roxie said.

'You're a good lass, Roxie.' She looked up at Mr Whittaker. 'I suppose I shall still have a limp?' she asked.

'Not if we can help it, but we can't guarantee that at this stage. I think you should know that Mr Morgan and I have worked together before. We make a good team, isn't that right, Jonathan?' he asked with a smile.

'If you say so, it is,' Mr Morgan said with a grin, which made him look almost boyish in spite of being a senior consultant here at the local hospital. He looked at Amy and her visitors. 'It is some time ago now, but I was fortunate to complete the last nine months of my training under Mr Whittaker. He is a fine surgeon and a good teacher. We shall certainly do our best for you, Mrs Baxter.'

'How long do you think I shall need to stay in here,' Amy asked anxiously.

'We must take one step at a time. I know you had intended to pay for the operation yourself so I have no hesitation in suggesting that if you make a good recovery during the early days, you could probably go home if you would agree to pay for the care of a private nurse to stay with you at your home, as well as your young companion.' He glanced at Roxanne. 'I can thoroughly recommend a nurse who concentrates on the care of her patient, but she does not undertake cooking or household tasks.'

'We could agree to that,' Amy said. 'Is she willing to travel each day? Roxanne lives with me. I can recommend her cooking and her company so there is no need to worry about daily chores.'

'In that case I shall introduce you to my friend, Mrs Anne Munro, when you have had a day or two to recover from the operation. You will probably have more attention at home than we can manage here, at the hospital, and Anne is a very experienced nurse if you should need to return.'

'I would be happy with that arrangement,' Amy told them.

'I shall be staying down here overnight,' Mr Whittaker told her. 'So that I can check on you this evening and again tomorrow morning, before I return to Glasgow. I have every confidence in Mr Morgan's judgement, but I shall come down again to see you before you are discharged into the care of the nurse and your friend here.'

'That all sounds good to me, Mum,' Ciaran said. 'Don't you agree?'

'I will agree to almost anything so long as you can ease this awful pain,' Amy said.

'In that case we must ask you two to leave now. We shall prepare you for the operation without further delay.' Mr Whittaker spoke briskly, noting the lines of pain Amy was struggling to hide.

Chapter 16

Amy's surgery took longer than anticipated, but both surgeons were aware that she should never have been sent home as she had been the first time and were determined to do their very best for her. Although Amy was heavily sedated, by the following morning, Mr Whittaker and Mr Morgan were pleased with their patient's progress and satisfied with the operation they had performed.

Ciaran wanted Roxie to stay with him at the farm — Don, Jenny and Peter having returned to their own home — until his mother was well enough to be back at the bungalow. She shook her head.

'I have the greatest respect for your mother. I would hate her to think badly of me and I think staying here together would be a temptation neither of us would find easy to resist. Am I right? Or is it only me?'

'You're right in my case, my darling Roxie.' Ciaran sighed. 'I am pleased to know you feel the same, though. I wouldn't be able to resist sharing your bed if there were only the two of us in the house.'

'I know your mother is very tolerant, Ciaran, but I think she might be disappointed in us if we stayed here on our own and set tongues wagging, as they certainly would. Anyway, I can never hide anything from her. She is a very perceptive person. Before we know it, the butcher, the baker and the candlestick-maker would all know.' She grinned at him. 'I don't think I could face the comments the butcher would make.'

'I know you're right, especially if Billy realises we're here on our own.' Ciaran sighed again. 'I do want you so very much though, now I know we love each other. It seems ages to wait until September for our wedding. It's only May! We are tentatively agreed on September, aren't we? Though it will depend on Mum, I know.'

'I agree, it does seem an age.' It was her turn to sigh. 'But early September works well. It will give your mum time to recover and I hope she will have a really good recovery this time, after all she has been through. Also, my friend Lucy will be up here on holiday then, and I would really like her to be at our wedding, and to meet you, Ciaran. If I'm back at the bungalow, rather than at the farm, I can focus on getting things ready for your mum's return from hospital, too, and allow me to give her all my attention when she first comes home, and we have the nurse visiting. I can prepare a few dishes for the freezer and I would like to fill up the tins too, for you, as well as us.'

'All right,' Ciaran said. 'I have some catching up to do myself. All the animals seem to be settling in well, though, after their long journey, but Billy is in a bit of a mood. You would think we had brought half a herd of extra milk cows and asked him to milk them all himself. He has not been very cooperative about anything since he was off with his broken leg. He doesn't seem to understand what a nasty shock it has been to arrive home and find Mum in hospital.'

'I guessed something was troubling you, as well as Amy's operation,' Roxie murmured.

'I shall always be glad I went to the sale and saw all your father's herd before it was dispersed, Roxie. I am pleased I met your brother, and your friends too.'

Roxie nodded. 'Yes, I'm glad, but I shall always feel guilty for leaving your mother as I did. Let's hope the cows all breed well for you.'

'For us.' Ciaran corrected her. He pulled her close for a lingering kiss. 'I had intended taking you to Edinburgh to look for an engagement ring as soon as we got back. I can't wait to show the world you're going to marry me. Mum's accident has delayed that.'

'The main thing now is that the operation is a success and she makes a good recovery. We know how we feel about each other, and that is what matters. Or at least it makes me happy and more relaxed.'

'Even so, if all goes well with Mum for the next day or so, perhaps we could go into town and look around the local jewellers to see if there's a ring you would like? I'm impatient to prove you're going to be my wife, my loved and loving wife,' he said with a boyish grin. 'We could go for a celebration lunch before visiting time at the hospital. I'm not convinced Mum really took it in when I introduced you to Mr Whittaker as my fiancée, but when she sees a ring on your finger I know she'll be certain and delighted. If the surgeons have been round, we might hear whether Mum will get home the following day. If she does, and I hope she will, you may be tied up for weeks. I can't wait that long now I have found the girl I want to marry. We can tell Don and Jenny once we've bought the ring and shown Mum.'

'Knowing Jenny, they have probably guessed how we feel already.' Roxie smiled, snuggling into Ciaran's chest.

'It will give me the greatest pleasure to confirm their suspicions.'

* * *

The following morning, Roxie got up early to cook some of the dishes she had planned for stocking the freezers. She wanted to get them all cooked and cooling by the time Ciaran arrived to collect her for their trip into town. She had never been acquisitive, or possessed expensive jewellery, but she couldn't help feeling excited about choosing an engagement ring, something she would cherish for the rest of her life. She wondered if she should buy Ciaran a gift in return, but she wasn't sure what would be appropriate. She knew he didn't want to wear a wedding ring because they had both heard of accidents if the ring got caught while they were working with heavy sacks or with animals.

'Mmm . . . Something smells good,' Ciaran said as soon as he entered the house to collect her. He drew her into his arms for a prolonged and very loving kiss. It was some time before Roxie could tell him her morning's work was for stocking the freezer, but she had made him a special meat pie so he would have a good meal to eat at the end of the day.

There were not many shops specialising in the quality of jewellery Ciaran had in mind. He wanted only the best for his wife-to-be. The first shop they tried was one he knew Amy had patronised a few times. It was obvious they dealt in quality and they had a good selection of rings, bracelets and necklaces, though not many watches. Roxie had it in mind to buy him a gold wrist-watch for a wedding present and she had hoped to gain some indication of the kind he would like. She was determined to get the best for the man she loved. She could afford it, especially now she had all of her inheritance.

The dapper middle-aged man who served them was eager to show off one of his most expensive trays of engagement rings, but he was a little disappointed when Roxie's attention kept returning to one ring that had caught her attention from the beginning. It was still expensive with two beautifully cut diamonds set together on a twist of gold as though they were snuggling into each other, as she and Ciaran had done on their way home in the lorry.

'See how they sparkle,' Roxie said in delight, holding out her hand to Ciaran as she tried the ring again after several others.

The owner of the shop was clearly keen to show them more expensive rings. 'Don't choose too hastily, my dear. You may be disappointed later. What month is your birthday? Maybe you would like a ring set with your birthstone. Many have diamonds, too, if diamonds are your preference.'

'Her birthday is in August, isn't it, Roxie. Would that emerald match her eyes?'

'No, I'm afraid not. It is a peridot.' Roxie shook her head. 'We do have three beautiful emerald rings, if you prefer green?' he hastened to add. 'Remember, my dear, this is a ring to treasure for the rest of your life.'

'We only get engaged once, so you may as well show us what other rings you have,' Ciaran said. As the man disappeared through a curtain, he whispered in her ear, 'I want you to have the ring you really desire, my darling. It doesn't have to be from this shop, if you're not sure.'

'But I really do like the two diamonds together. The way they're set reminds me of us snuggling together on the journey home when we discovered how wonderful it was to find we love each other. The diamonds are lovely anyway. I'll bet it will be expensive, but he does not display any prices.'

'We're not considering that aspect today. This is once in a lifetime for the only girl I have truly loved,' he said softly.

The man returned, bringing another tray of sparkling gems. Roxie patiently tried some of them, then she sighed.

'I really do like the one with two diamonds best of all, but it is rather loose on my finger and I would be afraid of losing it.'

'We can alter it to fit snugly,' the man said quickly, afraid they might go to the other first-class jeweller in town. 'We can do that today. If you have any shopping to do, we can have it done in a couple of hours, I think.'

'If you're sure that is the one you want, Roxie, we will leave it to be made smaller and come back after we have had lunch. Would it be ready then?' Ciaran asked.

'I guarantee it will, sir. If I could take your size, please?' He smiled at Roxie as he brought forward a ring sizer. 'I see you are a young lady who knows what she likes and you are not easily influenced once you have made up your mind.'

Back on the main street, Ciaran chuckled.

'I hope that applies to me as well as rings?'

'Well, I have never chosen anyone for a husband before, or even been tempted.'

'Then I know I really am a lucky man. We'll go and have a celebration lunch now, but we shall need to leave the champagne for another day when we aren't driving.'

'We will save that to drink when your mother comes home. That will be a cause for celebration.'

'Yes, so it will. Come on, we'll get the car. The hotel is the other side of town and we don't want to be late.'

'I thought we would be going to one of the restaurants in town. There seems to be plenty of choice.'

'They're probably all fine, but I wanted to give you a special treat.'

It was a delicious meal, even without the champagne. They had a table in an alcove screened by tall green plants so no one saw when Ciaran clasped her hand and kissed each of her fingers as he gazed into her eyes, sending silent messages of love.

* * *

Their high spirits were rather chastened when they reached the hospital and the nurse in charge waylaid them on their way to Amy's room.

'We tried to telephone you earlier. I'm afraid we may have to keep your mother in a little longer than we planned, Mr Baxter.'

'Oh? Has she had a relapse?' Ciaran asked anxiously.

'We don't think so, but she had a restless night so she is in low spirits today, not at all like her usual cheery self. She mumbled something about having a wonderful dream and she's been disappointed since she woke up. The nurse on duty thought maybe the medication had affected her, but we've checked in case she'd been given more than she needs. Some medication can have that effect, but she is on a low dose since she seems to tolerate the pain better than many patients.'

'Perhaps we can cheer her up,' Ciaran said optimistically. 'We have something to show her. I am sure it will please her.'

'I do hope you're right, Ciaran,' Roxie said worriedly. 'I would hate to upset your mother when she has had so much to contend with already. Do you think I should wait out here?'

'No! No, my darling girl. She will want to see you as much as she wants me, maybe more. She thinks the world of you, Roxie.' He took her hand and squeezed gently, aware of the nurse's sharp eyes watching them. 'Pin on your usual bright smile and we shall see for ourselves.' He turned to smile at the nurse. 'I promise we shall not stay long if Mum seems tired or upset.' The nurse nodded uncertainly.

Amy did look weary and pale as they entered her room. She turned her head listlessly to see who was entering and her eyes brightened immediately.

'Roxie! You have come back to us,' she said, unaware she was repeating her earlier greetings.' Ciaran pressed Roxie's hand and grinned. 'You see, it is you who matters more than her only son.'

'And you have come with Ciaran, my dear. How wonderful. I-I thought . . .' She frowned, looking confused. 'I thought Ciaran told me . . . and I was so happy. Then I knew I must have dreamt it when I woke this morning. You went a long way away . . .'

Ciaran bent and kissed her cheek.

'Dear Mum, I think you have been having bad dreams, as you did after your first operation, due to the medication. Roxie has been to Derbyshire to help her brother with the sale of his dairy herd — but you knew that. It was before you fell and were rushed in here. They allowed me to see you for a few minutes before they operated and I told you Roxie had travelled back with me in the lorry. I told you she has promised to marry me. You seemed pleased, but you were very groggy due to the medication they had given you for the pain. Maybe you don't remember?' Ciaran broke off uncertainly.

'I don't know what day it is or how long I have been here . . .'

'Not very long. It was a tricky operation so you must be patient.'

Amy looked from one to the other.

'You're both looking very smart. Is that just to visit me?'

'We've been for a celebration lunch, Mum, and to choose an engagement ring. We wanted you to be the first to see it so we can make it official and tell Jenny and Don. Show her your ring, sweetheart.'

Roxie held out her hand, smiling shyly. Amy clasped it with surprising strength as she looked up into Roxie's eyes.

'It is true? I didn't dream it, then? I thought you had gone away?'

'It is true,' Roxie said. 'We have discovered we love each other very much, in spite of our arguments.'

'Oh, my dear Roxie, I am so happy. No wonder you look so pleased with life, son.' She smiled happily up at Ciaran. 'You're a very lucky man.' She turned to Roxie. 'I can't tell you how much joy it gives me to welcome you as one of the Baxter clan, Roxie.'

A little while later, the nurse came in to do the usual checks.

'I think a visit from your family is proving better medicine than anything we can give you,' she said with a smile. 'But I think Mr Morgan will insist on you staying at least one more day with us. If you continue to improve, you will be able to leave the following day in the ambulance, complete with a wheelchair, which you will need for a while until the wound heals completely. The physiotherapist and your nurse will advise you on that, though.'

Both Roxie and Ciaran noticed how quickly Amy became weary in spite of her joy.

'I feel so guilty that we are both so happy while you are lying here tired and in pain,' Roxie said softly, leaning closer.

'Ah, my dear child.' She patted Roxie's hand affectionately. 'I would go through it all again to see you both so happy. Apart from any physical attraction, I believe you are well matched in your interests and the courage you show when coping with life's difficult times. These things are so important in a long and happy life together, yet some young people fall at the first hurdle.'

'I think you are getting tired now, Mum,' Ciaran said gently. 'I believe Don is coming to see you tonight, so we shall leave now and let you have a little sleep.'

'Yes, dear, I am a little weary, but I'm looking forward to seeing Don and thanking him for taking such care of me and for contacting Mr Whittaker so early in the morning. I couldn't have had better care even if we had gone to Glasgow.'

* * *

Later, as they approached Oaklands, Roxie said, 'I will make you a drink of tea before you go home for the milking, and I'll give you the meat pie for your supper, if you can eat it after such a lovely celebration lunch?'

'I'm not sure I can. Maybe salad would be better. In any case, my darling Roxie, as soon as we've finished milking, I thought I would cut across the field and join you here. I shall not be driving so we can drink the champagne I bought. We can have our own little celebration. Would that suit you?' he asked hesitantly.

'Oh, Ciaran, I would like that, if you will not be too tired after helping with the milking and everything else.' She didn't tell him she had nothing in the house to make a salad. She would manage to pop into the little greengrocer's in Thornielee before closing time. The butcher would surely have some of the delicious roast ham he cooked on the premises, and maybe some of his free-range eggs. Maybe she should get a crusty granary loaf from the little bakery too. She remembered how she had always worked up an appetite after milking the cows, taking them back to the field, cleaning the parlour and feeding the young calves, even when there were two of them, as there should be tonight with Billy working.

Back at Oaklands View, and with things prepared for their evening meal, Roxie decided to take a shower and wash her hair. It had been an unusually warm day, even for the end of May. She had plenty of clothes to choose from now she had brought everything back with her from Willowbrook. She settled for a summer dress that buttoned down the front. It was white with flowers in pink, yellow and blue, and sprigs of green leaves. She had always liked the material and the style. She picked up a fine wool cardigan in pale blue and took it downstairs with her in case it became chilly when the sun went down. She had a feeling Ciaran would not be in a hurry to leave this evening when they were both on their own. She felt a little thrill of excitement. They had spent so little time together just the two of them.

She glanced at the clock. It would probably be another hour before Ciaran arrived by the time he had washed and changed, and walked across the field. She knew how much he liked lemon meringue pie and the greengrocer had had some fresh plump lemons, which had tempted her. She sighed. She didn't feel like making pastry. Then she remembered the lemon duchess pudding her mother had taught her to make when she was quite young. It was the lightest of sponges with a tangy lemon sauce underneath when cooked. It would not be so filling and she was certain Ciaran would enjoy it.

Ciaran was whistling happily as he pushed open the back door with his shoulder. He was carrying a bottle of champagne and an empty ice bucket.

'I couldn't remember whether Mum has one of these or not, so I brought the one we always had at the farm.'

'You're looking fresh and clean, in spite of doing the milking,' Roxie said, taking the bottle from him. His skin was glowing and his hair still slightly damp from the shower. He had changed into a pair of beige chinos and a blue cotton shirt, which emphasised his blue eyes.

'Ah, Roxie . . .' He drew her into his arms. 'You look good enough to eat yourself, my darling.' He proceeded to kiss her as though they had been apart for days instead of hours. Eventually he broke away.

'The surgeon phoned to say they are not sending Mum home tomorrow, although he felt she was in considerably better spirits than she had been in the morning, and her mind appeared to be perfectly clear and alert now. He is going to introduce her to the nurse who will be coming here to look after her. Apparently she is Mr Morgan's sister-in-law. I hadn't realised that.'

'No, I didn't know that either.'

'He says she and his wife are twins, but she is a widow now. She has always enjoyed her work as a nurse. He guarantees Mum will get the best of care.'

'I do hope she will,' Roxie said with feeling. 'It is important that Amy has confidence in whoever is looking after her. Are you ready to eat?'

'I'm famished, but this all looks appetising and something smells good. Surely you have not had time to cook?'

'It is only a light lemon pudding,' Roxie told him cheerfully.

Ciaran grinned. 'You look as fresh as a daisy and far too desirable for me to spend time eating . . .'

'Even so, a hungry man needs to keep up his strength. I will bring the glasses ready for the champagne. I see you already have a bag of ice with you.'

They enjoyed a leisurely meal and toasted each other with generous drinks. Roxie felt relaxed and happy, and a little light-headed.

'Shall we go through to the sitting room and I'll bring us some coffee to dilute the champagne?'

'All right, but I'll take our glasses through and we can drink the rest of it later,' Ciaran said, his eyes sparkling.

It was much later and the beautiful day was drawing to a close as Ciaran gathered Roxie into his arms and pulled her on top of him as he stretched out on the long settee. He began to open the buttons on her dress down to her waist. She gave a little gasp of pleasure when his fingers pushed aside her lacy bra and began to stroke her breasts, his thumb caressing her nipple until it rose to greet his eager lips. Roxie felt the hardness of him against her thigh and knew that tonight nothing could keep them apart – she wanted this just as much as he did.

'Ciaran.' She gasped softly as his hands became more persistent in their exploration. 'We must . . .'

He paused and looked up into her eyes. She read the fleeting disappointment. 'We shall not have many chances to be on our own,' he said huskily.

'I know, but I think we should go up to my bed, rather than leaving any traces down here.' She saw the joy and desire return to his blue eyes. She tried to raise herself but he put his hands around her waist and lifted her and himself from the settee. 'My darling,

Roxie, I love you more with every minute that passes.' He lowered his head to find her mouth in a searching kiss.

'Put me down,' she whispered. 'You can't possibly carry me up those stairs.'

'I can, and I will, if it means you belong to me — only to me — my darling Roxie. I think I'm the happiest man on earth.'

'And I think we have both drunk a bit too much champagne to do weightlifting on the stairs. We shall get there quicker if you put me down.'

He set her gently on her feet but he kept his arm around her waist, holding her close as they climbed the stairs to her bedroom. Ciaran lost no time in opening the rest of her buttons and removing her dress, and his eyes blazed at the sight of her in her scanty underwear. He kissed her gently on every part he could reach then slowly removed the remaining bits of clothing before rapidly stripping off his own.

* * *

Much later, Roxie opened her eyes to see the full moon lighting her bedroom. She lay contentedly cradled in Ciaran's arms, as he had held her when they'd slept together in the lorry.

'Are you awake?' she whispered.

'I am, but I don't want to leave you, not ever.'

'I know. What time is it?'

'Two o'clock in the morning.' He nuzzled the silky warmth of her neck. 'I don't want to be walking home across the field when Billy arrives for the milking, but I can't bring myself to leave you, Roxie.'

'I-I never dreamed it could be so wonderful,' she murmured.

'Wonderful enough for us to do it again before I leave, my lovely lassie?' he asked, his voice husky with emotion. In answer, Roxie turned to him and kissed him with all the passion a man could desire from the woman he loved.

Sometime later, Ciaran pulled on his clothes with a sigh, thinking it was a long time to wait for their wedding in September, how tied Roxie would be once his mother was home and how restrained she would feel, knowing his mother was both observant and very perceptive.

'I will collect you tomorrow afternoon in time for visiting, Roxie,' he said softly, bending to give her one last lingering kiss.

Chapter 17

About three quarters of an hour before Ciaran was due to collect Roxie, he telephoned to ask if she would visit the hospital on her own.

'I'm waiting for the vet to come,' he said. 'One of the heifers has been calving too long and I can't help her. I think we shall need a caesarean. Will you visit Mum, Roxie? Tell her I will try to look in tonight before the end of visiting.'

'I'll tell her, Ciaran. She will understand. You must attend to the heifer first.'

'Thanks, Roxie. Can I — can I come round to you after visiting this evening?'

'Of course you can, if you're not too tired.'

She blew him a kiss and heard him chuckle, then whisper, 'You're a sweetheart and you're mine,' before he blew a kiss back to her. Roxie smiled and shook her head. She would never have believed that she, or Ciaran, would act like a pair of teenagers, but it was wonderful to be so happy. Wistfully she thought of her father. She was sure he would have approved of Ciaran and he would have encouraged him to upgrade his dairy herd, maybe even have helped him.

Amy understood Ciaran needed to be there for the vet, as they had known she would.

'I will phone him on my mobile and tell him not to come tonight,' she said. 'Jenny is coming for evening visiting. She says it is easier to see me here than at Oaklands when she lives in town. Donald doesn't mind babysitting in the evenings. Anyway, I shall see Ciaran when I get home tomorrow. He will be more eager than ever to join us for his midday meals, I suppose?' she asked with a twinkle in her eye.

'He will.' Roxie smiled. 'What would you like me to cook for your lunch to celebrate your homecoming?'

'Well, I have had a longing for caramel custard, so light and delicious. I know you make a lovely one. Could we have that? The nurse will be joining us for her meals too. She says we have not to call her nurse, though, because it sounds too official, especially in my own home. Her name is Anne. She came to see me this morning and to get her instructions from Mr Morgan. She seems very pleasant. I think she will be in her late forties or early fifties, perhaps. She has two children at university. I suspect she has had her own share of trouble because she has been a widow for eight years.'

'I suppose most people have troubles at some time in their lives, but I should think it must be hard to be left with two youngish children to bring up and educate.'

'Yes, I agree. Mr Morgan told me her husband was a GP and she worked with him as a nurse in the surgery. She still works there a minimum of eight days a month, filling in for other nurses when they are off. Will you mind making lunch for four of us, Roxie?' Amy asked anxiously.

'Of course I don't mind. I shall be cooking anyway. We can't live on caramel custard, though.' She smiled mischievously. 'What else do you fancy?'

'How about roast chicken? We still have some nice plump chickens in the freezer, haven't we? The ones the butcher got for us.'

'We have. I will take one out to thaw as soon as I get back.'

'I have not had much appetite while I am just sitting or lying all the time. Don't make a starter for me, but I expect Ciaran will be hungry as usual.'

'I expect he will, but he will manage very well without his soup if I make some Yorkshire puddings and roast potatoes to fill him up,' she said cheerfully.

'Ah, you're a good lassie, Roxie. You never say anything is too much trouble, or too difficult.' She reached for Roxie's hand and patted it affectionately. 'I can't tell you how much I am looking forward to being home and able to sit up at my own kitchen table again, even though I shall be in a wheelchair for a while.'

'Mmm, I'd forgotten about that. Your leg will need to be straight out for some time. I will remember and seat Anne next to you instead of on the opposite side of the table. It's lucky you have a decent-sized table in the kitchen.'

'Yes, I hadn't thought of that either. I expect we shall encounter a few little inconveniences until I can get the plaster off and manage to walk again, but I have promised Mr Morgan and Mr Whittaker that I shall not try to rush things. They have arranged for the physiotherapist to visit me at home to show me and Anne the exercises I should do and what I must avoid in the beginning.'

'Whatever the problems I'm sure we shall find a solution,' Roxie said reassuringly.

'Here we are chattering about me when all I want is to talk about you and Ciaran, and your wedding. Have you decided when it will be yet?'

'Not an exact date. We'll see you back on your feet and feeling like dancing, first.' Roxie chuckled.

'Oh, don't consider me, my dear. If I know Ciaran, he will want to make you his wife without delay. His father was just the same. Once the Baxter men make up their minds, they're very impatient.' Roxie hoped guilty colour was not staining her cheeks, after last night.

'Everything has happened at once. If you are making good progress, my friend Lucy and her family will be up here on holiday at the beginning of September . . .'

'Oh, surely I shall be well by then.' Amy smiled. 'And your brother? Have you heard from him since you returned?'

'I certainly have.' Roxie grinned. 'I phoned to tell them about your accident the morning we arrived back. They were shocked of course, but Ciaran was a real hit with the two women, Maggie and Beth, who were helping with the catering. They couldn't do enough for his comfort. He can be very charming.'

'Another Baxter trait.' Amy smiled. 'Did he meet your brother?'

'He did. I was so pleased. They seemed to get on really well, in spite of Tommy not sharing Ciaran's interest in pedigree cows. Tommy phones for a progress report every evening so he can tell Maggie and Beth how you are doing. He has promised to come up for the wedding to give me away, and he will bring Beth and Maggie with him. Ciaran has told him he must bring a busload of the friends who helped with the cattle-dressing too, but I think he was probably joking.'

'I'm pleased to hear it will be a proper wedding. I did hope he wouldn't want to rush you to a register office.'

'I don't think he considered anything like that. He does say it is a long time to wait until September, though, but he understands my first priority must be to see you fully recovered, and hopefully without any pain.'

'I have no pain lying here and it is wonderful. I know it might be different when I have to put weight on my leg again, but Mr Whittaker says he can almost guarantee I shall be able to walk well, and without pain. It will be like a miracle if he's right. But, Roxie, dear, I am delighted you will be married up here. Ciaran is my only son and you're already as dear to me as any daughter could be. Whatever happens, I want you to set a date for a September wedding, whether or not I am completely recovered. That is three, maybe three and a half months, depending on the date, but it is surprising how time flies when there are arrangements to make. It is so exciting. I can't wait to be home and hear all your plans. Oh! There goes the bell. It must be the end of visiting already.' Amy looked disappointed, but Roxie knew she must be tired.

'You should have a rest now, then you will be fresh for Jenny's visit tonight. I have not had a proper conversation with her since we came back, and Ciaran and I have not discussed any plans yet. I know my friend, Lucy, will want to be my matron of honour, because I was her bridesmaid. I thought Jenny might agree to be a matron of honour too, especially as Ciaran will be asking Don to be best man.' She sighed regretfully. 'I had better go now before the nurse throws me out.'

She bent to kiss Amy's cheek and felt her fingers squeezed in response.

* * *

Roxie had not been back very long when the phone rang. As she had guessed, it was Ciaran.

'Mum telephoned to tell me not to go in tonight. She sounds in good spirits?'

'Yes, she is. She is eager to talk about the wedding, and is pleased we shall be getting married up here and not in Derbyshire. So am I really. It would not be the same without my . . . well, without either of my parents.'

'I can understand that, but I am glad Tommy will be coming and bringing some of your friends.'

'Oh, yes, so am I, but I was not expecting we should have a big wedding. We'll talk about that later. How is the heifer?'

'She is fine, on her feet and chewing her cud, and the calf is a fine heifer calf so it has been a worthwhile afternoon.'

'I am glad about that.'

'Will you also be glad if I join you for our meal again, even if it is without champagne?'

'Of course I will, and I don't need champagne to make me happy.'

'You're a girl in a million, and you're my girl.' He chuckled. It seemed to have become his favourite phrase.

'Your mother is expecting to see you at lunchtime tomorrow. The nurse will be here too. Her name is Anne Munro and that is what we have to call her.'

'Mmm, we shall need to mind our p's and q's then, but I'm sure I shall manage to steal a kiss before I leave.' He laughed out loud. 'I can almost see you blushing so charmingly, my dearest Roxie.'

'I shall deal with you later, Ciaran Baxter. I am going to prepare some food for us now. See you later.'

* * *

Amy arrived home in the ambulance the following day with Nurse Anne Munro following in her own small blue Vauxhall. Roxie was concerned to see that Amy looked quite weary so early in the day, but perhaps it was the stress of getting ready and the journey. Ciaran arrived soon after. When he had greeted his mother and been introduced to Anne, he announced that he was famished. Roxie and Amy both shook their heads, but they smiled. They knew it was typical of Ciaran to hide his true feelings, but they could see he was relieved and delighted to see his mum home again.

'I will show you the downstairs bathroom, Anne,' Roxie said. 'It is a little earlier than we usually have our midday meal, but it is ready so we may as well eat now.' In the hall she lowered her voice. 'Amy seems quite weary compared to the way she was when I saw her yesterday.'

'Yes, but I shall persuade her to take a rest in her bedroom after lunch and I think she will be relieved to be home. They all said what a good patient she is.'

'She is a good person. She never moans, even when she must have been in pain.'

'That is good to hear.' Anne Munro smiled. 'She sings your praises too and she seems extremely happy to know you will soon be part of her family.'

'I will start putting out the lunch. Come through to the kitchen when you're ready. We usually eat in there anyway, but Amy said you have a blow-up bed and intend staying overnight for the first two nights at least, so I have made space for you in the dining room, if that's all right? That's the door straight across from the bathroom and Amy's bedroom.'

'That will be ideal. Most patients like their privacy, but I like to be close in case they need me in the night.'

Roxie was pleased to see Amy helping herself to a decent meal and she seemed to enjoy it. Ciaran certainly enjoyed his, including eating up the spare Yorkshire puddings.'

'That was delicious,' Anne Munro announced. 'If you feed me like this every day, I shall have put on a stone in weight by the end of the fortnight that I am booked to come every day. I am flexible, so we shall see what you need after that, Mrs Baxter.'

'Oh, do call me Amy. We don't stand on ceremony here.'

'No, we don't,' Ciaran said. 'So, no more Mr Baxter either if you please.'

The jolly exchange set the tone for Anne Munro's visits and they settled into a happy atmosphere during Amy's convalescence. Some healing could not be rushed, but Amy understood that. Even so, she was delighted when Mr Whittaker came down from Glasgow to see her the third week in June. She knew he would add the trip to his fees, of course, but he helped her spirits tremendously when he told her and Anne that they were making excellent progress between them.

'You have no idea what a difference it makes to have a well-organised happy household, both to me and to my patients,' Anne said to Roxie.

'Amy is certainly looking better for your ministrations,' Roxie assured her.

'Yes, and she is so excited about the wedding. I heard her telling her son he must take you down to the farmhouse to choose which bedroom you want to use for yourselves, then he must get the painter in to decorate both it and the sitting room to your own choice. She also instructed him to take you to choose new carpets for both rooms on the days I shall still be coming so she will have company. She said it would help you to feel it is your home and that you truly belong. Not many mothers-in-law are so kind and considerate.'

'Amy has been kind and welcoming since the moment I arrived,' Roxie said with a warm smile.

'And her son too, I imagine,' Anne said with a mischievous grin.

'Oh no! Ciaran and I almost had a stand-up quarrel the day I arrived. I suppose we both have a bit of a temper at times.'

'He's certainly making up for it now. He obviously adores you.'

Roxie blushed, but made no reply.

The physiotherapist turned out to be a young man named David Vey. He was very good at his job and patient with the people he was treating. He appeared to be late twenties and rather good-looking. He annoyed Ciaran from the first time they met, because he was obviously keen to gain Roxie's attention and entertain her with his jokes and teasing. Sometimes he joined them for lunch if his appointment coincided with their meal time. Roxie made a point of remembering his likes and dislikes if she knew he would be joining them.

'There's no need to make things specially to please that fellow,' Ciaran grumbled to Roxie one afternoon when he had finally got her to himself.

'I try much harder to please you,' she said, grinning cheekily.

'I wish we were married right now,' he said softly. 'It seems ages until September.'

'Don't worry about David, Ciaran. He is here to do a job and your mother likes him, but she let him know from the beginning that we are engaged and planning our wedding soon. I think he sometimes flirts with me a little to tease her, but she has realised that and she gives him a bit of cheek in return. He says she's one of the best patients he has had.'

'Mmm, that's all very well,' he muttered. 'I think it is time we spent an afternoon together to collect the wedding invitations and check up on the hotel to make sure everything will be organised for the evening guests, and those who are staying the weekend. I feel we should invite the clique Don and I used to go around with. Don and Jenny didn't have a very big wedding. Jenny was still missing her mother, so they had no evening guests.'

'I can understand that,' Roxie murmured sympathetically.

'Tommy has promised to invite your mutual friends and their partners, especially the ones who helped you with preparations for the sale. He expects most of them will be eager to come. He says you were very popular with them all. He thinks they might hire a minibus, but he is bringing Beth and Maggie in his car.'

'Goodness me! How do you know all that?'

'Ah, Tommy and I have had a few chats on the telephone. I think we should have got on very well, if we had known each other. We are both alone in the evenings, so it is a good time to chat and I like to hear about you. I could think of better ways to fill my evenings though,' he added with a wicked grin.

'Mmm, I know you could,' she said darkly. 'Our main concern is that your mother should be recovered well enough to walk without pain, or the need for her wheels.'

'She is expecting to send the wheels to the devil and dance down the aisle, if you ask me. She is more excited than we are. She keeps reminding me we are her only family, so ours will be the only wedding she can help with. I expect she has told you she is paying for the reception as she wants the best for both of us.'

'Paying for . . . ? Oh, no. Your mother cannot pay, Ciaran! It is up to the bride's parents to pay for the wedding. I know my father would have . . . would have . . .' She gulped down a sudden knot of tears.

'Oh, my darling Roxie.' Ciaran pulled her into his arms. 'I didn't mean to upset you. Both Mum and I know it is as hard for you as it was for Jenny, without your parents.'

'It is only when I stop to think about arrangements and guest lists. To tell the truth, Ciaran, I am glad the wedding is away from everything that was familiar, like the local church and so many people who have known me since I was a child. Even so, I must pay for our wedding reception . . .'

'I know you can afford to pay, Roxie, but Mum truly wants to do it. She regards you as a daughter and I am all she's got in the way of family. She wants to give us a day to remember. We can't spoil her pleasure.'

Roxie bit her lip and wiped away a few tears. She didn't think Ciaran had been aware how much she longed for her father to have been there, but it seems he had and so had Amy.

'I expect we'll work something out,' she said gruffly as Ciaran drew her close for a long kiss.

'Oh, I'm sorry, I didn't mean to disturb you,' Anne said hastily and immediately withdrew, leaving Ciaran to move reluctantly.

'I'd better get back to work.' He sighed. 'There's no doubt Billy is not as reliable about details as he ought to be. He was fine before he got so keen on following the local football team to all their matches and started helping to coach the youth team. He goes with his motorbike friends to all the matches. He is worse since he started coaching, wanting to rush the milking during the week so he can get away early. It is not as though he is their only coach.'

'I remember you weren't too happy with his work when you had been at the sale.'

'Yeah — and he made young Vic prepare and bed the sheds for the animals we were bringing back with us that night, despite me asking him to do it. He used to be so keen, and he seemed to take an interest in his work and which cows were due to calve, and how they were milking.' He didn't tell Roxie how irritable, almost resentful, Billy had been ever since the weekend she had done the milking for Ciaran when he'd had the food poisoning, and the teasing Billy had subsequently received.

'I tried to tell him you came because I was desperate and there was no one else I could call on.'

'I suppose some of his friends have easier jobs than he does. Few of them will start work so early in the morning, or work after five in the evenings,' Roxie said.

'That's true, but they work all day. They don't have several hours off in the middle of the day. Surely that makes up for the early mornings?'

'Sometimes it does, I suppose, especially if a person is truly interested in their work and the animals, but it depends on their interests and commitments, whether they are married with a home, a family, a garden to enjoy. Time off through the day is not much use if your friends all meet in the evenings, or at the weekends while you're working,' Roxie said.

'Are you saying I don't treat Billy well?' Ciaran asked indignantly.

'No, I'm not saying that. I think you treat him generously. Not many dairy workers in England have so much time off during the day, especially in the summer. I think it was being tied to a demanding routine seven days a week that Tommy hated.'

'I expect it depends what we want from life.' Ciaran sighed. 'Billy certainly likes the extra money for being a herdsman.'

'If you are really interested in your work, as Dad and I were with our animals, and trying to breed something better, you don't grudge the time it takes. I know you feel the same, but Billy seems to have developed other interests. Maybe he is finding he's not cut out to be a dairyman now, but still wants the higher pay he gets for unsocial hours.'

'I think you're right. Mum thinks it would be good for both of us to get away abroad for our honeymoon. I would love to do that with you, Roxie, but I'm not sure I could rely on Billy to look after the animals properly for one week, even less for the two or more weeks I would have liked for our honeymoon. Max, the tractor driver, is good at his job, but he would be no use at milking, or even knowing when a cow was calving or needing the vet. At least if we were in Britain, we could get home within a day if there was any kind of crisis.'

'You mean something like when Billy broke his leg?'

'Less than that even — anything that threw him off routine. I would have staked my life on him being reliable at one time.'

'Dear Ciaran, it's true I'm looking forward to getting away on our own for a few days, but I don't care where we go, if we're together. Anyway, I haven't got a passport, so you need not worry about going abroad. If we only get to Edinburgh or Blackpool, or wherever, it will suit me.'

'Ah, Roxie, no wonder I love you. I can't wait for September to come.'

* * *

Time passed more quickly than any of them had expected. After attending Amy every day for two weeks, Anne Munro started coming three days a week, mainly to help with bathing and dressing until the plaster cast was removed. Amy was relieved when she did get rid of it and she was diligent about doing the exercises which David, the physio, recommended. He had tried to keep her other leg and the rest of her muscles in trim and it was paying dividends. Eventually Anne was able to stop her official visits, but Amy asked her to keep in touch regularly and maybe call in for coffee and a chat every week if she had time.

'I feel you have become a good friend and Roxie agrees. We shall both miss your cheery company.'

'Yes,' Roxie said. 'And I would feel happier if I knew Amy had company when I need to go into town for shopping, at least until she has been able to practise walking for a bit longer.'

So, Anne got into the habit of calling in for coffee and a chat most weeks.

* * *

Amy wanted to buy a special birthday present for Roxie and she confided in Anne.

'I would like to buy her something pretty and it would be a bonus if it was blue. I know she wants to keep her wedding dress a secret, but it is ivory satin and she will be wearing her mother's veil. I overheard her telling Jenny she had something old, something new and something borrowed . . .'

'Ah I see.' Anne chuckled. 'But she has nothing blue yet?'

'That's right. She told Jenny she would just sew on a blue bow somewhere. She and Ciaran are so happy about everything I think they would have been quite satisfied with two witnesses in a registrar's office, but Ciaran has a lot of friends and Roxie's friends are hiring a minibus.' Amy sighed happily. 'I want them to have a wonderful day. Ciaran is my only chick and Roxie is like a daughter to me. That's why I would like to get a special birthday present.'

'When is Roxie's birthday?'

'In August, the fifteenth, I think.'

'What would you say if I drove us to Edinburgh? I don't think you would need a wheelchair if we plan things properly, but I can borrow a folding one to put in the car boot, just in case. You're doing so much better than any of us expected. I could ask Jayne, my daughter, and her cousin Hannah, to suggest a hotel where we can park and have lunch. They would enjoy scouting around the jewellers to see if they can find anything they like themselves. After all, Roxanne is not so much older than they are. If they find what they like, you might consider something similar. We can take a taxi from the hotel if it is too far to the shops. I would never want you to overdo things.'

'I would enjoy meeting Jayne and your niece. Perhaps they can have lunch with us, unless they will be home for the summer by the time we go.'

'They share a flat belonging to my brother-in-law, so they often stay there, even during the holidays if there is a show they want to see or things they want to do. Jayne is lucky. Jonathan is very generous that way. I am ready for a day away myself. I will phone Jayne tonight and ask them to scout around, then tell me when they would be free to meet us. I will let you know what can be done.'

* * *

The visit to Edinburgh proved very productive and Amy enjoyed meeting Jayne and Hannah.

'They would pass for twins!' she said as soon as she saw them waiting in the hotel lounge.

'Well, they both take after their mothers, and Jean and I are identical twins.' Anne smiled. As they ate lunch, the girls described some of the jewellery shops they had visited.

'We saw several bracelets and some of them with blue stones were very expensive, but there was one — what did they call the blue stuff, Jayne?' Hannah asked.

'Lapis lazuli. I looked it up later. It's supposed to aid calm and a focused state of mind. Maybe that's what I should have to wear during my exams,' Jayne said with a smile.

'You always do well, whether you're calm or not,' Hannah said. 'I saw a lovely blue topaz pendant with tiny diamonds surrounding it, but it was more than two hundred and fifty pounds.'

Jayne nodded. 'There were a few really lovely items with blue stones. I think some of them were sapphires on gold chains, but they had no prices. They were obviously expensive because they were in a glass cabinet, which was locked.'

'If they are good quality and value for money, I would quite like to see them,' Amy said. 'Apart from the fact that Roxie will be my daughter-in-law soon, she has been so kind and considerate to me right from the day she arrived. I have never seen Ciaran so happy either and that is worth everything to me.'

Anne nodded. 'Yes, she is a lovely person and a very capable young woman too.'

'I know she intends to wear her mother's pearls on her wedding day,' Amy said. 'But she has a lovely deep-blue evening gown she wore to the New Year's dinner dance, so she could wear a necklace with that.'

'Oh, she could wear it with anything!' Jayne said enthusiastically.

'Yes, she could — a summer dress or a smart outfit. The pendant we saw was gorgeous,' Hannah said enthusiastically.

'Well, girls, the least we can do is look at it when you have taken so much trouble searching the shops on my behalf,' Amy said with a smile.

* * *

'I understand you were looking for a bracelet in blue, but I am so sorry — the only blue one I have in stock is part of a set,' the jeweller said apologetically. 'I am most reluctant to break it up yet as we have not had it in stock very long. I do have a diamond bracelet or a very nice broad one in gold with engraving.'

'No, no, I would like it to be something blue,' Amy said. 'May I see the set, please? She glanced at the girls and saw Jayne chewing her lip while Hannah watched anxiously. She smiled at them. 'You have researched well on my behalf, girls, and I think I must bow to your knowledge of what is fashionable for a generation so much younger, and so different, to my own.'

The jeweller discreetly turned over the box showing the price ticket. Amy did her best to keep a neutral expression but she saw it was expensive.

'I believe the stones are sapphires?' she murmured, looking at the man. *At least I can afford it*, she thought, *and Roxie has no parents to buy her jewellery.*

'It is beautiful,' she said to Anne wistfully. 'Roxie is not a careless girl, especially with things she treasures. I could give her the bracelet for her birthday so she can wear it for her wedding, as well as her mother's pearls, if she wishes. Then I will keep the pendant and earrings to celebrate her first Christmas as Mrs Baxter.'

'I'm sure Roxie will appreciate how very generous you are,' Anne said.

'Yes, I will take the set,' she told the jeweller, waiting patiently. She heard the girls give a faint gasp.

'Your new daughter-in-law will love it, and you,' Jayne said with a wide smile.

'She will love you for ever,' Hannah said. 'I know I would.'

'It seems you have done a good job then, girls.' Anne smiled at them both.

'You have indeed. I shall not forget how helpful you have been,' Amy said. 'Maybe you will call to see me when you come down for the holidays. Now, I would also like to buy a small gift for my good friend here.' She smiled at the jeweller and indicated Anne. 'I thought perhaps one of these gold brooches in the cabinet. She indicated three brooches neatly displayed on a crimson velvet pad in a glass cabinet.

'Oh, no!' Anne said. 'You can't possibly buy anything for me. I have been well paid, not to mention well fed, for doing my job. What is more important, I have truly enjoyed it. Few of my patients are so easy and pleasant, or so grateful. It has been a pleasure.'

'Even so, I do want to give you a small gift. Think of the time I would have had to spend in hospital if you could not have come to nurse me. I had intended to have the operation done privately in Glasgow and that would have cost me far more, too, so please choose one of these brooches, or something else if you prefer? Earrings, maybe?' Seeing Amy was in earnest, the jeweller drew out the pad for closer inspection and when Anne selected a pretty leaf-shaped brooch, he was well pleased.

'Madam, I shall give you a ten per cent discount on your purchases since you are taking the brooch as well as the complete set.' Anne and Amy looked at each other, eyebrows raised in a humorous glance.

'Thank you very much,' Amy said with a smile as she paid. 'I believe we have had a worthwhile afternoon.'

Chapter 18

On the way home, Amy told her new friend that Ciaran was planning a special birthday for Roxanne.

'He is taking her away for the day, either to the coast if the weather is good, or maybe up here to Edinburgh, as she had not visited Scotland before she came to Oakfield. Her only close family now is her brother, so Ciaran has invited him to come for a surprise visit so that we all meet before the wedding. He has also asked the two ladies who looked after him so well when he was down there for the sale of the dairy herd that belonged to Tommy and Roxie's father.

'Now that I am beginning to feel like my old self again, I have promised to invite them to my home in the evening for a buffet meal, but I shall have to wait until Ciaran has collected Roxie in the morning, or she will feel she should stay and do the preparations. My niece and her husband and baby are coming too. Jenny is coming early to help. She is bringing some quiches. I believe you know her husband, Donald. He is a dental surgeon.'

'Oh, yes, I do! I have met his wife, too. I am a patient there and they are both very pleasant and reassuring.' She grinned. 'We medics are more nervous patients than most other people, I suspect.'

'That is good if you have met Jenny already, because I was going to ask if you would like to join us. I know you and Roxie get on splendidly.'

'We do indeed. I never felt there was a generation gap, as one often does with people so much younger.'

'I suspect Roxie has had her share of life's less pleasant aspects. That usually strengthens character and broadens the mind. I never met a young person whose company I value so highly.'

* * *

The evening before Tommy and Maggie were due to set out for Scotland and Roxanne's surprise birthday, Tommy telephoned Ciaran.

'Do you remember the young herdsman I had at the time of the sale?' he asked.

'I certainly do,' Ciaran said. 'Harry, wasn't it? Harry Dunn?'

'That's right.'

'I was impressed with the way he looked after all the animals, right to the end, and he seemed to know most of their breeding too. Roxanne was amazed that he recognised the individual cows and how they were performing. She said he was really keen to learn everything about preparing them for sale.'

'Yes, Roxie was pleased with his willingness to work and to learn everything he could. He came to see me this morning to ask if I could store an oak corner cupboard and a Welsh dresser, plus a few other small pieces of furniture he wants to keep. They belonged to his mother who died recently. He is selling their house — in fact, he has already accepted a really good offer for it. I invited him to stay overnight. He hasn't enjoyed working for the dealer in spite of very good pay. He didn't like the system and never getting to know the animals. He plans to see something of the country before he settles down to another job. He intends to sell his motorbike and buy a small car. He was talking of going to Wales because six of our cows went to two herds there. I believe he hopes to come your way sometime too, so I wondered whether to suggest bringing him with us tomorrow. I haven't mentioned it to him, but I've looked up a Travelodge and it seems in reasonable distance to you, but if that is too much of an imposition please say so. I do understand.'

'Of course, you should bring him with you if he wants to come,' Ciaran said. 'I'm sure Roxie would be pleased to see him again.'

'I'm sure Harry would like to see how the cows you bought are doing.'

'Don't even think about the Travelodge,' Ciaran said. 'So long as you don't mind making do, that is. I told you I don't have a housekeeper, but Iris, my cleaning woman, has already made up two beds. One of the rooms has twin beds so she could easily make up the other bed in the morning, if you don't mind sharing a room? I am really looking forward to getting to know you better, Tommy. It will be a lovely surprise for Roxie.'

'Yes, I'm looking forward to coming. I have a lot to tell Roxie, too. Some things are easier face-to-face, rather than on the phone. Maggie is like part of the family so she knows most of what has been going on with my affairs and the solicitor. The reason I will not bring Beth on this visit, is due to Gilda's wild accusations about me having an affair with Beth.' Tommy sighed. 'She will be coming to your wedding, though, and she is really looking forward to it.'

'In that case, we shall look forward to seeing the three of you tomorrow. I have not breathed a word to Roxie. Mum wants me to take her away for the day so she will have plenty of time preparing a buffet for an evening meal for all of us. She wants to meet you before the wedding. My cousin has baked a birthday cake and she will be helping her prepare. They all love Roxie. I told you where to find the key to let yourselves in if you arrive before we return from our day away. Make yourselves some tea and toast until we return, and you'll find biscuits in the tin.'

* * *

It was a bright summer morning and Roxanne had woken early. She lay in bed for a while, relaxing and listening to the birds singing. She was looking forward to spending her birthday with Ciaran. He had said he would collect her fairly early. The forecast was good so they planned to head for the Galloway hills and the west coast, and find a nice place for lunch near the shore. It was all new country for her, so she was looking forward to it.

Roxie hummed to herself and put on a pretty floral cotton dress. It had a full skirt and was sleeveless, but it had a little matching bolero that could be removed if it became very warm. She put on her sandals, but collected her comfortable shoes and a jacket in case they decided to take a walk anywhere.

Amy greeted her in the kitchen. 'Oh, Roxie, how pretty you look. I do wish you a very happy birthday.' She moved round the table to give Roxie a warm embrace. 'I have made your breakfast for a change since this is your special day.'

'You're spoiling me . . .'

'Now, don't protest. You are worth it, and it is wonderful to feel more like my old self again and be able to do things without hobbling around with those horrid wheels. I hardly even need my stick when I'm in the kitchen with most things in reach. Ciaran said he might join us for breakfast, if everything was going well, but we don't need to wait for him. You know how quickly he can demolish a meal if he is hungry.'

They finished bacon and eggs, and the toast and honey, and moved onto their second cup of coffee, but there was no sign of Ciaran.

'I expect there is a cow calving or some other animal in trouble.' Amy sighed. 'Anyway, that is no reason why I should wait to give you your birthday present, Roxie.'

'I thought you were inviting Jenny, Donald and baby Peter, and making us a buffet supper as my birthday present,' Roxie said.

'Oh, that wouldn't be much of a present.' Amy smiled broadly. She passed Roxie a lovely card and a small parcel wrapped in silver paper. When she unwrapped it and opened the jeweller's box with the white silk lining, Roxie gasped aloud.

'Oh, this is beautiful, absolutely beautiful, b-but it is far too much. Oh Amy . . .' There were tears in her eyes as she looked up. Amy shook her head.

'You deserve that, and more, lassie,' she said warmly, her voice husky with emotion. 'I was not sure about the choice but . . .'

'It's truly lovely, but it looks very expensive and — and I — I don't know what to say . . .'

'Try on the bracelet. I thought that might be something blue you could wear on your wedding day if you wanted.'

'You're right! I had nothing in blue. Oh, Amy, you are so thoughtful and far, far too generous.'

'Roxie. It will give me the greatest pleasure to know that my new daughter-in-law is wearing a small gift from me on her wedding day.' Roxie stood up and hugged Amy warmly.

'You have been kind and generous to me since the day I arrived.'

'Anne's daughter and niece did some shopping research in Edinburgh before we went so that made . . .'

They both turned as Ciaran came through the back door looking hot and disgruntled, still in his working clothes.

'Sit down, Ciaran and calm yourself,' Amy said. 'Your breakfast is ready and keeping warm in the bottom oven. I will just add a couple of eggs to the frying pan and make some fresh toast, while you drink your fruit juice.'

'Don't rush, Ciaran, we have all day,' Roxie said calmly. 'Presumably something is wrong with one of the animals?'

'No, there's nothing wrong with the stock. It's the stockman.'

'Billy, you mean? Didn't he turn up for the milking? You should have pho—'

'Oh, he turned up this morning all right. He has known for weeks that I planned to go away today, but he has still arranged to go with the youth team to a football match up in Ayrshire this afternoon.'

'Ah, so he will not be here for the afternoon milking?' Roxie asked. 'Never mind, we'll have most of the day together. We shall have to come back a bit earlier than we planned, but I'll bring my jeans and a T-shirt and help you,' she added amiably.

'What a shame, son, today of all days, and when you had made plans,' Amy said, looking troubled because she knew Ciaran had planned Tommy's surprise visit too. 'Had Billy forgotten you had made arrangements to go away for Roxie's birthday?'

'No, he hadn't forgotten. He thinks he should do as he likes lately.' He couldn't tell either of them of Billy's spiteful comments about his forthcoming wedding, and that they would both have a woman for a boss once she got a ring on her finger.

'I'm afraid I lost my temper this time,' Ciaran muttered. 'I told him he needs to consider what is more important to him — his job or the football club. We both got rather heated. He said he was sick of the bloody cows and fitting his life round their routine. Then he said if a day out with "a bloody woman" was so important to me, he would come back and milk the cows at two o'clock this afternoon and get away by four thirty.'

'Two o'clock!' Roxie gasped. 'The cows will not be ready for milking again by then. Tomorrow morning some of them will have so much milk they will have painfully swollen udders . . .'

'Precisely,' Ciaran said grimly. 'Even young Vic would realise that. I told him we would come back earlier than planned and I would do the milking myself.' Ciaran took a deep breath and grimaced. 'I'm afraid I was so angry, so frustrated with him, I told him that since his job means so little to him he could take a month's notice and look for a job to suit his own pursuits.'

Roxie and Amy spoke in unison. 'Oh, dear.'

'A month!' Amy continued in dismay. 'But that gives you no time to look for a new herdsman before the wedding. Your honeymoon . . .'

'I didn't consider anything in the heat of the moment. I was so angry, and disappointed in him. Anyway, I'm not sure I could trust him if I go away and leave him — even for a few days, much less the fortnight as we had hoped.'

'Oh, Ciaran, that's terrible. You must have a honeymoon. Couldn't you apologise?' Amy asked.

'I'm sure we shall survive,' Roxie said calmly. 'Maybe we shall manage a weekend on our own, even if you have to book the man from the relief agency?'

'I'm sorry.' Ciaran gave a sigh and rubbed his brow. 'Do you still want to marry a man who loses his temper, Roxie?' he asked dejectedly.

'Oh, Ciaran, of course I do. I would make a poor wife if I fell at the first problem.'

'Thank God you appreciate what's involved with caring for animals, Roxie.'

'Let's get away and enjoy what we can of the day — *after* you have showered of course,' Roxie said with a smile.

'Yes. I'll do that, sweetheart. Mum, we shall come back here as planned after I have done the milking. We'll try not to be too late.'

'Don't worry about that. It will be a buffet so nothing will waste.'

'Thank God I have two understanding women in my life.' Ciaran finished off his last piece of toast.

'One very understanding and reasonable young lady, I'd say,' Amy said drily. 'You forgot to wish Roxie happy birthday.'

'Goodness, so I did! Roxie, I'm so sorry. My decent clothes are in the car. When I have showered and changed, I shall give you a big birthday kiss and all the good wishes in the world — and maybe even a wee present,' he finished with a grin. Roxie shook her head and grinned back at him.

'I will bring in your clothes. Then I shall collect my jeans and wellingtons so I can change and help you with the milking when we get back.' She didn't see the exchange of glances or Amy's eyebrows raised in anxious query. Ciaran shrugged, knowing there was nothing he could do about their surprise visitors.

'I reckon, from what I saw of him at the sale, Tom will understand that these things happen,' he said in a low voice when Roxie went out to the car to collect his clothes.

* * *

They drove through Dumfries and took the road to the Galloway coast, stopping off at one or two points where the tide came right in because Roxie was fascinated by the sea, the sand and the tides, and the shells and rocks at the different inlets. Having lived all her life in Derbyshire, she had rarely been to the seaside except for a rare day trip when she'd been at school.

'My parents were as tied up with milking routines as you are,' she told Ciaran. 'I never felt I was missing out on anything. We had a very happy childhood until Mum became ill, and, even then, my parents did their best to appear cheerful and happy.'

'You seem to have a calm and happy outlook on life, Roxie, in spite of the terrible loss of your parents. I know what a dreadful shock your father's death has been, and how grief stricken you were when you first came here. They must have set a fine example. I am thankful for that, at times like this. I was just so — so angry and disappointed in Billy this morning. The strange thing is, it is often the people who lack for nothing who seem to grumble most.'

'You could be right about that.' Roxie mused, thinking of people she had known who never seemed content. 'I love the scenery and the sea all the more now I am here,' she continued. 'We must enjoy it while we can. It is a beautiful day. We couldn't have asked for better.'

'Except a dairyman who is reliable,' Ciaran muttered drily.

'Do you think he will look for a similar job with animals?'

'I doubt it. He seems ready for a change, even though it will mean less money. I'm sorry I lost my temper, today of all days. Mum is right, it will not be easy getting a reliable worker before our wedding, but I must book the relief worker for a long weekend at least.'

'It is not the end of the world. We could stay in a nice hotel somewhere like this area. It is all new to me, and we would not be far away if anything goes wrong and we need to hurry back.'

'Mmm, I suppose so. It's not what I had expected us to do for a honeymoon, though.'

'Let's forget about everything else and enjoy our day,' Roxie said, then added with a smile, 'I'm getting hungry.'

'We have not much further to go,' he said with a chuckle. He winked wickedly. 'We're going to a hotel near the sea where they have really good food.'

* * *

It was more than two hours later when they came out of the hotel, both feeling happy and replete.

'It was worth waiting for,' Roxie said as they got into the car. 'The menu was extensive and everything I selected was delicious.'

'Yes, I agree. It was Don who recommended it. I must tell him how good it was.'

'Speaking of Don and Jenny, I hope no one has gone to too much trouble over a buffet meal. I don't think I could eat another thing until tomorrow morning.' Roxie tentatively patted her stomach.

'It is a long while until then and lots to do. I had planned to take you to Logan Gardens, or to the lighthouse today. You could see the

Isle of Man, as well as parts of England, Ireland and Scotland if you climb to the top. Blast Billy Brewster for spoiling my plans,' he said, but his tone was not so bitter now and Roxie was glad.

'Never mind, Ciaran, I have already had a lovely birthday as well as beautiful gifts from you and your mother.' She glanced down at the lovely gold watch Ciaran had given her. 'There will be other times when we can get away for a day once we're married. I thought Tommy might have sent a birthday card, but I expect he's forgotten.'

'I wanted to make this an extra special day for you, my darling,' Ciaran murmured. He drew her into his arms for a passionate kiss, before reluctantly drawing away with a sigh. 'I'm afraid we must start on the homeward journey now or I shall be milking when we should be eating supper.' He was tempted to tell her about the unexpected visitors he had arranged for a birthday surprise, but he kept silent in case anything else should go wrong.

Much later, when they turned into the Oaklands farmyard, Ciaran was glad he had not spoiled Roxie's delight. She gasped incredulously as she recognised her brother's car, and then at the sight of Tommy in the big farmhouse kitchen at Oaklands. On the other side of the table, drinking tea, was Maggie West. At her side, smiling shyly, was Harry, the young stockman who had worked so hard to help her make the Willowbrook sale such a success.

'I can't believe it,' she said when she had finished hugging both Tommy and Maggie, and had told Harry how good it was to see him again. Ciaran grinned, relieved the visitors had found their way all right.

'We made better time than we expected,' Tommy said. 'So, we have made ourselves at home as you instructed, Ciaran.'

'Yes, we have just made a pot of tea,' Maggie said. 'I hope you don't mind?'

'Of course not. I'm glad you could come, all of you,' he said, smiling at Harry to reassure him he was welcome. 'I told Tommy to feel free to make yourselves at home.'

'We didn't expect you back so early, from what you told me of your plans,' Tommy said, eyebrows raised in question.

'No, I had intended showing Roxie a lot more of the Mull of Galloway but . . .' His mouth tightened. 'Things don't always go to plan. My stockman told me this morning he had other, more important things on today, so we had to come back early to do the milking before we all go to my mother's for a buffet meal.'

'Ciaran, can I get them anything to eat? Toast, perhaps?' Roxie asked. 'We have had such a delicious lunch, so all I want is a drink of tea. You three have had a long journey.'

'We left early and stopped for lunch on the way,' Tommy said. 'But I wouldn't mind something to eat if it will be a few hours before we have our evening meal. We don't want to look like gluttons when we get there.' He grinned at Ciaran.

'Don't worry about that. Knowing my mother, there will be more than enough to eat. She is thankful she is on her own two feet again and able to make a decent spread.'

'I did bring a Victoria sponge,' Maggie said. 'And I made a batch of cheese scones this morning before we set out.' She smiled at Ciaran. 'I remembered how much you enjoyed a sponge cake when you were down for the sale and it is very kind of you to invite me to your home, too.'

'I am pleased to see you again, Maggie,' Ciaran said with a smile. 'And I knew Roxie would be thrilled to have you here. Is this your first visit to Scotland?'

'It is, and I've been that excited,' Maggie told him eagerly.

'You must have got up early to bake before you set off, Maggie. You shouldn't feel sorry for this man.' Roxie winked at Ciaran. 'He spends most of his time getting fed with us at the bungalow.'

'Did you leave the baking in the car, Maggie?' Tommy asked. 'I'll bring them in. I have a huge parcel in the boot for you, Sissy.'

'And instructions from Lucy!' Maggie reminded him hurriedly, shaking her head in exasperation.

'Oh! I forgot I was supposed to keep it a secret.' Tommy gave a repentant grin as he went out to the car with Ciaran and Harry.

'I don't know what kind of a surprise that can be,' Roxie said. 'And now I can't wait to see.'

Maggie was standing behind Tommy and Ciaran so they didn't see her mouth silently, 'Wedding dress,' and put a finger to her lips. She looked alarmed, but Roxie nodded and smiled. Then Maggie whispered, 'There is a smaller box with a bridesmaid's dress and a squashy parcel for your birthday, but she said I should warn you not to open that either in front of Ciaran and his mother, or you might feel embarrassed.' She giggled like a girl and Roxie gave her a suspicious look. 'She didn't tell me what it was, but I'm guessing she's made you a sexy see-through nightie.' Maggie chuckled.

'Oh, gosh.' Roxie blushed. 'I'm glad you warned me. I will drive up to the bungalow with Tommy in his car and leave you and Harry to come with Ciaran, then I can dash upstairs to my bedroom with the parcels while you are all being introduced to Amy and Jenny.'

Chapter 19

'I must go and change now to get on with the milking,' Ciaran said ruefully. 'I am really sorry about this.'

'The best-laid plans and all that,' Tommy said drily. 'We understand.'

'Can I come with you?' Harry asked eagerly. 'I would love to see your cows and the farm.'

'Do you think you will be able to pick out the Willowbrook animals we brought back with us?' Ciaran asked with a grin.

'I don't know. I would like to think I still know the cows, though not the young calves. They will have grown a bit by now. I have a spare pair of jeans and a T-shirt.'

'You can change in the downstairs cloakroom then,' Roxie said with a grin, seeing how eager Harry was to go with Ciaran.

'I wouldn't be surprised if he ends up helping with the milking,' she said, when both Ciaran and Harry had gone to change. 'The milking parlour is very similar to the one we had at Willowbrook, and I'll bet he recognises at least three of the cows.'

'Do you really think so?' Tommy asked dubiously.

'Yes, he cared for them like many people care for their pet dog. His interest was genuine.'

'In spite of the extra money, he certainly hated working for that dealer and having strange cows coming and going all the time,' said Tommy. 'He stuck it because it was convenient and allowed him to be with his mother when she needed him. He had done a lot to their cottage and he tried to make everything comfortable for her. He has sold it now and got a far better price than he expected. Over the years he had built a staircase and put in two dormer windows upstairs, as well as a small bathroom with a roof light. They had a very large garden that had been his father's pride and joy. That is what attracted the man who bought it. He is a GP and has joined the local doctors' practice. He is engaged to the district nurse who has been very kind and caring with Harry's mother, so she knew how much Harry had done to improve the house and that he intended to sell it and move away.'

'He was lucky to get it sold with so little trouble,' Roxie said.

'I suppose so, but the nurse had lived in the same village all her life and her mother and Harry's had been good friends when they were younger.'

Roxie nodded. 'Ciaran says he will have to modernise one of his cottages before he gets a new stockman. He thinks it would be more convenient to have a stockman living close by, as they used to have when he was young. Billy preferred to live in the village where he grew up, but it is a few miles away so not so handy if there are cows to calve when Ciaran is away from home, or working in a distant field.'

'You do seem really happy together,' Tommy said. 'You appear to have so much in common with your interest in the cows.'

'We are very lucky,' Roxie said with a happy sigh. 'I never thought I would ever meet a man who shared my interests as Dad did.'

'If you don't mind,' Maggie said, interrupting them. 'I'd like to go to my bedroom, and have a little rest and change my clothes ready for this evening. I hope I shall fit in all right, Roxie,' she added anxiously.

'Oh, Maggie, of course you will fit in. You will love Ciaran's mother. She is so homely and kind. She made me welcome from the moment I arrived. But you go and have a rest, and you'll feel better after such a long journey. I can't tell you what a lovely surprise it is to see you both, and Harry too. Ciaran never breathed a word to me. Amy must be in on this as she is preparing a buffet meal for us.'

When Maggie had gone upstairs, Tommy and Roxie were alone in the kitchen.

'Ciaran invited Beth to come with us, but I couldn't bring her,' Tommy said a little glumly.

'Is she too busy with the catering? I hope she will manage the wedding?'

'She would have come this time and I know she is looking forward to coming to your wedding, but there will be a whole lot of our friends coming then. I didn't feel she should come with only me and Maggie. Gilda has been trying every trick she can think of to blame me for the divorce proceedings.'

'Surely she can't do that when you're not even the father of her baby!'

'Money is all she wants. Her and her father,' he said scornfully. 'So, any excuse will do to pass the blame and make a claim. She tried to make out that Beth had been looking after me before we married and that we were still having an affair.'

'But that's ridiculous!'

'She's trying to make a big thing of Beth doing my shopping and providing meals for me. She invents all sorts of inferences and stories. Fortunately, the people at the petrol pumps, and other locals who have always known us, realise they are all lies, but it doesn't mean to say a court would see things that way so we are being careful.'

'I'm so sorry that's happening, Tommy,' she said. 'I have always liked Beth and she used to hero-worship you when you were at school.'

'I was an impulsive, blind fool,' Tommy said bitterly. 'I don't know what I would have done without Beth's help before Maggie came back. Dad was so right.' He sighed. 'Gilda is an evil woman. Hindsight would be wonderful if only we had it before instead of after.'

* * *

Harry Dunn was in his element helping Ciaran round up the cows and bring them in from the field. Ciaran had fitted him up with a waterproof smock when he realised he was keen to come into the parlour, too. It seemed natural to Harry to start washing the udders and putting on the milking machines as they chatted. He had recognised all but one of the six cows Ciaran had bought at the sale. At the end of the milking, Harry grinned happily.

'I have enjoyed being back in a normal milking parlour and seeing each individual animal properly. I can't tell you how much I hated the rotary parlour and seeing strange cows passing by me almost every day. Money is not everything, even though the dealer did pay us well. Can I come with you to the milking in the morning?'

'Billy will be back to work tomorrow morning, or at least I am expecting him.' Ciaran paused and took a deep breath. 'I'll tell you what, though, Harry, now I have seen you at work and I see you're as keen as ever about the cows, I would give you a month's trial if you want to give it a go. I can understand you might not want to move as far north as this, of course. I need to improve a cottage to provide accommodation, but I intend to do that anyway for whoever replaces Billy.'

'I'm not bothered where I live, but I do want work I can enjoy and find some satisfaction in. The problem is, when would I be able to start? I have sold our house and the new owners would like to move as soon as I can move out.'

'I'll show you round everywhere tomorrow, including the cottage, and we'll see what can be done. You could start work in two weeks, but I can't promise to have a cottage ready by then. Maybe I could make it habitable, though. Billy is on a month's notice, but he is due two weeks' holiday and I know he will take them as part of his notice, if only to be awkward. He is not in the mood to put himself out these days.'

'Two weeks would suit me fine, and I've done plenty of decorating and plastering at home. I quite enjoy a bit of woodwork in my spare time, too. The evenings will still be light to get things done.' Harry sounded enthusiastic.

Roxie had been looking out of the kitchen window so she saw the cows making their way back to the field for the night.

'I think Ciaran must have had Harry helping him milk. They are finished quicker than I expected. I'll go and chase the cows into the field while Ciaran, Vic and Harry clear up and wash the parlour. Do you want to come for a short walk, Tommy, or are you tired after the long drive?'

'I could do with a walk. I would like a look around the farm, if Ciaran has time tomorrow morning before we leave, and so long as he doesn't mind. Just because I don't like dairy farming, it doesn't mean I'm not interested in everything else.'

'Ciaran will be happy that you're interested, I'm sure,' Roxie said as they crossed the farmyard to gather up the cows and drive them to the field.

Harry and Ciaran joined them on the way back to the house.

'Ciaran, you cheated!' Roxie chuckled. 'You must have had help to get done so quickly. Is everything washed up as well?'

'It is. Harry has been a great help in the parlour and Vic stayed on to do the hosing down of the collecting yard.' He stopped walking and faced them. 'Could you manage to stay another night, Tommy?'

'We could, but wouldn't that be overstaying our welcome?'

'I would like you to stay. After all, we shall soon be brothers-in-law.' Ciaran grinned. 'As a matter of fact, I have asked Harry to come to work for us on a month's trial to see whether he can settle this far north. If you can stay tomorrow, we can all have a good look around the farm and the area. Most importantly I need to improve the cottage. I know it needs a new bathroom suite and the kitchen needs a lot of work. It has not been occupied for some time, but there is a firm of cleaners who would come and give it a thorough clean from top to bottom before Harry arrives here in two weeks, though he would need to put up with the tradespeople working around him to make the improvements and do some decorating. Could you do that, Harry?'

'I'm used to that,' Harry said. 'I have modernised my mother's cottage from top to bottom. I could hire a van to bring up the bits and pieces of furniture I want to keep, including my own bed. If I hire from a national hiring firm, they would let me collect it back home and allow me to return to a branch up here. Then I could look for a small car in this area.'

'You sound very enthusiastic, lad,' Ciaran said. 'That all sounds sensible to me, but I hope you will not be disillusioned with the area.'

'I'm sure he will like the area,' Roxie said enthusiastically. 'And the people are really friendly.'

'You wouldn't be biased about that aspect of course,' Tommy said teasingly and winked at Ciaran.

'I'm sure moving to a different area will not worry me,' Harry said seriously. 'I know this is the kind of work I can enjoy and take a real interest in, but there are some things I have no experience in yet. I mean, I know when a cow has milk fever and I could give it an injection of calcium under the skin, but if it was urgent I couldn't inject into the vein and I know Tommy's father could do that himself.'

'If you know what is needed, and when, you can call the vet if I'm not at home,' Ciaran said reassuringly. 'Lots of farmers can't inject into the vein anyway.'

I — er . . . I don't think I could calve a cow on my own either, not if she was in real trouble. Like if the calf had a foot turned back or if the calf was coming backward.'

'It's something you learn with experience,' Ciaran said. 'I am usually around and you can get me on my mobile. If I'm not here, you would phone the vet. We have a good veterinary practice in this area. They usually come quickly if it is an emergency.'

'The important thing is, do you recognise when a cow has milk fever, Harry, or if a cow is taking too long and having difficulty calving?' Roxie asked.

'Oh, yes. Anyone who knows them and cares about their animals must sense when there's something wrong,' Harry said earnestly.

'Aye, I can vouch for him on that sort of thing,' Tommy said drily. 'He seemed to anticipate which cows would need help calving.'

'By the sound of things, we shall get on splendidly,' Ciaran said. 'It all depends whether you get homesick for your friends and family.'

'I wouldn't have liked to move away while Mum was alive, but she has gone now. She was an only child, and so am I. I have no close relations left, other than a cousin in Australia on my father's side. I know I shall settle if I have a place to call home, rather than moving around. I like to have a go at doing things. I don't mind a bit of decorating or joinery work in my spare time. I have kept my father's tools,' Harry said with a smile.

'Right,' Ciaran said decisively. 'We had better get washed and changed, and go for our meal. They can't start without the most important birthday girl.' He grinned affectionately at Roxie before saying to Tommy, 'My mother is looking forward to meeting you, Tommy.'

* * *

Roxie managed to run up to her bedroom with the parcels as planned, while Ciaran introduced everyone. As soon as she put her head in the room, they all sang 'Happy Birthday'.

Jenny and Donald came forward to kiss her cheek and give her a gift, and even Anne Munro had brought her a peace lily in a beautiful plant pot.

Roxie turned to look at Harry, sitting shyly in a corner beside Maggie.

'You see, Harry, how friendly and lovely the people are up here. I am sure you will soon settle at Oaklands and make lots of friends too.' Harry smiled back, but he didn't say anything.

'I haven't told Mum the news yet,' Ciaran said. He turned to Amy. 'I met Harry at the sale when I went down to Derbyshire. He was Tommy's herdsman. His mother died recently, so he is looking for a job with some satisfaction. He helped me milk tonight and he is going to come for a month's trial to see whether he likes living up here.'

'That is a surprise. You were always a good judge of people, son. So, young man, I do hope you will be very happy here.'

'Both Tommy and Roxie have a good word of him, so that means a lot,' Ciaran told her. 'I could see while he was in the milking parlour how natural he is around cows. I am very hopeful.'

'Isn't it time to eat now?' Donald asked with a cheeky grin. 'I haven't been out for a posh lunch like our birthday girl and I'm famished.'

They all trooped through to the dining room.

Roxie gasped. 'Oh, my goodness! What a huge spread you have made, Amy. I feel terrible that . . .'

'No, no, lassie. I'm not responsible for all of it. I mainly made the salads and cold meats. Anne has brought the pizzas and sausage rolls; Jenny brought quiches and the birthday cake; they both made a sweet as well. Now, draw in your chairs and pile up your plates.'

Everyone tucked in and there was chatter and laughter, with Harry and Maggie being drawn into the conversations.

'It has been such a happy evening,' Jenny said with a sigh when she heard baby Peter begin to stir. 'It's a pity you don't have a birthday every week, Roxie, but I'm afraid it's time we went home now before this young man lets you all hear how loud he can shout for his food.'

'Like his daddy, then.' Ciaran grinned, giving Donald a poke in the ribs.

'The next big celebration will be your wedding, old boy. I, and several others, can't wait to get our own back for all the cheek you've given us.'

Ciaran looked at Roxie. 'Maybe we should dash to the registrar's, Roxie, and thwart them all?'

'I think you will survive.' Roxie smiled serenely. 'I expect you have had your fun at their expense in the past.'

Anne wanted to help tidy up the dining room, but Roxie insisted she had done enough already and she would do it after having such a lazy day. Maggie eagerly offered to help, so Amy made a box of food for Anne to take home. There was certainly plenty left.

Ciaran had already told his mother that his guests were staying another night so that he could show them around the farm, the cottage where Harry would live, and the district.

'I think you should come here for your lunch tomorrow to help us eat everything up,' Amy said. 'In fact, you could drop Maggie off here to chat with us while you men go your own way. I'm sure Roxie and Maggie have plenty of news to catch up on.'

'All right, we'll do that, if you make the lunch a bit later for once, maybe one o'clock. Then we will all go out for a meal at the local hotel in Thornielee in the evening. It will let Harry see we are quite civilised.'

'Oh, yes, that is a good idea,' Amy said. She smiled at Harry. 'It is not a very big town, but we have an excellent butcher and a good baker. In fact, you can get most of what you will need, but there are several supermarkets further away in Dumfries. Can you cook at all, young man?'

'Oh, yes. I enjoy cooking meat and vegetables, pasta and rice — savoury meals. That is why I don't want to stay with a landlady. I cooked for my mum, but she didn't have much appetite,' Harry said soberly. 'I can't bake like Beth and Roxie do, but I manage for myself. When Mum became very ill, I learned to organise my time, and the food, as she used to do.'

'I think you will do very well, then. I hope you will be happy here once Ciaran has improved the cottage. It is needing to be lived in again. Houses get forlorn and deteriorate when they're empty.'

'I asked Jenny for the phone number of the firm they used to clean their house before they moved in,' Ciaran said.

Amy nodded in agreement. 'Oh, yes, she said they were very efficient. They brought a whole team of people and cleaned it all in a day. It was a three-storey Victorian house, so the cottage will be child's play in comparison.'

* * *

Both Tommy and Harry enjoyed looking round the farm. Tommy was especially interested in the arable side and he discussed his own plans with Ciaran. Harry was immensely grateful to his former boss for including him in this visit and he felt very lucky that Ciaran was willing to give him a month's trial. He was confident that settling in a new area would not be a problem for him, once he had bought a small car to get around, and especially when he had seen the cottage, which would give him his own space and freedom.

'This is very similar to the way my mother's cottage used to be when I was young. It was part of the estate where my father worked. Everything was sold off when the owner died in 1980. He had no wife or family. Dad had used all their savings to buy it.'

'He did well then,' Tommy said.

'That was just before I was born,' Harry added. 'I know my father made a lot of improvements over time, but he was a good joiner. I remember he made the washhouse and coal shed into a proper kitchen.'

'He was obviously a thrifty man,' Ciaran said. 'And that's a good quality to have.'

'Yes, they were both thrifty. Mum had saved every penny I sent her from my wages since I started working.' He shook his head in distress. 'I'd hoped she would have a few comforts for herself. Anyway, I used it to make things easier during her last year. I made a shower room downstairs and put in central heating.'

'You're a good lad, Harry,' Tommy said sincerely.

'The present condition of this cottage doesn't put you off coming, then?' Ciaran asked.

'No, I am looking forward to living here. I can bring my mother's Welsh dresser for the kitchen. It comes into two parts so it should fit in a Transit van. I have a microwave, a grill and a kettle. I shall soon buy a kitchen table. If you are getting cleaners in, I expect they will clean inside the existing cupboards?'

'I shall make sure they do,' Ciaran assured him.

'If you decide I can stay, I shall paint them and emulsion the walls. Maybe if I'd had a wife, things would be different,' he said with a grin.

'You can say that again!' Tommy muttered, thinking of Gilda.

* * *

Later that evening they all had a pleasant meal at the local hotel, with a good deal of banter and laughter. Tommy was leaving early the following morning, so they all said goodnight outside the hotel. There was more teasing when Ciaran seized Roxie in his arms to give her a lingering kiss. As usual, it brought the ready colour to her cheeks.

Maggie hugged her and whispered, 'They're lovely people, lass. I'm sure you will be very happy.'

'I think so, too. I am looking forward to seeing you all again at the wedding. That is not so very long now.'

'Long enough,' Ciaran mumbled.

* * *

Two weeks and a day later, Harry drove into the farmyard at Oaklands. He had loaded the hired van the night before with the help of friends and neighbours who had known his family for many years. Consequently, he was able to leave at the crack of dawn, making the most of the quieter roads. Ciaran was surprised to see him as he was finishing his mid-morning coffee. It was Iris's day for cleaning, but Ciaran asked her if she would cook bacon and eggs and toast for Harry.

'You must be hungry and weary if you have come all that way without a stop!'

'Oh, I did stop once for the toilets. I had a cup of coffee then, but it was from a machine and it was terrible.' Harry grimaced. 'I'm pleased to be here. It helped that I've been here with Tommy or I might have taken a wrong turn once or twice.'

'Well, eat up now, then Vic and I will help you to unload and to fix up your bed, and anything else you need a hand to fix.'

'Maybe the Welsh dresser?' Harry suggested diffidently.

'Of course, we'll help you with that, too. Max, he's the tractor driver, and Vic you've met. They will both help. Billy doesn't finish until tomorrow night, so take your time settling in. I managed to get the plumber to install a new bathroom suite with a shower. We were lucky. He was booked to install one in a newly built house, but the builder was not quite ready for him. It is all clean but I'm afraid the bathroom still needs decorating, and I don't know when we shall manage to get the decorator we usually use.'

'I shall enjoy doing a bit of decorating. I have never had a job when I am free for a couple of hours during the day, so I shall get things in order a bit at a time.'

'During the summer, when the cows are out at grass, you could be off several hours, unless you choose to earn some overtime helping us with the silage. In winter, the cows are inside and that makes more work feeding and cleaning, as you already know. It can be a long day with maybe a couple of hours after lunch.'

'That will be fine for me. I like to have a walk around all the animals in the summer, especially if any are due to calve. I like to get to know the heifers too, so I'm familiar with the ones that will be coming on as replacements.'

'That's good,' Ciaran said with satisfaction. 'I try to keep a fairly closed herd with our own animals providing replacements. I don't often buy in as many animals as I did at the Willowbrook sale, but they were very good and, anyway, I wanted to please Roxie,' he added with a boyish grin. 'Usually, I only buy one if I fancy the breeding.'

'I'm glad you did buy the ones from Tommy's herd. They were all fine animals,' Harry said wistfully.

'Yes, I'm pleased with them so far. I couldn't afford to buy any more, but I was tempted. Now then, I'll give Vic a shout while you eat up and we'll get you unloaded.'

'That will be good. The sooner I can take the van back to the hiring firm, the less I pay. I have to take it to a depot at Dumfries.'

'In that case I will tell Roxie. I think she will be free to follow you to Dumfries and give you a lift back.' Ciaran smiled suddenly. 'The only thing is, you might find you get Mum too. She enjoys a run out, especially now she's recovered her mobility.'

'Do you think they will wait while I buy some food?'

'I'm sure they will. Don't buy eggs and milk, though. You get them as a perk.'

'Gee, thanks. That's super! Tommy did the same, but not many places do. Not many keep poultry anyway these days. There were no perks at all at the dealer's place, not even a waterproof apron or a pair of rubber gloves.'

'Protective clothing is not a perk — it should be provided for every dairy worker. I know some employers never think about safety, though, but some are plain stingy.'

'I think the dealer simply didn't think about anything except the next deal.' Harry smiled. 'I really do appreciate you giving me a trial. I promise to do my best.'

'Yes, I think you will, Harry, and nobody can expect more. I don't suppose you have learned to do artificial insemination yet?'

'No, I haven't. Tommy mainly used two bulls his father had bred, but when we did use AI, a person from the company came and did it.'

'Well, if you're still here six months from now, and you would like to have a go, give me a reminder and I will arrange for you to go on a training course. Billy never wanted to do anything like that. I usually do it myself, but it would be handy to have someone else who could do it if I was away, even for half a day. It's important to get the timing right.'

Chapter 20

Ciaran had rarely acted on impulse when it came to his business, especially the care of his dairy herd, but he had been impressed by Harry's knowledge and caring at the Willowbrook sale. Then he had seemed genuinely eager to see the cows when he came with Tommy for Roxie's birthday surprise. He had automatically helped with the milking without any prompting, so it was clear he was not lazy. Now the month's trial was over and Ciaran knew he would be very disappointed if Harry decided he wanted to move back south.

During the first two weeks, Ciaran had made a point of being at every milking with Harry, but he had no doubts about his ability, or about his hygiene, something which had sometimes irked him with Billy when he was in a hurry to get finished. Fortunately, Harry seemed happy and settled, and an added bonus was that he got on well with seventeen-year-old Vic, answering his questions, and encouraging the youngster to use his initiative and learn to drive the tractor now he was of age for a licence.

'I'm sure we could have a honeymoon abroad, Roxie, now that we know Harry intends to stay,' Ciaran said. 'I feel instinctively that I can trust his reliability. Do you think it would be worth trying for a late booking?'

'We can't do that. I don't have a passport,' Roxie said. 'In any case, I have seen so little of Scotland I am looking forward to exploring, just the two of us.'

'Oh, I'm looking forward to exploring too, just the two of us, but it's not the countryside I have in mind,' he said with a wicked grin. 'Ah, Roxie, I do love the rosy colour rising in your cheeks. I wonder if I can get you to blush all over?' he said teasingly.

* * *

Roxie's colour deepened when she thought of the birthday present Lucy had made for her. It was the finest pale blue silk, alluringly transparent, or almost, with only lace ruffles for the tiny sleeves and edging the low neckline. She had not shown it to anyone, even Jenny when she had come one afternoon to try on the dress Lucy had made for her as matron of honour, but she had been full of praise for Lucy's ability as a maker of stylish dresses. Roxie had proudly showed Jenny and Amy the lovely wedding dress she was borrowing from Lucy.

'Oh, my word, lassie, this is beautiful.' Amy had gently stroked the heavy slipper satin. 'It looks very expensive.'

'It was,' Roxie said ruefully. 'Lucy said it would be a shame to only wear it once so she was pleased when I told her I would be honoured to borrow such a dress if I ever found a husband. She said she would put it away for me when my turn came. I didn't think she had really meant it until she reminded me. She said it was probably the most expensive wedding dress her mother could find. I think she was a little hurt because she felt it was to make up for her mother not coming home to help her make the wedding arrangements.'

'Oh dear.' Amy frowned. 'Were her parents not at the wedding, then?'

'Yes, they arrived home two nights before the big day, with a very expensive double string of pearls.' Roxie's tone was dry. She felt no amount of money could make up for a mother's love and her presence on such an important occasion. 'Lucy never moaned or criticised, but I sensed she would have preferred to have had her mother's help and support. She had to arrange the reception and all the wedding arrangements and invitations on her own. Fortunately, Steve and his parents helped wherever they could. Her grandmother was too frail by then to be any help. In fact, she died three months after the wedding. She left her house to Lucy, and a lovely tribute saying what a blessing her cheery company had been in her declining years.'

'Ah, that was nice,' Amy said warmly. 'She would have been grateful for Lucy's youthful presence in her home.'

'Yes, Lucy really appreciated it.' Roxie smiled. 'But she suspected her mother was quite miffed. She took it as a criticism of herself because she rarely spent time with her mother. Most of her time was spent travelling abroad with Lucy's father as soon as Lucy was old enough to go to the grammar school, and could stay with her grandmother. I'm not sure what his work is, but it is something for the government. They are quite wealthy.'

'Oh, dear, I hope it didn't cause any estrangement between mother and daughter.'

'No, I don't think so. Lucy and Steve are very happy together anyway. That is the main thing.'

'I am looking forward to meeting your friends when they come on holiday, Roxie. I hope you have invited them for at least one meal with us.'

Jenny chimed in. 'Oh, yes, you must do that. I'd love to meet them, too, and their little girls. They are wearing the same cornflower blue as us, aren't they?'

'Yes, they are.'

* * *

It was a beautiful autumn day at the beginning of September and Roxie was a mixture of excitement and nervousness. The wedding was far bigger than anything she had ever contemplated. Tommy told her that all their old friends from their Young Farmers' Club days were keen to come. There were too many for a minibus, so they had hired a small coach and booked themselves and the driver in at the hotel. She knew Tommy had done the same for himself, Beth and Maggie, but the three of them were coming up the day before and spending the night with Ciaran so that Tommy would be on hand to travel with Roxie to the church and give her away. Ciaran, Donald and most of their friends were wearing their kilts. Lucy had been delighted when she'd heard that. Donald's parents were also booked in at the hotel for the night. They planned to take care of Peter and put him to bed in their room when he got too tired to watch the dancing.

'Everything seems to be falling into place,' Amy said with satisfaction. 'I am so happy to be here and to be able to enjoy Ciaran's wedding day at last.'

As a tribute to her, and also in appreciation of her remarkable recovery, the ladies of the church had asked if they could decorate the church for the wedding and preserve many of the floral decorations towards the harvest thanksgiving the following week. Both Amy and Roxie were overjoyed by the results and the effort they must have put in to transform the little stone church into a glorious floral splendour. Most of the regular members of the congregation knew this would probably be the largest wedding they had witnessed for several years. The Baxters were well respected in the parish and had always been generous supporters of their local church.

When Roxie caught a glimpse through the open doors, she was stunned to see the church filled to capacity.

'Where can they have come from?' she whispered to Tommy, her hand trembling on his arm. 'Neither of us have many family members.' Tommy covered her hand with his firm warm grip to steady her.

'You both have many friends, sis, all wishing you happiness,' he whispered back. 'You should be proud. Walk tall, walk straight . . .' He hummed softly, close to her ear, and grinned. Then she recognised Mr Jamieson from the carol service. He was one of the two elders welcoming them in at the door. He gave her a big smile and all his good wishes before she and Tommy began to walk slowly down the aisle towards Ciaran and Donald, who looked smart in their kilts. As they drew near, Ciaran half turned towards them. His eyes widened, his tense expression softened, filled with love and wonder at the beautiful vision walking towards him. Watching them from the front seat, Amy smiled happily, even as she wiped a tear from her eye.

When Ciaran clasped her hand in his, all Roxie's nervousness disappeared and she gave him a radiant smile.

The country hotel where they held the reception afterwards had been Amy's choice. Roxie remembered how Tommy had tried to persuade Amy to let him pay for the reception, as their father would have done, especially when so many friends of his and Roxie's had travelled north to attend.

'Laddie, this is the day I have longed for. It is my privilege to pay for the reception. I could never have dreamed of a better daughter than Roxie. You can see for yourself how happy the pair of them are together.' Tommy had to give in gracefully and agree that they made everyone smile to see their happiness.

The meal was delicious and Donald made them all smile with his speech and a few humorous anecdotes of his and Ciaran's youthful exploits. Eventually, more people began to arrive for the dancing and an evening buffet later on. Harry and Vic arrived together, with Max and his wife. Iris and her husband came, too. Anne Munro and her daughter and niece had also come for the evening as Anne had had to work during the day. There were several people Roxie didn't recognise, but they all wished her and Ciaran great happiness.

Roxie and Ciaran opened the dancing with a dreamy waltz, but after dancing with Donald, then Tommy and also Steve, she and Jenny and Lucy disappeared to help her change into a summer dress of turquoise silk with a swirling skirt, and a matching jacket to put on at the last minute, ready for going away, although they had no intention of escaping for a while. They had booked a hotel not too far away for the first night of their honeymoon, but they had not told anyone, even Amy, where they would be. Roxie was pleased to see Ciaran had persuaded his mother to have a go at a quieter dance, then Donald danced with her, too. Much later she saw Mr Jamieson getting Amy up for a waltz.

'I can't remember seeing such a happy crowd of people at a dance before. They are all mixing so well together,' Jenny said.

'The friends from Derbyshire are all people Tommy and I knew when we were in the Young Farmers. I expect a lot of Ciaran's friends are Young Farmers, too, so they will have something in common.'

'Yes, I wouldn't be surprised if there are one or two matches after tonight.' Jenny chuckled.

Roxie thought there would certainly be a match between Tommy and Beth. They had danced almost every dance together, and they looked so at ease and happy together. It was as though a huge weight had been removed from Tommy since the latest astonishing development. The wife at the Chinese restaurant in town had been convinced baby Liam was her grandson from the first time she had seen him. She didn't like the bad-tempered way Gilda often treated him so the couple had visited Tommy to ask if he would agree to them adopting him. He had promptly put them in touch with Mr Robson, the solicitor, but before the latest DNA results were available to prove the connection, Gilda had seized at the chance of adoption. She wanted her freedom back, and to go travelling. She was suddenly eager to agree to a divorce in return for a reasonable sum from Tommy.

Roxie hoped her brother could find happiness as she had done.

Eventually, as they had prearranged, Ciaran came to ask her to dance again. They got nearer the door, intending to make a dash for their car, but Donald and Tommy had been keeping a sharp eye on them and they pounced before Roxie and Ciaran could get out of the hotel. They were showered with confetti, amid a lot of laughter and teasing, before they could scramble into the car.

'It has been a wonderful day.' Roxie sighed happily as they drew away from the crowd of laughing friends.

'I can confess now,' Ciaran said. 'I felt very nervous waiting for you to arrive at the church. Don didn't help either. He said he had forgotten to pick up the ring. He hadn't, of course. The wretch was just pulling my leg. Everyone seemed to mix well and enjoy the day, though, most especially my mother. When I danced with her, she said it was the happiest day she could remember since her own wedding day.'

'I was dreadfully nervous when I saw the church so full of people and so many waiting outside, too. I didn't expect that,' Roxie said. 'Tommy was very good, though. He kept me calm.'

Ciaran stopped the car as soon as they turned into a quieter road out of town. He turned and drew Roxie into his arms.

'It feels as though I have waited all day to give my new wife a proper kiss,' he murmured tenderly and proceeded to give her several proper kisses. 'Isn't it great?' he whispered, lifting his head. 'We are on our own at last. We can go to bed together without my mother or anyone making us feel guilty.' He grinned and started the car.

The hotel suite was luxurious. Ciaran pulled off his evening jacket and undid some of his shirt buttons as he sprawled over the chaise longue, flinging his arms wide, while his kilt displayed a fine length of thigh.

'Whew, I'm glad we can have peace at last,' sighed Roxie. 'It was warm work all that dancing, much as everyone enjoyed it. I was pleased to see Harry getting Maggie on the floor a couple of times, and then Max asked her to dance and introduced her to his wife.'

'Yes, I saw that. Vic seemed a bit shy, but maybe he doesn't dance. Harry danced with Beth, too, but, of course, she knew most of the others from home as well, when Tommy gave them a chance to claim her.'

'I think I could do with a drink of tea, more than any of the other drinks,' Roxie said with a laugh, as she switched on the electric kettle left ready on a side table with everything for tea or coffee. She gently slapped his bare thigh as she passed.

'Right, dear husband. When the kettle boils, you make the tea while I have a quick shower.'

'Oh, Roxie, you can't . . .'

But she had already disappeared into the bathroom. When she reappeared a short time later, wrapped in a huge pink bath sheet and with her hair still wet, Ciaran had made them both a cup of good, strong tea.

'There, my dear husband.' She chuckled. 'You can have the shower if you want it, while I dry my hair. Thanks for my tea.' She smiled at him over the rim of the cup.

'Such cheek for a brand-new wife! We should have showered together.'

'There's a huge bath with sprays coming out of the sides we might try tomorrow, but the shower is barely big enough for one. I felt hot and sticky, and I wanted to wash my hair after having it lacquered into place all day.'

'I'm tempted to pull a corner of that sheet,' Ciaran said teasingly, making Roxie grab the big towel closer. 'I'm ready for a cool shower myself. The ballroom got quite warm.' He divested himself of his kilt and made for the bathroom in his underwear.

When he returned with a small towel round his waist, Roxie was sitting in front of the dressing table, finishing drying her wavy hair. She was clad now in the near transparent negligee. Her eyes met Ciaran's shyly as he came quickly towards her.

'Oh! Oh . . . What have we here?' He threw aside his towel and came to her, placing his hands on her shoulders as he met her eyes in the large mirror. 'I thought you looked like an angel coming towards me in church, but this is something else.' He reached for her hands and drew her to her feet. 'Now, my darling wife, you look like a water nymph.' He held her arms above her head to do a pirouette while he admired. As he turned her full circle to face him, she felt her cheeks flushing with a desire to match his own.

'Oh, my Roxie,' he murmured huskily. 'You're the sexiest vision I could ever have dreamed of.'

'Do you like it?' she asked.

'It is really lovely, but not as beautiful as the woman inside.' Ciaran lifted her in his arms and carried her to the bed. He drew her on top of him and growled softly in her ear. 'My woman! I'm the luckiest man alive,' he whispered as he covered her with kisses, arousing a passion in Roxie as only he knew how.

The End

Acknowledgements

Dear readers,

I thank you for reading, or listening to, my stories. I hope some of them have given you as much pleasure as they have given me when writing them. Without you, I would have no incentive to write.

I am happy to say *A Scottish Love Story* is being published for the first time by Joffe Books and I am pleased to be one of their authors. I thank all members of the Joffe team who have played a part in getting the manuscript ready for publication: Becky, Sarah, Kate and Tia. Thanks also to copy-editor Suzy Clarke and cover designer Jarmila Takač, and to those whom I have not yet been in contact with personally. Every stage is important and I appreciate you all.

www.gwenkirkwood.co.uk

The Joffe Books Story

We began in 2014 when Jasper agreed to publish his mum's much-rejected romance novel and it became a bestseller.

Since then, we've grown into the largest independent publisher in the UK. We're extremely proud to publish some of the very best writers in the world, including Joy Ellis, Faith Martin, Caro Ramsay, Helen Forrester, Simon Brett and Robert Goddard. Everyone at Joffe Books loves reading and we never forget that it all begins with the magic of an author telling a story.

We are proud to publish talented first-time authors, as well as established writers whose books we love introducing to a new generation of readers.

We won Trade Publisher of the Year at the Independent Publishing Awards in 2023 and Best Publisher Award in 2024 at the People's Book Prize. We have been shortlisted for Independent Publisher of the Year at the British Book Awards for the last five years, and were shortlisted for the Diversity and Inclusivity Award at the 2022 Independent Publishing Awards. In 2023 we were shortlisted for Publisher of the Year at the RNA Industry Awards, and in 2024 we were shortlisted at the CWA Daggers for the Best Crime and Mystery Publisher.

We built this company with your help, and we love to hear from you, so please email us about absolutely anything bookish at feedback@joffebooks.com.

If you want to receive free books every Friday and hear about all our new releases, join our mailing list here: www.joffebooks.com/freebooks.

And when you tell your friends about us, just remember: it's pronounced Joffe as in coffee or toffee!

www.ingramcontent.com/pod-product-compliance
Lightning Source LLC
Chambersburg PA
CBHW020320200626
46814CB00006BB/2344